A NOVEL

RICHARD FOXX

DISCLAIMER:

Spirit Ranch is a work of fiction. No real people are portrayed and no real events described. Nothing like this ever happened. Most of the scenes arose from the fevered brain of the author, usually late at night, usually with the only light in the house from the computer.

Any resemblance to any persons living, dead, or otherwise is unintended and is purely coincidental. The author also makes the same claim for himself.

That's a good thing.

Spirit Ranch, the polo club, Indio, the desert, the date groves, and most of the other places are real and existed just this way in the late 1990's (and back in the 1930's).

Except for the polo club, however, don't look for them. They disappeared in the housing boom of 2004.

Too bad…

DEDICATION

For JoAnn
The Real Spirit of Spirit Ranch…

1

June 1933

The sound, the insistent metallic clatter, grated against the stillness and she drew a breath and looked up, the VANITY FAIR *she had been paging through forgotten in her lap. The noise became the sound of a slightly out of tune automobile engine, and even though they had been expecting it, waiting for it in the oppressive heat for what seemed like an eternity, the sound terrified her and she suddenly wanted to run but she checked herself instead and tried to catch his eye, trying to look cool, and dying inside for an answer.*

Scott, for his part, stopped pacing and froze, hardly breathing.

After a heartbeat, he moved to the low doorway and cracked the sagging screen door as if it would help him hear. Finally, he thought, and he flipped the butt of his next-to-last Lucky Strike out over the patch of sparse grass and on to the sand. He watched it arc and watched it as it continued to smolder there, where it landed, barely hotter than the heavy air. And then he pushed the screen further and went outside.

The breeze had stopped and the air seemed to grow at least ten degrees hotter. Nothing moved. The car was louder now, and seemed to slow at the corner of 50th, about two, maybe three hundred yards away, the sound carrying easily across the flat sand and scrub vegetation. It sounded like a small car, a Ford roadster, maybe. The times he had met Rolando the man had been driving a Packard and that sounded different, more important. Still, this was the only car they had heard in a half hour or more so maybe it was him.

He thought he could see the car through the dense bushes that ran along the road at the south end of the property. It was definitely a Ford, ugly and black. For a moment it looked as though it would slow at the gallus gate at the entrance to the ranch, but it continued on by, gradually fading into the heat. He exhaled, aware for the first time that he had been holding his breath.

"I'll be glad when we can go." the girl said softly, almost afraid to break the silence. She had been trying to ignore the trickles of sweat that were forming between her thighs since they had begun their vigil but it was impossible, and she hiked her skirt higher, looking for a breeze that didn't exist, glad that she never wore underwear. When Scott didn't answer, she continued: "I swear I'm going in that pool dress and all as soon as we get there. You did say they have a pool, didn't you?"

Scott held his hand up, a silencing gesture. He had long since shed his suit coat and unbuttoned his vest and loosened his tie but he continued to wear his trim fedora pushed back on his head. It had become his trademark. It was what he had intended when he had lifted the affectation from his father back in law school. That, and the vest, and his white shirt with the sleeves rolled up, made him look like some kind of gambler, a croupier, perhaps, with a big, impossible bet on the line. And in a way, he was.

"He had a Packard." he said, to no one. "That was a Ford. Shit." He patted himself down and when he found the wrinkled pack of Lucky Strikes he took the last one out and crumbled the now-empty package and tossed it into a box that lay near the stove. The cigarette he lit with a wooden match, took a long drag, and then walked over to where the girl sat and held it to her lips. She inhaled deeply, her eyes searching his face, but he was oblivious, still listening. "Shit," he said again.

She had only begun to smoke since she had met the lawyer and it seemed to her sometimes as if she had always had the habit. She exhaled the smoke slowly, trying not to choke, and went back to idly flipping pages in the magazine. It was the February issue and she had seen it when it first came out but when she discovered it in the trunk of Scott's new Auburn roadster after they arrived she was grateful for the distraction. She wanted suddenly, desperately, to be somewhere else. Going to the desert with Scott had been a last minute decision, a whim, and in the back of her mind even now she wondered whether she had done the right thing. He had certainly not been much company once the waiting had started. Now he came back inside and leaned just inside the door where he could keep an eye on the driveway, arms folded, legs crossed. He studied the girl again. He never tired of it.

The white cotton dress she wore clung to her damp skin, revealing everything. The skirt was up far enough so that he didn't have to use much of his imagination to picture the curve of her thighs, the hair between her legs the same reddish-brown as the hair on her head, the color of a fine old porto. She wore her luxuriant hair understated, cut close to her head, and played off the color with a dark lipstick that she applied to set off her lips like a bow. Her eyebrows were accented with the same dark-toned color. The effect heightened the smattering of freckles that dotted her perfect nose just so. He could almost smell the warmth of her from here, the faint hint of the lavender that she favored. Even against the high standards of L.A. and Hollywood she was beautiful.

It probably wasn't the best idea to bring her with him, he knew that, but he hadn't been able to resist the idea of a few days at one of the new casitas that had been built at the La Quinta Hotel not far from where he had to meet the Mexican. They had only dated a short time, had only made love once in fact, and he couldn't believe his luck when she agreed to go with him.

Rolando was supposed to show at two. Now it was almost 4PM. A bad idea under the best of circumstances, to come here instead of meeting him out in Riverside, or one of the places in L.A. where he usually did, and in this heat it was turning out to be a really bad idea. Shimmers of hot air rose from the reaches of sand to the south and east, where ocotillo and scrub and creosote and tumbleweed defined the alien landscape. Two hawks that lived in one of the nearby palms swirled and dipped, weaving their shadows together on the ground. In the distance, the mountains seemed to be fading away, Santa Rosa almost invisible, a trick of the haze. Across the road and down a little way, a grove of date palms loomed and he could imagine the cool darkness in the shadows. All around there was silence, a silence so deep it made its own sound.

He looked at her again and thought: The hell with it. Rolando can keep his goddamn money. It was a lot for him, two thousand dollars, and out of law school barely a year with debts and all that, he needed it, but the truth was he had never felt comfortable working for the Mexican. Out here, away from L.A., Scott knew he was in way over his head. It was more than a bad idea. It was probably real stupid.

"Okay, sugar," he said, suddenly making up his mind. "We're out of here."

She was out of the chair before the words were out of his mouth and looking around to make sure she hadn't left anything, The screen creaked as Scott opened it and held it open for her, but even above the creak they could hear the car noise again and they looked at each other and why the hell did it have to come back now?

The car stopped at the driveway, still a few hundred yards from the ranch house, then made a right turn and began to crawl up the dirt road in their direction, the engine noise echoing off the oleanders. "Go inside." he said to her, suddenly aware of how vulnerable they were in the open. She hesitated. "Now!" he breathed, and he moved *protectively in front of her as the car came closer, up the driveway, past the small pasture, empty of horses now, past the citrus trees.*

The driver was small, with a dark-olive complexion, a thin moustache the only break on a face that could have been young or old or anything. Scott had never seen him and he watched as the man opened the door and got out and squinted at a piece of paper that he held in his hand. Maybe he was lost. That was it, he was lost. He wore a dark jacket with a rumpled white shirt and dark tie, and he looked nothing at all like the braceros *or the illegals that populated this part of the Coachella Valley.*

When the man looked up, Scott was suddenly, discordantly aware of how black his eyes were, coal black, and so dark the pupils didn't show. "Señor Carruthers?" he said, but the way he said it, it was clear to Scott that he knew who he was. Scott felt like a deer caught in the headlights and he thought frantically, irrationally, of trying to get to the Smith & Wesson under the seat of his treasured Auburn roadster but that was parked back behind the ranch house and suddenly it was too late for that because the man was walking toward him. Carruthers felt the hair on his neck rise.

"You are Señor Carruthers, the abogado. *You know," he whined, mixing English and Spanish, "what means the* abogado, *you are the lawyer. Señor Gutierrez, my* patron, *he ask me to give you something." He tapped his jacket pocket meaningfully.*

April watched warily from the kitchen window, the glare from the bright sky on the dirty glass making her invisible to Scott and the Mexican. The two men were speaking and as she watched she felt herself relax, as though maybe it would be alright after all. The driver didn't look all that bad, at least from a distance, not at all like the gangster types she had seen in the movies. Then there was a black pistol in the man's hand as quick and as slick as a picked card in a marked deck and there was no time for her to scream a warning, no time to look away, no time for anything. It was like watching an awful silent movie, until the world exploded with an unbearable noise as first Scott's head disintegrated, and then his chest seemed to burst into a red mushroom. He hit the ground hard and his legs kicked the dirt with a jerky running movement while his hat rolled away on the sand. The birds that had been feeding quietly nearby evaporated like smoke.

Then she heard herself scream.

2

1996

The gunshots jerked him awake and he rolled off the side of bed nearest the adobe wall and crouched there, alert for anything that moved, while the sounds reverberated around the room, echoed and died away. How quickly the moves came back. He could see Max in the hazy light that filtered through the plantation shutters but the big yellow Lab only turned a sleepy eye in his direction and thumped his tail as though rolling off a bed in the middle of a quiet afternoon nap was something the man did all the time, strictly for the dog's amusement.

But for the man there was no mistaking the smell of cordite that hung in the air like a cloud over a firing range. The shots sounded as though they had come from a small weapon, a .38 maybe. Nothing moved but still he waited, hardly daring to breathe. After a while he moved toward the nightstand, eased the drawer open, and closed his hand around the familiar cold of his 9 mm. Glock. There was a round in the chamber and he slid the safety off. Only then did he chance a look outside through the shutter slats. Nothing had changed since he had closed the shutters a scant 15 or 20 minutes before. The heat was still raising mini-thermals from the expanse of green lawn out back and the house finches were still fighting with the pigeons over the bird feeder that hung from an eve on the bunkhouse. Nothing was out of place.

Out beyond the lawn, beyond the oleanders, where the coyotes and the owls hunted at night, the giant tamarisk trees spread their gauzy branches silvery gray-green in the harsh afternoon sun. Underneath it would be dark and cool, a place for scorpions and rabbits and fieldmice. A roadrunner cruised past not far from the window clicking to himself, looking for an unsuspecting lizard or better still a snake.

He was about to chalk the whole thing up to some bizarre auditory hallucination, the kind you have when you're falling asleep and you hear someone calling your name and no one is there, when the third gunshot went off next to his head. He hunched his shoulders and dodged reflexively. This time it was even closer and louder and it rang in his ears the way it did when he shot his pistol without ear plugs.

The dog never moved.

"You didn't..." he mumbled to the dog, and shook his head to clear it of the noise. "No, you didn't. Maybe I didn't. Maybe I've been out here too long by myself. Maybe it's this freakin' heat. Still..."

He moved to the bedroom door and opened it crouched low and off to one side where someone on the other side would not expect him to be coming from. But the old, one-story adobe was quiet; the air conditioner's anemic wheezing the only sound. A dust mote here and there lit up in the afternoon sun where the light came in reflected off the windows in the bunkhouse, and here and there a fly buzzed. "No..." he hissed a warning to Max when the dog went to the door with him.

There was no one in the living room. The pictures, his precious old New Mexican pottery jugs, the few rare Navajo saddle blankets, lay undisturbed. Beyond a passthrough in the wall the kitchen rested quietly with only the hum of the refrigerator and the machine noise of the water cooler. On the arm of the couch in front of the cold fireplace a large black cat dozed.

He went from room to room, bedroom to kitchen to dining room to office, pistol barrel up, the gun at the ready. The house was built in the old style, open, the rooms big, and there were no closets for an intruder to hide. There was nothing. In each room he looked out the window but the small ranch stretched quietly away in all directions.

He let himself out the front door still in a half-crouch and this time when the big dog tried to follow Morgan made no attempt to stop. The extra warning would be useful, he thought, but Max just looked around disinterestedly and lay down near the pirul, the old pepper tree that dominated the middle of the back lawn and watched with ill-concealed dog-amusement as Morgan looked around. The man was taller than average, and angular, sparely built, not young, but with an obvious physical power, and he moved with a restrained intensity.

The house occupied a low rise, the way they built houses in the desert years ago, so that it would be above the water the next time there was a hundred-year flood. It had originally been adobe but the additions had been done with stucco so except for the thickness of the walls, there was little to give away its original construction. The building was barely visible from the road with fruit trees close on all sides, a few bearing date palms, and an impossibly tall, impossibly ancient eucalyptus that towered over the whole thing. The green of the lawn and the trees against the sandy brown of the house and the quiet, gave it all the effect of being some kind of mystical oasis. He had been unable to get it out of his mind since he had first set foot on it not quite three months before when he decided that somehow, someway, he would make himself be able to afford it.

There was another house, smaller, not ten feet from the first, set back and hidden by it from the main road. It was the same adobe style, but older, built, they said, on a foundation that dated back to the 1920's. Here and there, where the foundation stones were visible, were streaks of black that might have been soot from some long ago fire but the records from those days, if any indeed had ever existed, had long since disappeared. In an attempt to lighten the place a previous owner had put in some new windows that looked out over the swimming pool and Jacuzzi, and French doors to the west but with it all it remained a little dark and a little reserved, as though withholding some secret thing for itself.

Nothing was moving and he whistled the dog up to walk the perimeter of the small ranch with him. And then what? Call the police and have them come over for an auditory hallucination? "Yes, officer, this is Nicholas Morgan. I'm the guy that bought the old Stevens' ranch at 50th and Jefferson just down from the polo club and I just heard three shots in my bedroom. No, I can't see anything unusual. No, there are no dead bodies."

Sure. The Indio police would shake their heads at the weird antics of the Hollywood types who were moving into the area and the next time his alarm went off it would get something less than front burner attention. Not a good idea.

"Screw it." he said to no one and reset the safety and tucked the Glock behind his back into his waistband where he could get it if he needed it. No one could see onto the property, but still, he'd have a tough time explaining why he was walking around like Rambo. Max got up carefully, tested each leg and stretched it elaborately, and then ambled over to Morgan but Morgan was already walking down the long driveway.

The further down he walked, the more relaxed he became until before long he found himself almost strolling, struck with the absolute absurd normalcy of the day. The weather was perfect, a little too warm in the midafternoon perhaps, but it was the desert and it was late Spring and already the temperature had begun to climb into triple digits on a regular basis. It would be a hot summer. He liked that, or rather liked the fact the heat drove out a lot of the visitors and left the desert for the regulars, the desert rats as he thought of them. It was one of the big reasons he moved there. That, and the polo.

In the distance he could see a couple of rabbits on the other side of a rise but they weren't visible to the dog who just then was deeply involved sniffing out a mole hole, being a dog, totally involved in the moment.

The ranch was quiet in the way it was quiet most of the time, with the kind of silence that reminded him of the curtained wings of a stage, absorbing, expectant. Even though it was a scant three acres it abutted the desert at the far reaches of Indio and La Quinta, and with a foot in two worlds it was almost the last outpost of a too-rapidly encroaching civilization. The natural traffic of coyotes, hawks, road runners, bobcats, and rattlesnakes still outnumbered the cars even as he wondered how long that would last.

There was a green cocoon of old-growth oleander bushes that surrounded the place on all sides and formed a impenetrable barrier. They towered more than 12 feet tall in some places and gave the ranch a sense of being apart from the world. The mountains towered away in all directions with

Santa Rosa to the south and they formed an endlessly changing hypnotic tapestry, appearing clear and close enough they could be a painted scene in a movie at times and almost fading into the haze at other times, going gray to green to purple to brown from moment to moment to moment at the whim of the ever-changing light.

An expanse of green lawn, a luxury in the desert, rolled down to the road from the house. In the midst of it, a three-rail white fence enclosed about a half-acre pasture, empty now, the water trough dry. The asphalt drive curved down in front of it and ended at a large, wrought iron gate under a gallus arch constructed of logs. Over it all an ancient wooden sign hung that said: "Spirit Ranch" and on the back, where you could see it when you drove out, "Vaya con Dios", painted in whitewash in a casual script, someone's old, offhanded blessing against the dangers of the world. Large saguaros guarded the two front corners of the ranch, set in cactus gardens that held nopals and ocotillos, agave and barrel cactus. The gate was still closed, the bolt rammed home.

All that was left to explore was the older building, the guesthouse, and he skirted his way around the pool and the Jacuzzi to the front door of it. The poolmotor hummed in the silence, a peaceful counterpoint to the bubbling sound the water made where it trickled down from the spa into the pool. The quiet was palpable. By this time, he thought fatalistically, if someone wanted to kill him they could have had a clear shot. Several, in fact. He turned the handle on the door and pushed it open and the cool chill that enveloped him was so noticeable that his first thought was that he had left the air conditioner on but he knew he hadn't. Inside, the only sound came from the loud ticking of the old schoolhouse clock and it sounded as it once had when it had hung on the wall of his house in Dillon when he had been a boy. The space in front of the massive stone fireplace was dominated by an ancient pool table and in front of that a brown and white cowhide, the brand still visible, lay on the terra cotta pavers.

Except for a persistent uneasiness he had about convinced himself the sound had never happened but till he held his breath while he stepped softly inside and made his way from the old kitchen to the living room and then to the bedroom to the right of the fireplace. The bedspread was flat, taut, the way he knew the cleaning lady would have left it.

The room on the left was cold. Not cool, cold. He shivered involuntarily. That was what he had noticed about it before but there had always been something else going on that distracted him from paying attention. Now that he thought about it, that was what had been nagging at him since the real estate agent had left after the walkthrough. Tentative, unsure of what he would find, he stepped further in and stopped at the warm smell of lavender that embraced him. He had smelled it before on the ranch and he had hunted in vain for the plant he was sure had to be the source of it, and now here it was again, around him, part of him, strong enough so that he couldn't ignore it.

The bedroom windows looked out onto the most secluded part of the ranch where a one story two-horse barn and small corral had been built long ago. The twisted limbs of an old orchid tree draped over the fence in a macabre pattern that riveted his attention. Even though the room was filled with an orange-yellow light from the afternoon sun he was still cold and then he realized that he was hearing breathing, regular, not panting, a deep sighing in and out and he turned and looked for the dog that he was sure had come in the room without him noticing but there was no dog. He checked through the window in the other bedroom and he could see that Max had taken up his post outside on the grass under the pirul tree. Still the breathing continued.

He walked back to where he had stood but the breathing was gone now and the uneasiness was gone and he remained in front of the window like that with an unfamiliar longing, trying to recapture what he had been thinking, what he had been feeling. The scent of lavender enveloped him.

"I need you help." The heavily accented voice came from behind him, so unexpected and so sudden that Morgan almost felt his heart stop beating. He spun and reached for the gun in his waistband in one movement.

3

With his finger tightening on the trigger, Morgan saw that the weapon was pointed right into the middle of a round, brown face. It was a face he knew almost as well as his own, and he realized with a sudden chill that he had almost blown it away.

"*Madre Dios. No balazo! No balazo!* It's me, Amado."

"Son of a goddamn bitch, I told you before not to sneak up on me. You were gonna get your ass killed." Morgan lowered the Glock, aware of the faint tremor that remained as the adrenaline ebbed from his body. "You know, you're gonna get yourself killed someday doing that." he repeated. "Dammit, say something next time before you surprise me, will you?"

"*Lo siento, amigo…*"

"Say something like 'hey Nick, how're you doin?', or something like that before you get up behind me." Morgan waved the apology away and saw the look on the man's face. "Ah, don't worry about it. It's okay. You're probably too much Indian to make any noise, even if you wanted to."

"*Que paso?* What's goin' on?"

"I wish I knew. All I know for sure is that I was in the middle of a nap not 30 minutes ago and thought I heard pistol shots and I've been trying to figure out where they came from."

"You think they come from in here?" He eyed Morgan with suspicious eyes that darted from one corner of the room to the other, a trapped animal in the presence of the loaded gun. "Why you no call the *policia?*"

"I don't know and now I'm not even sure I heard them at all. Max didn't even move and now he's acting like nothing's wrong."

"*No entiendes.* Where you hear them?"

"In the main house. That is, I think they came from in there, in the bedroom. I searched the ranch and wound up here. I don't know why." He pressed the clip release on the handle of the weapon and worked the slide until the unused round spun out of the chamber and he caught it off-handedly as it tumbled in mid-air, an old trick. He replaced the round in the clip and slipped it into the back pocket of his jeans.

Amado's coal-black eyes were wide open, and he stared at Morgan's hands, like a kid watching a magician do a close-up card trick. "How you know to do that?"

"Do what?"

"You know…with the bullet…"

It had been something he had practiced long ago, in another place, when things like that seemed important, but now he shrugged the question away impatiently. "*Olvidalo.* Don't worry about it…c'mon, we both need a Corona."

They moved into the kitchen where Morgan retrieved two Coronas from the ancient Frigidaire while Amado leaned against the pool table, arms folded, trying to strike a nonchalant pose. The refrigerator was probably from the 40's or earlier, and like the rest of the kitchen, the dark cabinets, the tile countertops, it seemed suspended in time, never aging, as if waiting for something or someone to come back.

It was the same feeling he had had about the place when he first walked in just a few months before. And the same feeling he had had when he first saw the old ranch from a distance five or six years before that. The place resonated with him. It drew him. He had gotten into the habit of timing it when he drove past on his frequent jaunts to the polo club in Indio so that he could slow down just enough to look through the gate between the oleanders and see the house, on the low rise, back maybe a quarter mile from the road. There was an old wooden sign that someone has hung on the gallus gate and the sign read: "Valley Ranch" but that made as much sense as anything else about the place. There was never anyone around, not even at night, and no lights, and he didn't know anyone who knew who owned it. So it became his own private thing, looking at it as he drove by.

After he came out on top in his last arbitration with WGA at the beginning of the polo season last November, he had suddenly found himself with enough money for a down payment on something, and he and his long-time girlfriend Alexis had begun to spend Saturday afternoons after his game house hunting all over the desert near the polo club. He knew he wanted to live there. Alexis was happy in Beverly Hills and so they found nothing, by mutual understanding. Places were either too old or run down or too Palm Springs cum Rancho Mirage cum golf course kitchy. Then, back in March, when he had all but given up on finding anything they liked, he and the dog had driven down from L.A. on a whim on an off day, a Monday, when there was no polo. The dog was stretched out in the back of his silver '71 SEL, and when he rounded the corner at Jefferson the "For Sale" sign was the first thing he saw even though it was half a mile away. Morgan hit the brakes and the dog almost slid off the back seat and gave him a baleful stare but by noon man and dog were prowling through the house with a realtor.

There was about the place the sense of graceful age, the feeling of long-forgotten stories, and all of it, the views of the mountains especially, reminded him of Montana, of home. Not the true appearance of it, of course, but the sense of it. When he left he couldn't get it out of his mind, as if it had become a new lover.

Alexis was in Las Vegas at some kind of fashion show and he told her about it that night when they spoke on the phone and when she came back he brought her down and they made an offer that weekend, and it was in escrow by the following Monday.

The place hadn't been lived in for a few years. It had been owned by a restaurateur from L.A. and he had had cosmetic work done to it, tile work mainly, and he had updated the bathroom and the kitchen in the main house, laid in the Mexican pavers throughout. And then, suddenly, he moved back to the city and as far as anyone knew he had never been back and no one knew why.

Morgan couldn't wait to move in, and he had finally moved in just a few weeks before, in late April, when Alexis was gone again, this time to Europe on a buying trip. Since then he had been there with only the big dog and the black cat for company and he had never felt anything but comfortable there by himself and at peace. Except for the guesthouse. It always seemed chilly in there somehow and he found himself looking for reasons to stay out of there.

He snicked the beertops off and handed a bottle to Amado and the two of them went outside and sat on the rocks that rimmed the Jacuzzi. Obviously a city person, the previous owner had gone to great expense to truck in some granite rocks and cluster them between the spa and the front door of the bunkhouse not realizing how much rattlesnakes loved cool granite rocks near water. They had already killed a four-footer in the oleanders near the garage and it was only May. There would be snakes around until at least July.

Not far from them, at the corner of the bunkhouse, birds covered the feeder and where they sat they could just hear the hum of the pool pump. Somewhere in the not-too-far distance, a tractor worked and now and then the scent of freshly cut grass came to them. The mountains seemed etched in the clear air and the sky was an achingly beautiful cerulean blue. The very gentlest of breezes moved the tops of the four tall date palms that surrounded the pool and the movement of the fronds produced an almost imperceptible hissing sound like some kind of beaded curtain being gently moved across a beckoning door.

"Funny place this is, *amigo*." Morgan said, finally. "It always feels cold in here." He indicated the bunkhouse with his head.

Amado started to say something, thought better of it, then started again. "This bunkhouse, *amigo, es muy extraño lugar.* Since I first come here I know it. When I wait for you the other day, I hit some pool balls. I alone, and I hear voices from the bedroom."

"You sure?"

"I sure."

"English or Español?"

"English, I sure."

"Women or men?"

"Both, I think. But I don't think anyone is here and so I walk in. And nobody is here." He cast his black eyes to the heavens and felt of the heavy gold St. Christopher medal he always wore. .

"What else?" Amado was quiet. "C'mon, don't give me that *feo, fuerte*, formal stuff. I know you well enough to know that something else is on your mind. What else?"

"Breathing. I hear breathing when I in here myself. And Connie say she hear things once in a while."

"The cleaning lady? What did she hear?"

"Breathing, too."

"And, what else?"

"She say that last week she put something down in one room and she go out of the room and when she come back it moved."

"Drugs, right? She takes drugs." Morgan laughed. "And I thought we finally found a good cleaning lady."

"I no think so. She no take *drogas*."

"So what do you tell her?"

"*Nada*, Nikko. That *cabrona* would be out of here so fast. And then you'd never get her back in. And that kind of stuff, she tell all her *amigas*, and no one want to clean here."

Amado was half Mexican and half Indian, Yaqui, or Mayan, or something close. He didn't know. All he knew was he was part Indian, "*indio*", he called himself. His skin was the color of oxblood loafers, smooth and unlined although he was at least in his late 30's. He tended to be overweight but even with it he moved with the grace of a natural horseman. His father, so he always said, had been a *curandero*, a healer, and one day he had sat Amado down and told him he was going on a long journey and he wouldn't be back and he wasn't. Amado was expected to follow in his father's footsteps but his love for horses had been even stronger than the love for his father and when he was 16 he left and went over the border to the U.S. by himself, the dangerous San Ysidro route. After that he never went back but he sent money regularly every month to his mother and his brothers and his sisters.

"So what are you telling me?"

"No se."

"What d'ya mean 'you don't know.' You're tellin' me the bunkhouse has *espiritus*?"

"*No se...*" he held up a hand and shrugged and rolled his black eyes. "*pero...es possible.*"

The way he spoke about it, the ease with which he discussed it, was beyond the experience of Morgan and he listened curiously, disbelieving. Amado had worked for him for almost ten years, worked closely with him on the horses, and yet Morgan was constantly surprised at how little he knew about the Mexican.

"You don't actually believe in that stuff, do you?"

Amado tipped the Corona back and took a long pull. My *abuelo*, you know, my grandpapa, die when I was maybe 10, or 11. He always like me, and everyone say I was his *favorito*, his favorite. He always tell me stories about the Norte. He no want me to come here. Then after he die, I wake up late one night and there was my *abuelo* standing by my bed. He wear the same *campesino* clothes, the white guayabera he buried in, and he was say something to me. His lips were moving but I don' hear nothing. And then, after a while, he left." He was quiet.

"What happened then?"

"The next night my *abuelo* come back. This time I hear him and he say me don' go to the *Norte*. I tol' my mother and she told my *tia* and she sprinkle some holy water And then my *abuelo*, he never come back." He sighed.

"You weren't happy about that."

"No. I love my *abuelo*."

For Amado there was almost no difference between alive and dead. He loved the old man and that was enough. He hadn't been frightened but he was absolutely sure it was real and he was just as sure it was real sitting in the sun outside Morgan's bunkhouse 20 years later as he had been then, in the half-light of the small bedroom with the dirt floor in the tiny house outside of Guanajuato, in the mountains near Guadalajara, where he had been born.

But Morgan wasn't. "Garbage." he said with finality until he saw the crestfallen look on Amado's face and then he added: "Garbage for me, anyway. You're an Indian, maybe even a *curandero*. You can believe anything you want. But for me...*basura*...*garbage*." Morgan drained the last of the Corona, underhanded it into the garbage can, and got to his feet. All the same, there were some things that he had begun to think about as Amado had been talking, things that he had passed off or ignored or failed to acknowledge like the lights in the bunkhouse that had come on when no one was in there and the water that he had found running one morning in the bunkhouse kitchen when it had been locked all night and he felt just then as if he were standing in front of a door that he didn't want to open but that he couldn't avoid just trying the handle anyway, just to see what would happen.

It was not an unfamiliar feeling. The times he had known it before he had shook it off and had invariably been sorry. But in spite of that he shook it off again. Too long in the desert, maybe, he was used to things not making too much sense. Besides, it was too nice a day to think about that right then. "What kind of help you need?" He asked the Mexican.

"I need your pickup. We need bran and couple bags of 4-way and Juan is using the truck." The horse community that had grown up around the polo club was run, for the most part, by Hispanics, *Latinos*, Mexicans, Argentines, Chileans, Guatemalans, he was never sure what to call them. They formed a close-knit community that worked together during the day and partied together during the night and shared cars in a sort of third world motor pool wherein anyone could take anything that ran and had keys in it. Some, the unregistered ones, could not be taken off the club property, at least not during the day, but for local runs it was one for all. It worked, until someone needed a pickup and there was nothing around.

They called themselves *caballerangos* or *peticeros*, words that defied translation but implied someone who cared for the spiritual as well as the physical needs of horses, and they spoke a language that had roots in Spanish. It was not the Castilian Spanish of Spain, but a bastardized amalgam of English, Spanish, and South American they used, and it worked most of the time except that sometimes the Argies couldn't make themselves understood to the Mexicans and the Mexicans couldn't make themselves understood to the *anglos*, the *Norte Americanos*. More than anything, they used the language as a curtain to enable them to retreat into a world from which most of the *anglo* community was excluded.

Morgan was an exception.

For years they had watched him, watched how he worked his horses. He rode like one of them except he rode straight up where they tended to slouch with their legs forward. They had watched as he worked his green horses and had picked him up off the ground riding horses that most of the other polo players wouldn't have gotten on and they had seen the horses that he had made and they knew he was different, a *caballerango*, the ultimate compliment, a horseman. He wasn't a soft touch, but he was always ready with a car or a few bucks that he never seemed to want back, not at all like the Mexican *tiburones* from *la familia* that always charged heavy interest. There grew a bond between them and cautiously at first they invited him to their fiestas and *asados* and their *baptismos* and into their baroque churches in Coachella and slowly he became someone they trusted. They veil of invisibility they dropped over themselves when an *anglo* came around didn't drop around him.

"Sure." Morgan extracted his keys from the back pocket of his jeans and flipped them in a long, lofting arc. Amado raised his eyebrows. "You come?"

"*Porque no?* I'm finished writing for the day." Actually it seemed to him that he had been finished writing for some time now. Sure, he had no problems with the scripts and the contract work he had, the stuff that paid the bills, but he had been unable to budge at all on the book. He had been stuck on it for years. The book, it had become "THE BOOK," in caps as he came to think about it, had gradually become one of the more important things in his life. Too many unresolved issues, he thought, too many things that he couldn't look at even though most of a lifetime had passed.

There was the book he had written 20 years before, BULLETPROOF he called it, when he had first gotten out of the army and he could still smell the jungle on the fatigues that hung in his clothes closet, but that had been easy and he had sold that and the script for it so quickly he thought there was nothing to it. He always figured there was time for the other book that burned in him but now he was beginning to think that time was running out and the harder he tried to reach down and dig it out, the deeper it seemed to retreat. "Yeah, I'm comin'."

He whistled the dog into the main house, shut down the computer in his office, settled his gray Resistol on his head and twisted the deadbolts to make sure the doors were locked. Then he walked down the long drive and waited at the gate while the Mexican turned the once-silver-and-and-now-grey Ford pickup around and drove out the gate. The last thing Morgan did was swing the gate shut, pass the chain around the upright, and lock it. Then he climbed into the truckcab.

They rode in silence east down 50th. The road stretched ahead, die-straight, past horse pastures and groves of date palms that towered 70 feet or more, their heads glittering in golden sun and their bases wreathed in perpetual darkness and dark shadows and gloom that no one broke except the date workers and then only a few times a year and then only armed with machetes against the rattlers and whatever else lurked there. They passed the polo club after a few minutes but with the season winding down and the days growing warmer the games took place mostly in the morning and at this hour the huge fields, the endless expanses of green grass, seemed to stretch to a horizon broken only by heat shimmers and an occasional dust devil that swirled along the dirt exercise track like a whirling dervish from the Arabian nights.

A little further and houses appeared, some little more than one story, one room shacks with parts of cars and parts of toys scattered around the front and no one visible in the heat, no children, no old ones, like some kind of surreal post-world war III scenario. It was like they were entering another country.

Indio was the county seat of the east end of the Coachella Valley, the ancient sea bed that stretched from Palm Springs in the west to Thermal and Mecca and the mysterious Salton Sea in the east, but once off the main east-west highway the influence of the self-consciously pretentious court house and city hall and jail fell away and it was Mexico as far as the grooms were concerned. "Mexico," they would say, "If I wanted to live in Mexico I would have stayed home." Amado's friends and cousins, *primos*, he called them sometimes, Angel and Juan and Borrego agreed, shaking their heads disdainfully. Amado seemed to have an endless extended family of "cousins."

Coachella, the next town to the east, blended seamlessly

into Indio on one side and Thermal on the other. It had changed little during most of the century, and it was still a cowboy town complete with raised wooden sidewalks and storefront businesses and dusty streets and if there would have been a shootout one day at lunchtime, two men facing each other in the middle of the street when the taco shops and the restaurants that advertised "*Comida China*," Chinese food, had been full, no one would have been at all surprised. They would merely have shrugged, and moved off.

They drove in near the front of the feed store that was a converted gas station, dodging potholes and pieces of asphalt, and they parked in the shade of the pressed tin roof that sheltered the concrete islands where the pumps once stood guard. "Tijuana." Amado said, clucking like a disapproving hen. "*Chinga* TJ." He and Amado humped the 50 pound sacks into the back of the truck and headed back in the direction of the club.

Morgan's eight horses were stabled near the front and they picked up their heads as soon as the pickup rounded the oleanders. Macarena, the big chestnut mare noticed them first and nickered and the rest stopped foraging and watched the men unload the sacks.

They were a team in the true sense, all ten of them, eight horses and two men. They were dependent upon each other for the most basic elements of their existence — the horses for food and water and exercise, and the men for sustenance of a far different but perhaps more compelling sort. Morgan believed them to be rare creatures that God had put on earth in a moment of infinite kindness and wisdom — proof, he often said, that God loved man and wanted him to be happy — and he and the Mexican looked on themselves as caretakers of those creatures and, on a good day, possessed of the merest understanding of that divine purpose. From the time he was a kid they seemed so beautiful to him it made his eyes hurt just to look at them and when he looked away even now there were times when he wasn't sure he hadn't just imagined them, that he had conjured them out of his imagination, out of the books he read as a kid, about the Arabian Nights, and that they didn't exist in flesh and blood at all.

He knew the Mexican felt that way, but he locked it down deep, behind hundreds of years of impassive denial. One night, years before, when Amado had first begun to work for Morgan, the writer had come back to the barn after midnight, unable to sleep, and had found Amado asleep in one of the white plastic chairs, stocking feet propped on a saddle. After a while, he admitted to an argument with his live-in and after another long while he finally admitted to Morgan that he had come back to the barn so the horses could comfort him and Morgan nodded, and as was his nature, said nothing more about it. Neither ever mentioned it again.

Over the years he had bred a few horses and bought many more and rode them from green horses, trained them, and turned them into polo ponies, made horses, as the players put it. Amado had been right there. He had sold some, some for good prices, so that he and the Mexican enjoyed a reputation in the polo world of turning out good ponies. It was the ultimate compliment to their collaboration. But beyond that, and in spite of all the time they spent together, they shared little else.

Morgan's grandfather had been born in Eastern Europe and when he was barely old enough had signed on as a mercenary in the Austrian cavalry. He had fought in several small skirmishes, anachronisms even in those days, and had been shot off his horse and then decorated for bravery when he remounted and when Morgan heard the story he always figured that's where his stubborn trait came from.

After the fighting Morgan's grandfather had taken his family and moved to the United States, and wound up, for some reason even he hadn't known, in western Montana, Dillon, South of Butte. Morgan adored him and absorbed his love for the great animals and believed his grandfather when the old man told him that the soul of the horse could only be known in battle. When he was young, Morgan believed that the closest he would ever come to that was working cattle. But then, years later, when he found polo, he discovered the truth of the ancient game, the essential secret of it, that everyone who ever played from the cavalrymen of Alexander the Great to Winston Churchill to Cecil Smith and Memo Gracida had known, that it was the finest thing a man and horse could do together. There was a wild freedom about it, a controlled mayhem that in truth could only have been duplicated in battle and it was then, when he played, and only then that his eternally restless spirit was stilled. From his first scrimmage he was hooked.

Macarena was in the pen nearest the tackroom, the one they reserved for his best horse, and Morgan folded himself through the pipe rails and walked up to her. He had almost sold her a year before during a time when he was desperate for money but the sale fell through and even though he was out of money for a while longer he knew it was the best thing that had ever happened to his polo and one of the best things that had ever happened to him. He bent over and ran his hands over her lower legs. There was the merest trace of thickening on the left front where she had been injured the season before. While he did that he talked to her softly and called her "Diva" and whispered to her that she was as fast as the wind and that she had the agility of a prima ballerina and that if they managed to get into the Finals of his tournament on Sunday that she would be his fourth chukker horse and maybe his sixth and that she should sleep soundly and rest up. She arched her great neck over his back and kept it there until he stood up.

"You want to ride?" Amado asked from his perch on a chair in the sun. He had been waiting for Morgan to emerge from the stall.

"Yeah, but...I have to meet the painter at the house and give him a check." The painter had actually finished painting the inside of the bunkhouse the day before but had misconnected with Morgan. Now he was due at 4PM and Morgan wanted him to talk with him about some other work.

"...but it shouldn't take long. I'll be back around 5. How 'bout I take *Perla Negra* and hit a few balls? I've got to be up in L.A. tomorrow so I can't ride in the morning."

"And the Finals are Sunday. *Recuerdas?* "

"As if I could forget..."

Amado dropped him at the front gate and took the truck back to the club and Morgan went up to the house and let the dog out and the two of them walked the perimeter of the ranch again, the man with a careful eye on the dog, calling him out from under the oleanders when he went in too far. He had already begun to hear the rattlesnake stories. Amado had killed one in the back of the stables the week before and Borrego had killed one behind the cantina at the club just the other day. The warm weather brought them out, and the thick underbrush with shade and sprinklers was a natural snake magnet. The dog had never been bitten, but Morgan knew of a dog that belonged to an English player, an Australian shepherd named Tom, that had been hit by a six footer and had been dead by time they got him to the vet.

The painter was late as usual and when he showed, Morgan saw again that the man fulfilled the criteria of his long-dead grand uncle who had been a housepainter and had always told him never to hire a painter who showed up in clean clothes. The man's name was Felix and he looked to be in his 70's, thin weight hair over a thin, pinched *anglo* face. He managed a wry grin when Morgan handed over the check. "Do you have time to look at the bathroom in the main house and give me a quote on a new paint job?"

The painter shook his head as he tucked the check in his shirt pocket. "Not a chance." He shook his head again and started to walk toward his car but after a few steps then turned back with a deep sigh. "This place is haunted, ya know."

"Sure, and I'm William Jefferson Clinton."

"Ya might be, for all I know. Still don't want the job."

"How do you know? That it's haunted, I mean?"

"It's cold in that bunkhouse. Not a real cold, ya know, a damp cold, the kind you never get in the desert, and the whole time I'm paintin' in the back I'm hearin' a knocking in the wall. Not a tappin', believe me, a knockin'. And when I go over to get a good look, the knockin' stops. Just like that. And when I painted in the back bedroom, this face is in front of me." He held his right hand at arms' length, palm toward his face. "Not an evil face, a pleasant face. Maybe a woman, but it's there, plain as day. So if it's all the same with you, I'll pass on the main house."

"You can't be serious."

"'bout as serious as a heart attack."

"Why did you stay?"

"Once I start a job, that's it. I finish it, ya know. But I don't want it again."

"And you think…?"

"No, I know. So…sorry. Hope you find someone."

After the painter left, Morgan walked in to the bunkhouse and sat on the stone ledge in front of the massive fireplace and let himself feel the damp cold. Softly, like a whisper, he became aware once again of the scent of lavender and it swirled around him, warm, sensuous, and he let himself go into it and it was oddly soothing and comforting. He leaned back and closed his eyes and he remained there what seemed a while until the phone rang. The cordless handset wasn't on the phone base and he searched for it for moment before seeing it on the pool table.

"Mister Morgan, this is Delores." It was the decorator he had hired, the chubby one in her 50's from Palm Desert who still wore Go-Go boots and came out with her white Cockatiel and who Amado had quickly christened "Gordita," the fat one. She was an unlikely person for Morgan to hire but she had found him the painter and she was good for deals on furniture and she was well-recommended and he hated to think about details like that. When she spoke, she ended every sentence with an upward inflection of her voice, as if she was asking a question. "Mister Morgan, I have sort of a strange request."

"Yes?"

"I have a friend. She's a psychic and she lives in La Quinta and she passes your ranch all the time and she asked me if she could come by and look around." Her voice up-inflected. "Do you think that's okay?"

Synchronicity was one thing, but this, he decided, was more than that. He felt the hair tingle on his neck.

"Why? Why would she want to come in here?"

"Now I don't rightly know. She said she just felt something up there was calling her."

"Calling her." He repeated, his voice flat and soft and very skeptical. "Right...something is calling her. What do you mean?"

"Like I said, I don't know. Look, is it alright?"

"When? I mean, sure."

"Sometime during the week."

There was a time when he would have just laughed at himself and at Delores but now, for some reason, he found himself saying: "Sure, why not?...but have her call first, though. I'll be up in L.A. tomorrow."

He hit the disconnect on the handset and stared at it and tried to go back to where he had been but the lavender scent was gone and after a while he gave up and let himself back into the main house.

4

June 1933

The Mexican watched without emotion as the back of her head exploded, blood, brains, hair sheeting the window and the wall behind her with a red curtain and she slumped with the softest sighing of her last breath. She lay now on the ground at his feet, her dress hiked up, exposing her long legs, revealing the hair on her pubic mound. Yet even in the midst of all the gore, the vulgarity of death, a soft, unspoiled sweetness lingered around her and it affected him in a way that he could not express.

He had to do it, had to kill her, and quickly. She was screaming and tearing at the window in the bedroom, trying to escape, her hands bleeding where the nails had torn off on the wooden casement.

She had been beautiful. Perhaps, he thought, if there had been time…but he knew the patron was on his way, would be there in less than a half hour, in fact. He had wasted all that time looking for the ranch, and now he had to rush. He would have liked to play with her for a while before he killed her, would have liked to make her wish, even, for death, but he knew in some primal place that would have been out of the question as well. He holstered his gun and grinned a yellow-toothed grin and licked his lips. Suddenly he bent down and took the neck of her dress in his hands and ripped it down the front, all the way down in one motion. Mierda. *Her body made him catch the breath in his throat. Her breasts were beautiful, full, the areolae slightly ruddy-dark as he knew they would be.* Que lastima.

Still, it was a job. He would get his five hundred from the patron in a few minutes. Then he could send some money back to Guanajuato so his madre would think him successful and he'd have something left over in his pocket again.

Reluctantly he left her and walked out the door, back to where the dead gabacho *lay. Flies were already covering the lawyer's mortal wounds, their buzzing a tuneless hum, and he stepped over the body and went around to the back of the house. Just as Ramirez had said, there was a perfect area to bury them, a small orchid tree in front of a small, two horse barn. He retrieved a long-handled rusty shovel from his trunk, propped it against his car, and then he removed his jacket and then his tie. And then, as if packing a suitcase or preparing for a trip, he folded the jacket neatly, once, twice, and then placed it on the front seat of the Ford and the tie on top. He shrugged out of the bulky shoulder holster, added it to the pile, and tucked the murder weapon into his belt.*

In the perfect stillness of the afternoon, the shovel made a soft, chuffing sound but as soon as he got through the first few inches the sandy soil yielded quickly and before long he had something that resembled a pit in front of him, roughly rectangular, about three or four feet deep. He stepped back with a satisfied expression and pulled his shirt out of his pants to get cooler, and fanned himself with his shirttails.

Now came the part he dreaded.

The lawyer was a big man, about six feet tall. He wasn't fat, but he had to weigh about 190 pounds, and the Mexican went to the trunk of his car and stared at the contents aimlessly for a second until he saw a thick cotton rope. With this he roped the lawyer's legs together, the same way he used to tie the legs of the calves together when he roped them as a young man in Jalisco, years ago, before he had come north and thrown in with the patron. And then, by alternately pulling on the legs and pushing and pulling, he manhandled the body down the slight incline to the hole beneath the tree, and then he rolled the body over. It landed on its side hard, and the dead lungs exhaled the air they had contained with a sound that startled him and he noticed off-handedly that most of the man's back was the consistency of salsa, the shirt blown back. He was really sweating now, his own shirt a wet, dirty rag.

The girl bothered him more than he anticipated. She wasn't that big and he tried at first to carry her but stumbled badly, unnerved by how close his face was to her body. He tried to pull her by her legs but what was left of her dress wound up around her shoulders so he settled on tying her arms together over her head and pulling her that way. The smear of blood that he left was as wide as the stripe on a highway, and about as hard to ignore. The patron would be angry. The ranch belonged to Ramirez, the patron's driver, and he was not to have left any traces. Even Ramirez was not to have known about the lawyer, not to mention the girl.

When he rolled the girl's body on top of the lawyer, he stepped back and took up the shovel and then he paused, his eye attracted by the silver gleam of a brooch encrusted with stones in the shape of an initial on the left side of the girl's dress. It looked like it could be expensive. He could put it in his pocket and sell it to Ramos later for a couple of dollars, depending on the mood of the fat moneylender.

He tore it off what was left of her dress and was about to put it in his pocket when he heard the sound of the car.

5

1996

To the south the highest peaks of Santa Rosa had just
begun to turn a bright orange-red in the light of the not-yet-
visible sun while the Indio Hills to the north slowly emerged
from the darkness, shedding shadows and secrets like so
many outgrown skins. Ahead to the west the massive bulk of
San Gorgonio loomed, at its top the remains of the winter's
snow reflected an otherworldly crimson from the night's low
clouds that even as he watched thinned and disappeared. So
immense was the scale, so overwhelming the perspective, he
could almost hear the world turning on some huge, grinding
axis as the line of sunlight crept down the mountains one after
another and oozed across the dead sea bed.

He drove easily, casually, one hand on the wheel,
mesmerized as always by the sheer beauty of the mountains.

The magic ended abruptly when the sun cleared the
horizon behind him and the light went flat and bright and
only then did he take a sip of his coffee and begin to scan
across the radio dial, trying to pick up a traffic report on an

L.A. station and not having much luck still two hours out. The big dog was asleep stretched across the back seat, the speedometer soldered at 85, and the coffee still warm. All in all, not a bad start to the day.

The radio volume from KFI in Los Angeles rose and fell as they passed electrical wires and bored through overpasses, teasing, but stronger, always stronger, the closer he got. It was as if he was circling a vortex and he was going down into it.

He was driving the silver car, the SEL that he had acquired from another polo player ten years before, just before the man disappeared. It was said the man was a drug dealer but he was a 2-goal player with some nice horses and he paid his bills with cash that he took out of an elegant Louis Vuitton attaché case so no one really cared and no one checked too closely. Since Morgan had moved to the desert full time the car mostly sat covered in the garage and when he rolled it out now it was almost exclusively for trips to the city.

He was dressed in his meeting gear, his camouflage, as he thought of it, the clothes that enabled him to move around the industry and blend in — Cole-Haan loafers, pressed dark-gray slacks, and black t-shirt. His Zegna blazer was neatly folded in the trunk next to the black boots and the jeans and the fringed buckskin leather jacket and new tan Resistol cowboy hat that he planned to change into as soon as he could. Next to him, on the floor on the passenger's side lay his slim leather dispatch case, in it his latest creation that he envisioned as a vehicle for someone like Keanu Reeves or Nicholas Cage, a cerebral Robert Ludlum-type plot. Not WAR AND PEACE, to be sure, but if he could get it picked up it would keep him in mortgage money and hay money and allow him to keep playing polo for a while longer. Perfectly worthy goals.

It had been a quiet night but for the dream. He hadn't remembered it at first but after he had been up for a while it came to his mind and since then he had kept turning to it, a tongue probing a missing tooth, experiencing it over and over again against his will until he could recall every detail with crystal clarity.

In the dream he had been walking alone through a wooded area on the side of a steep hill covered with rocks. The trees were stunted, bare of leaves, deformed, and he was looking around and picking his steps carefully when he noticed a cougar crouched near a rock. At first he was certain that he was the intended prey but after an anxious moment he realized the cougar was riveted on a small wild boar. Tail quivering, the cougar charged with a great roar and took the boar in his teeth and claws but as the boar struggled, screaming, the cougar lost his footing and cougar and boar began to roll down the hill. The hill grew steeper as they rolled faster and faster, shale, rocks, twigs, tumbling and each creature unable to stop the plunge. A large red-tail hawk or an eagle soaring on a thermal above saw the struggle and swooped down and sank its talons into the still struggling boar and with a great flapping of wings lifted off. Still the cougar held on, refusing to let go though heading for certain doom. As he watched they grew smaller and smaller in the distance until they disappeared, hawk, boar, and cougar.

The dream was the reason for the vague sense of dread he noticed when he had awakened and when he remembered it he tried to place himself in it again, symbolically trying each character on for size, cougar, boar, and hawk, until he realized, at last, that he could be, indeed had been, all of them at different times.

But which was he now?

He had almost put the experiences of the day before out of his mind by the time that he began to prepare his coffee that morning. Measuring the beans into the grinder, counting half-awake spoonfuls, his back to the kitchen and the small family room beyond, he caught the movement almost without realizing what he was seeing. On one corner of one of his stereo speakers, a single silver candle holder began to move slowly from one side to the other. It was so subtle that for a moment he wasn't sure that it had happened, a trick of the light, or the dog bumping against the speaker. Maybe one of the constant earth movements that were forever rippling through the Valley, down through the San Jacinto fault.

He stopped grinding, not believing what he had seen, aware suddenly of the profound silence that seemed to suck the air out of the kitchen as he walked over to the speaker. It was a Paradigm tower speaker, black all over, one of a pair that he had purchased not long before and as he stood there looking down at the top of it he saw in the fine layer of dust the unmistakable track of where it had moved. Bullshit, he thought, and he moved it back.

He finished making the coffee and just before he walked out the front door about a half hour later he glanced over at the speaker top again. The candle was back in its new location and now he wondered if he had moved it back when it happened the first time or if he had just meant to move it back and had gotten distracted. Parlor tricks, he sniffed.

Now, in the bright sunlight, it was easy to rationalize. Max must have walked by and banged against the speaker and he meant to move it back and forgot. Simple. He quit obsessing over traffic reports and dialed up KUSC on the car radio. They were playing a Chopin piece and he immersed his thoughts in that and tried to put everything else out of his mind.

From the west side of Kellogg Hill, L.A. shimmered in the distance like the towers of Camelot and it all appeared so easy and beautiful and controllable from here, like the Rhine maiden's song must have seemed to the men who were ultimately lured to their doom. He had turned his back on living in L.A. long before buying the ranch but he needed the contacts there and the undercurrent of creative energy that even the dickheads in the industry could not eradicate. Bottom line it was the need for work that drew him back over and over again so that he had formed a push-pull love-hate relationship with it all, the city, Hollywood, the industry. He managed a smile. Sutton's Law it was. For sure.

He picked up the cell phone and dialed the familiar number and Alexis answered on the second ring with a barely awake "Hello?"

"Glad you're on your feet," he teased, but he felt his heart leap when he heard her voice. "When did you get in?"

"'bout 11 last night. And I'm not on my feet. I would have called you but I knew you'd be asleep. It's good to hear your voice. Are you okay?"

"Always. I'll be near the Boutique in a little over an hour. You have time for coffee?"

"The corporate types are going to be around until noon. They're going to pounce while I'm still jet-lagging. You don't have to go right back, do you?"

"It's your lucky day. I'm meeting Charlie at The Grill at noon, it'll take about two hours to dump him, and I'll come over to your shop then. If you're nice, we can do dinner and if you're extra good I'll spend the night."

"You have your nerve. You must think I'm a wanton woman."

"I know you are."

"Only for you, cowboy, only for you. You know I'm a sucker for country boys."

"Good to have you back, Sunshine."

"Good to be back, cowboy. It is sooo good to be back."

"Even with all of Paris at your feet?"

"Even with my perfect room at the Lancaster complete with an endless supply of chilled Veuve. Can't wait to see you."

Tucked away on Dayton off Rodeo in Beverly Hills behind an unpretentious sign and an even more unpretentious door, The Grill exuded a timeless quality, an essence that reeked of deals made and broken, of dreams created out of whole cloth and destroyed by an unreturned phone call, elements as strong in their own way as the rich smells that flowed from the kitchen in a steady stream. For every consummated deal, there were scores who had waited in vain for lunch partners who never showed. It was the kind of place where old-time actors and agents and producers rubbed luncheon elbows with young up-and-comers, and where you could see actors like Warren Beatty and Robert Wagner tucked away in the snug booths that lined the walls along with news anchors and starlets, all of them oblivious to the tourists that nudged each other knowledgeably and gawked at them from the streets as they walked in and out.

Morgan's agent, Charlie Margolis, had set up the meeting with someone from New Line, and Morgan had specified The Grill, knowing that it was just down the street from Alexis and that it was a chance to stick his agent for lunch and that was something Morgan always looked forward to with great anticipation. He figured over the years Margolis had made enough money from him.

It was a little early for the peak crowd when Morgan left the car and the dog with the valet. He paused at the door to give his eyes a chance to accustom themselves to the low light, caught the attention of the maitre d', asked for Margolis, and was shown to the booth they were already settled in toward the back of the long room. Sharon Stone and someone who could have been a producer were visible over the partition two booths away, and Morgan looked and looked away, so aware he was of invading their space. A strange place, this L.A., he thought for the bazillianth time. He had been in the town for almost 20 years, had enjoyed a degree of success, had worked with and played polo with more celebrities that he could have ever remembered, and there was still something of the voyeur that remained, something that looked at people like Sharon Stone and thought "celebrity". No matter where you were in the scheme of things, the celebrities were special, atop the great pyramid of publicists, stylists, writers, directors, the engines that propelled the shiny toy shop called Hollywood, that allowed grownups to deal in fantasy. Everyone dignified it by calling it an industry, but in many ways it was still the senior class high school play and just as much fun. If, of course, you were in the production.

After introductions, Morgan ordered an iced tea and a Cobb Salad and before they were brought to the table he managed to run through a short pitch of his latest idea. The New Line producer might have been genuinely interested and Margolis might have been suitably pleased and Morgan walked out encouraged. Which, of course, meant nothing in his business except that he would be back in front of the computer in the morning. To a writer, he remembered with a wry grin, heaven and hell were the same except that in heaven they bought what you wrote.

He pulled the car around to the back of Giorgio Beverly Hills and parked next to the new red Mercedes C320 that belonged to Alexis. Max caught sight of it and wagged his tail and looked crestfallen when Morgan left him in the car with the windows carefully cracked. She was on the phone when he spotted her from the parking lot, her black Armani blazer and short black skirt and crisp white shirt perfect foils for the blond hair that fell softly around her classic face. A shoe dangled from a perfectly-shaped crossed leg, provocative for its total lack of guile or affectation, and she tapped a long yellow pencil on the blotter on her crowded desk. She was in her mid-30's, that marvelously magical age, her beauty no longer the endowment of unthinking youth but a triumph of diligence, effort, and breeding. The back door to the Boutique was open and he went up the back steps and entered her office and when he came around to the front of her she rose, still talking, gave him a quick kiss without missing a word, and held up two flawlessly manicured fingers. Not at all surprised at how she looked, he nevertheless marveled that she had flown in from Heathrow not 12 hours before and still could be so well turned out.

The Boutique had been remodeled two years before and behind its new, two story yellow-and-white façade it now enjoyed a status on Rodeo that it hadn't known since its early years and he knew it was in large part due to Alexis. It looked good to him but it always looked good to him and he knew he was as far out of his element as it was possible for a human to be and he was glad when she finally put the phone down. He went to her and she gave him a hug and squeezed his hand and he inhaled the essence of her. "Let's get out of here. Twelve hours back and I'm ready to go nuts."

"Looks really good here. You look really good here." And then he whispered: "But I think you'd look better out of those clothes."

She gave him a playful shove.

"Find anything exciting in Europe?"

"New designer. Two guys, in fact. In Paris. I'll tell you about it."

"I can't wait."

"No one likes a smart ass, you know. These guys are really talented. You'll see. I know you'll get it."

The minute they cleared the big glass Giorgio doors her demeanor morphed like a computer generated image. Corporate executive, international buyer, once out of the Boutique she became his girlfriend again and they walked close to each other, holding hands, arms pressed close, catching up. She had been in Europe for almost three weeks, Milan, Paris, London, and even though they had spoken several times a week, it felt to him as though she had come back from outer space.

They walked up Rodeo hand-in-hand. The fabled street, shopping destination of the world, was polished and shined up for spring, fresh flowers planted in the center divider and around the front of most of the stores. From Bvlgari to Harry Winston and Ralph Lauren to Hermes and Gucci, Rodeo was lined end to end with the choicest stores in the world. Tourists rubbed elbows with Beverly Hills matrons and rock stars, and producers and agents and wannabees and the celebs moved freely among them, their "people" close by, cell phones at their ear or at the ready. On the corner of Brighton a VIP TourBus was disgorging a load of Japanese tourists and they were lined up in front of Giorgio Armani endlessly snapping pictures.

She asked about Amado, and about Max, and about the horses by name, and he had to give her a detailed report on each one, how they were doing, and how each had played in the games the weekend before. As always she asked him who his best horse was and as always he answered Macarena. She asked about the ranch and he thought about telling her of the gunshots and the candle and the painter but thought better of it and wound up telling her nothing of the strange happenings. She had only seen the place once, on the afternoon he made the offer. There would be time enough.

"I'll be down on Friday night. But late."

"I think I'll be around. May even have dinner waiting for

you."

"For me?"

"Yeah. Lucky girl. Fact there's a party over at Amado's that night but I've already blown them off."

"You could go."

"Right. My one true love comes down to the ranch and I'm gonna take her to a party. How old you think I am?"

"Timeless, my love. Hey, we've got to look in here." Alexis said suddenly, stopping in front of the new Chanel Boutique. "They just remodeled this place and there's a replica of Coco's studio on the top floor that I really want to see."

They walked in, past the handbags and glass cases, and as they were passing the fragrance counter Morgan suddenly stopped, a look of absolute puzzlement on his face.

"What's the matter? You look like you've seen a ghost."

Interesting choice of words, he thought. For a vertiginous second he was transported back to the ranch, back to the bunkhouse and the damp cold and the back room. But all he said was: "What's that smell?"

"What smell? That's fragrance. Perfume. You know. Haven't I taught you anything?" She tried a laugh but with the way he looked it came out forced.

"But what kind?"

"Smells like a lavender base to me. It's one of the classic old fragrances."

"Is it popular now?"

"Not really. Hardly anyone wears it straight. They keep it here for historic value. It was really big in the 1930's. Why?"

"Because I've been smelling it back in the desert. A lot."

"You probably have been smelling some wild lavender. Did you look around?"

"All over. And I had Ray the *brujo* look for some as well when he was doing some gardening for me. There's nothing."

"Not to worry. When I get down, we'll look around together. Deal?"

"Deal."

"C'mon." She glanced at the petite gold watch on her wrist. "Walk me back to the Boutique, give me a half hour or so to finish my work and I'll meet you home."

The small apartment on Charleville felt like home in a way that had not yet happened at the ranch. It was a one bedroom with a den and he was not surprised to see that no evidence of suitcases or the detritus of a long business trip remained. That was her style and some things never changed. Max bounded in and looked for his water dish in the same spot and made a bee line for the patio as was his habit once he had satisfied his thirst. Morgan hadn't been there in almost a month and he was surprised in the way that the little place pulled at him but at the same time he knew what pulled him was not the place but the woman who lived in it.

She was as close to him as any woman had ever been. Their commitment to each other still surprised them both and the five years or so that they had been together had brought them even closer than most of the married couples they knew but that is as far as it had ever gone. They had both been married and for now that was enough. When he thought about it, Morgan felt sometimes that going any further would destroy what they had, as if it would somehow resurrect a past he would rather leave unexamined.

Alexis liked the desert and liked the animals and liked to ride. She was, in fact, a good natural rider and enjoyed being up on his polo ponies. Like a typical Taurus, when she was around she assumed the role of earth mother to the horses and Morgan freely surrendered those details of his life to her. But her job as buyer required her to be away for three or four months a year, and much of the time she was around she was involved with business in the city, and the corporate types that owned the Boutique were in and out of town and required hand-holding attention and the net result was that she wasn't around very much and lately hardly at all.

She was always going to spend more time in the desert but somehow, something always happened. At first, when he was still renting condos around the polo club for the season he had tried to entice her into quitting and moving down to the desert with him but after years had gone by and he realized that it would probably never happen he quit asking. When the ranch came on the market she was the first one he told about it and he only made an offer on it after she had seen the place. When the sale went through he even put her on the title.

He set his laptop on the kitchen counter and spent some time tweaking his current project but after a while he succumbed to the lure of the bed and he was asleep on top of the bedspread with the television on, the sound muted, when she finally came in two hours later. Traffic on the street was irregular, and the occasional car noise was barely perceptible so that it was the sound of water running in the shower that finally woke him. Her black suit was draped on the back of the chair in the corner of the bedroom and her white shirt hung from the knob on her closet door. He slipped out of his clothes and opened the bathroom door.

Steam filled the tidy bathroom and he could just make out a figure behind the glass-doored shower enclosure and a head of wet, blond hair. He slid the door and moved in. "This the Bates Motel?" he asked.

"Down the street."

"Sorry. Look, as long as I'm here…" and he held out a hand and she took it and was in his arms shivering, as close as she could get to him and he as close as he could get to her. Their kiss was long and wet and steamy and when they broke for air, her makeup and eyeliner and lipstick long gone, he looked closely at her. "You're gorgeous and I missed you like crazy and I'm just plain crazy in love with you."

She reached between his legs and circled his penis with her hand. "Is that a nightstick you're carryin', officer, or are you just glad to see me?" she said, in a fake Mae West drawl. He laughed and drew her close, a hand on each of her buttocks and she put his penis between her legs and he could feel the hot wetness of her hotter even than the steam and wetter than the water and he put his head on her nipple and ran his tongue around the tautness of it and touched her clitoris and she moaned and held on to him to keep from falling. And then she drew him inside of her and began to thrust against him and in a millisecond she came and he a moment later.

They threw some towels across the bed and he laid her across them and began to kiss her breasts again and she slowly began to touch his penis. When her nipples hardened, he moved his kisses down slowly, past her navel, past the mound, down between her legs, and he drew his tongue across her labia and around her clitoris and he marveled for the uncounted time that the wonder of their relationship was not in the newness of the sex but in the knowing what pleased her and the pleasure he got from the way she writhed beneath him. He was hard by the time she was ready and this time when he penetrated her he could feel all of the parts of her and he cupped a hand beneath each buttock and moved her strongly against him and he could feel her legs tight on the back of his thighs and her feet on the back of his calves and this time, after they came, they lay still, exhausted.

He was out the door in the morning, in the gray light of false dawn, having left a note that said "I love you" on top of the thermos of coffee he had made and filled and the sun was already almost two hand's breadth above the mountains when

53

he neared home.

He had been listening to KCLB and Tom Petty had just come on doing "Runnin' on a Dream" and the sound of his guitar was a counterpoint to the tires of the Mercedes as they slapped concrete at the top of the off ramp at Jefferson. There he was, looking forward and looking back again, Janus, sure of where he was going but wishing somehow that it could have been just be a little different this time and that he could have taken a little of what he left behind with him when he went.

6

As soon as he was off the freeway he let the window down on the driver's side and let the sense of the desert into his pores. He had missed it almost from the moment he left it, as if he was somehow incomplete away from there and altogether too vulnerable for the deficiency. There was a hypnotic sense about it, the way it immersed you against your will in a shadow world that pulsed to an alien, edgy rhythm, a sandy jungle. There was a sense that it functioned on its own terms just out of control and he sensed you accepted that or were pounded to pieces on it.

But perhaps more than anything it was the horses that drew him back. He could be away from them for only so long. They had always been his secret antidote to the world; had always been there and carried him through so much. They saved him when he was a kid, and saved his sanity after he came back from Central America when he had seen more than he ever wanted to remember and he knew, somehow, that he and they were pieces forever balanced in a cosmic enigma.

When he made his left onto 50th it was coming seven and

he went past the ranch with scarcely a glance and headed directly to the barn. Most days Amado would have had a set on the trail by now, riding one and leading three others, but this morning he had most of the tack spread out all over the small porch, saddles on the railings, and bridles and reins hanging from the j-hooks that were fastened to the rough 4 x 4 columns on the porch. The soft sound of Ranchero music surrounded him and the Mexican had a large pail with a bar of saddle soap and a small, well-used sponge and he followed the same routine on each piece, rinsing the sponge, squeezing it out, passing it across the bar of saddle soap a few times, and then massaging it onto the tack until it glowed as if from somewhere deep inside, the color of old mahogany or oiled teak. A Circle K coffee cup was close to his hand, sweet with lots of sugar and pale with creamer, and the crumbs of a *pan dulce* in a crumpled napkin.

"You been out already?" Morgan asked, unfolding himself from the Mercedes. He was in his jeans and boots and he wore a plaid shirt fastened at the neck and at the wrists and as he got out he retrieved his hat from the front seat where it had made the journey brim up, of course, so the luck wouldn't run out.

"No, I'm wait for you."

"I wasn't supposed to get back until noon."

"Que?"

"How'd you know I'd be back early?"

"*Inteligente.*" He smiled, tapping the side of his head with a finger.

"*Hoy usted un brujo?*"

"No..." He said, drawing the word out, suddenly self-conscious. "I no witch." Amado was uncomfortable with that in his own way and he looked down at what he was doing and deftly changed the subject. "*Tu estas listo, amigo?*"

"I was born ready."

The moment was lost in their banter and they split the eight horses evenly into two groups and with Morgan on Perla Negra and Amado on Guerrero they walked them out on the dirt road that ran along the edge of the polo fields and skirted Donegal Farms and Empire, and went on that way into the desert that lay on the other side of 52nd. The sun had only just begun to warm the air and pink up the mountains and in the long morning shadows it cast, the prints of coyotes and the tracks of the Sidewinders that had passed the night before stood out as if in relief, a hard reminder of who the lawful inhabitants were. Two red-tailed hawks soared not far away, catching thermals. Along the base of the mountains in the distance, the line that had been the level of the ancient sea bed was clearly visible. In the quiet, the horses took advantage of every bush that rustled or rabbit that scampered by to jump and flutter and blow through their noses in mock alarm and there was a constant rearranging of lead ropes and horses as they jockeyed for position like children on a recess from school, pushing and shoving and laying their ears back and taking half-serious nips at one another. Morgan rode erect, his legs close behind the shoulders of the horse the way he had ridden bareback as a kid, and it was the way Amado had come to ride from watching him so that even from a distance it was possible to tell him from most of the other pros who rode back in the saddle.

They were out that way for more than an hour cantering laps around the exercise track and when they got back Morgan was finally ready to sit down at his computer. There was time enough to tackle the project he had pitched in Beverly Hills. His sixth sense told him that was a done deal and there was not too much it would need to be in almost final condition. What he really wanted to do now was make some headway on

"THE BOOK." He had taken it out and put it away so many times during the last ten years he imagined he had been stuck on it forever. The story was simple enough, the outline sensible, the characters well-drawn, but try as he might the writing of it failed to ring true. Objectively he knew it was a tribute to his father, how the man had constructed his life, and the frustration he knew he had felt when his business partners looted the company and left him to take the rap. Morgan had buried it under memory for so long, denied it so well, that it was no longer accessible to him. All that was left of it were the defenses and not even he suspected they existed.

In moments of candor he admitted to himself that writing another book had become something of an obsession. The idea that he only had the ability to write one book in him nagged at him more than he liked to admit. He had no such trouble writing other things, and fixing scripts, and reworking dialog, and such, but on this it was like he had run into a wall and he knew that there would be no second book until he addressed the issues of his father.

When he had sat long enough without writing a word, he pushed back from the computer and went into the kitchen, popped the cap on a cold Corona, and then went outside and lit the propane grill he kept not far from the front door. The beer was gone when the grill was hot enough, and he threw a dozen of the long green Anaheim chiles on the grill and opened another one.

When the chiles had turned a purple brown on the heat, he roasted two small tomatoes, and then he put them in plastic bags to steam, and after a while he was able to slip their skins off and seed them, and when he had a pile on the carving board he chopped them carefully into small pieces and before long there was a decent pile on a Mexican plate that probably had enough lead in the glaze of it to poison an entire platoon of OSHA inspectors. He carefully added the herbs, the cilantro and oregano and marjoram, and then the olive oil and the cider vinegar and tasted it with his finger. It was something that Alexis loved, a salsa verde he had picked up in Santa Fe, from the owner of the Coyote Café. When he heard the phone ring he let the answering machine pick up and he eavesdropped on the message leaning against the jam at the door to his office. "Hi, darlin'," the voice said, and when he heard Alexis' voice he wiped his hands on a dish towel and lifted the handset, full of anticipation.

"Great. An obscene phone caller. I thought you had gotten over that." She laughed a rich, sultry, sensuous laugh. "What time you gettin' down anyway?" He couldn't help asking.

"That's what I'm calling about. I've been gone so long and the boutique is a mess and I've got some work to finish up and I called to see if you wouldn't mind if I came down in the morning. You wouldn't mind, would you." she crooned.

"No, I was trying to figure out how to tell you that I had a hot date tonight. You've solved the problem."

"Smartass. You know how much I wanted to come down."

"I don't know if you don't come down. C'mon…it's Friday night. Look, all that other stuff will wait until Monday, won't it? The boys are beginning to talk that maybe I'm weird."

"Well I'll vouch for you."

"No need. Look…come down tonight, leave Sunday night."

"I always say I'm going to and then I wind up staying until Monday morning. Really, I wouldn't be able to enjoy myself if I came down tonight. Please understand."

"I do. Of course I do. It was just…"

They stayed on the phone a few more minutes and before Alexis hung up, she asked: "What time do you play tomorrow?"

"Ten."

"I'll track you down at the club."

"You don't have to come to the game."

"I'll be at the game. It's not that I don't like to watch you play. It's just that…"

"…you've picked me up off one too many polo fields."

"I worry. I can't help it."

"It's okay, Sunshine. I understand. I'll see you *mañana*."

"Be careful."

The silence that surrounded the small office after he hung up was deeper even than it had been before she called, and the muted sounds that were the ranch, the well pump kicking on, the hissing of the air vent in the water holding tank, the occasional sound of a car or pickup going by on 50th, only served to point up to him how much he craved her company. He was perfectly content in his own company or with the horses or with Amado and the boys and some of the professional players, but when Alexis was around even the colors seemed brighter. He had felt it almost from the first when they started to go out and now, after all these years, nothing had changed.

He stashed the salsa verde in a plastic container, thinking how much he had been looking forward to seeing her. After a while he rounded up the dog and fed him and from the back of the house, outside the bedroom, he watched as the sun kissed the top of Eisenhower Peak. What was left of the beer grew warm in his hand.

There was an unopened bottle of Conmemorativo in the liquor cabinet, and he got it and tucked it under his arm, set the house alarm, and drove over to Amado's. When he turned onto the dirt road through the polo club, the short cut, the air had already darkened, and become still and filled with the sand that was stirred up every evening by the thousand or so horses that were stabled there and it sparkled when the light hit it just right like so many millions of sequins or diamonds.

Like many of the grooms, Amado lived in Coachella, not far from the club but at the Eastern end of the valley, near the border with Thermal, and it was particularly at night that the further East he drove, the farther back in time he went. Sidewalks, streetlights, traffic, all dropped away and before long all that was left was the velvetiness of the night broken here and there with the yellow glow of fly-specked porchlights and it felt like driving the back streets of Cabo or of Mazatlan or Las Mochas, the engine noise echoing off the unseen houses and the unseen palm trees. At last he made a right onto Highway 86 and after a few moments, a left at the Rancho Grande Market, its lights a landmark in the darkness. Couples strolled along the sides of the darkened road, shapes, and there were groups of young boys, *cholos*-in-training, and here and there a young mother and father pushed a stroller.

The houses were set low and close here, most of them attached units, like old motels except that they had never been built as motels but as cheap residences for the undocumented workers, the *mojados*, the wetbacks that worked the grape crops and the citrus and the dates many years ago. This was the other side of the desert, the side away from the countless golf courses and exclusive gated communities, where there was no Jensen's Market or El Paseo Drive.

There were no streetsigns and no numbers and no mailboxes, and Morgan idled the pickup along until at last he glimpsed the glow of a fire at the far end of an alley on his left and he could see cars that were familiar and then he pulled in and wedged the truck between Juan's lifted Ford pickup and Pepe's rebuilt Camaro with the headliner that sagged like the top of an ancient prairie schooner. The boys, grooms and players, most of them, were gathered around the fire, some standing, some hunkered down on their bootheels. A few loitered along the chain link fence that ran along the side of the alley and their faces glowed in the firelight making their skin a rich golden brown. In their boots and jeans, with their straw ten gallon hats and jackets drawn against the chill of the evening they looked like the wranglers and cowboys and *peticeros* he had once known and that they were. There was music from inside one of the rooms, mariachis and salsa, and the sweet smell of burning *colillas* drifted over from where some neighbor kids were smoking dope next door. The grooms waved to him and called his name as he got out of the truck and he opened the bottle of Conmemorativo and handed it to Borrego and it went from hand to hand all around, a sort of chalice at a communal baptismal font. "*Eso patron.*" a few of them said. "*Gracias.*"

On the left, in chairs drawn into a straight line, the women and girls sat, hands in their laps, engrossed in soft conversation as if in some kind of stylized receiving line and he nodded to them and smiled and touched the brim of his black Stetson and they smiled back shyly.

Amado emerged from where he had been, somewhere perhaps back in the shadows that clung to the corners of the house and with an elaborate flourish twisted the top off a bottle of Corona and handed it to Morgan who took it with a half-salute and tipped it back. Amado waved a response and went back from where he had come while Morgan joined the group around the fire and they made room for him. They differed only a little from the groups of men that had worked the cows with him back in Montana. Here he was just another cowboy.

The fire crackled and spat and when someone added a few pieces of mesquite, inserting them into the fire like carbon rods in a nuclear reactor, sparks rose into the black sky and

Morgan's heart with them and he was back there in his mind, sitting on his heels, watching the fire long after the other wranglers had gone to sleep, looking for answers to questions that had no words.

He had left his mother and his sister that summer after high school, after that hollow year when father had lost everything including his life to his business partner and he had promised himself that trust was folly. Nothing had happened since to change that. Only to reinforce it. He went West out of Dillon and joined up with a group of cowboys on a ranch near the East side of the Rockies in the Horse Prairie Valley that belonged to the father of a friend, working for expenses and the joy of being on a horse.

The answers hadn't come, not even after, not even in Central America, with all the things he saw. The questions had merely been put away.

"*Donde esta, usted?*" Amado said softly, having returned as quietly as smoke.

"Where am I, indeed. A good question, my friend."

"And you have an answer?"

"I don't. Somewhere."

"*Largo tiempo antes?*"

"Si. A long time ago."

After a while a very old copper kettle at least three feet was set across the fire, perched on cinder blocks, and at the right moment, Ramon, Ray the *brujo*, the acting chef, unwrapped four large packages of white *manteca* that resembled bars of Crisco and he put them in the pot where they began to melt and then sizzle and when there were four or so inches of steaming fat he began to add the pieces of pig, chunks of meat with the skin attached. When things were boiling to his satisfaction, he straightened up and noticed Morgan. "*Hola, Señor!*" Morgan greeted him in kind.

Even in an area like the desert, where bizarre characters were the stock-in-trade, Ramon stood out. Barely five-two, given to pudgy, with hair on his face that would have been a goatee if it could have or would have received the most minimal of ministrations, Ramon nevertheless exuded a presence that defied anyone to overlook him. He spoke rapidly and intensely but he had had a harelip repaired years before and he was almost equally unintelligible in English or in Spanish and as if to overcome that he stood very close when he spoke to anyone and fixed them with his dark brown eyes and he gestured emphatically with hands thrust into the air, hands that were oddly soft for someone who used them to make a living. His deformity cast his features in a peculiar skew and gave credence to the theory that he was something of a *curandero*, a *brujo*, a warlock as it were, and he was held in high esteem as a person who could do anything, from fix a sore back to gardening, from repairing a car to cooking.

"You want to ask him." Amado said from behind.

"Want to ask him what?"

"About the spirits."

"You know, *amigo*. In the bunkhouse. *Los espiritos*. Ask him. He tell you."

"Jesus. Did you tell everyone?"

Morgan glanced over at Ramon who had taken a shovel and was using the handle to stir the pot, an expression of unrestrained glee on his face. With the steam from the boiling fat swirling around him and the crackling embers from the mesquite, in the darkness and backlit by a lone porch light in the distance, Ramon had become a witch from Macbeth, a satanic follower and it seemed perfectly plausible just then for him to be an expert on such matters. Morgan shrugged and tipped up his beer and walked over to where Ramon was standing.

"You want to know what I think?" Ramon began.

"So you are a mind reader, too?"

"No…" he laughed, giggled, actually. "No…Amado…he tell me *un poco*. But I know myself. I am there once or twice." Ramon stuck the blade of the shovel in the ground while the dripping fat ran down.

"And…*que piensar?*"

"I don' like to be there. For you is okay to be there. They no bother you, the *espiritus*. For me, I no want to be there. I think maybe for Amado, the same."

"You're sure there are spirits there."

Ramon put his face close to Morgan's and said in clear English in a voice that raised the hair on Morgan's neck. "Aren't you?"

"I don't know, frankly. You tell me."

"*Si, es posible.*" Ramon shrugged, about to turn away, lowering the curtain of communication once again. "But what do I know? "

"Wait a second." Morgan put a hand on the *brujo's* shoulder. "Why are the spirits still there?" Morgan surprised himself that he was even asking the question.

"*Escucha*. Listen to me. When you die and you sick a long time, you spirit, you *alma*, it has time to prepare and it leaves. *Pero cuando* you die sudden, is no time for the alma to be ready and the *espiritu* no leave. It is confuse. It stays. Sometimes because there is work for it, it has to do something. Sometimes because it is no meant to die, no listo, no ready."

"What could…"

"Maybe something bad happen there a long time ago. *Quien sabe?* But you find out in time. We always find out. They tell us, *los espiritos*. Be patient. You patient with horses but you no patient with yourself and no patient with *personas*. Now it is time to be patient. *Ahora necesito cocinar.*" And he grinned and he cackled around his goatee and his hairlip and then he upended the shovel and plunged the handle into the bubbling cauldron and stirred the meat around and around, oblivious to the dirt that had lodged in the fat, until he was satisfied. One more time he walked over to where Morgan watched and drove the blade of shovel in the ground again and he said something softly to him, his face serious. Morgan missed what he said the first time and asked him: "*Que?*"

Ramon put his face close to Morgan who bent to listen. "Be careful, amigo. *Tenga cuidado*. If you look too hard at this, too strong, I see trouble for you. The spirits, they no hurt you. *Las otras cosas...no se.*"

"What other things? What do you mean?"

Ramon started to turn away. "I don't talk about it any more..."

Morgan was about to laugh and then thought better of it and merely nodded, then watched as Ramon took a long swallow from a cold bottle that someone handed him out of the darkness, wiped his mouth with the back of his hand, reversed the shovel and resumed stirring with the handle, preoccupied, privy to a hidden world that Morgan would never, could never completely understand.

Morgan finished his beer, long gone warm, and left with a word to Amado. He had a ten o'clock game and a lot on the line in the morning.

That night he might have heard three shots again but they were not so loud and not so clear and he stirred only a little. Later he thought he dreamt of an auburn-haired girl with skin the indescribable color of light cinnamon, what the Mexicans called *canela*, in a diaphanous dress that swirled in the desert night wind that rang the wind chimes that were just outside his bedroom window. When she turned a certain way the light appeared to sparkle from her and he could see how the structure of her cheekbones was made but of her face he could see nothing.

They were in the last chukker, holding on to a one goal lead by the grace of two more lucky breaks than they deserved when Morgan finally spotted her red Mercedes during a penalty time out pulled in next to his truck at the side of the field where Amado had all of the horses lined up at one of the tie rails. Even from mid-field, even 150 yards away, he could make out her face and her hair and how delighted she was and how she hugged Amado and he her in a giant *abrazo* and he could see that she walked over to the horses next as if they were old friends. And then time was in and Adolfo who was playing up front for the other team suddenly had the ball and began to drive for goal.

Morgan was playing Back, defense, and saw the switch in the momentum a millisecond too late and he touched Macarena's reins and tapped on her right flank and she came to a sliding stop, planted, and spun to the left on what felt to be one leg and in two strides she had reached her top speed and in two more strides the chestnut had matched Adolfo's bay. They were 80 yards from goal and closing fast but Morgan, on the left of Adolfo, let a beat go by, took the time to get a leg up on the other man, and then gave some left leg to Macarena and she responded, laying her ears back, hunching her back, and then horse and rider slammed into Adolfo, a thousand pounds of horse and rider, and many, many more tons of pure horse heart. Morgan had timed it just right, and Macarena gave him just the advantage, and together they moved Adolfo off the play and then Morgan leaned off the left side of the horse still with Adolfo pressing him from the right, drew a bead on the ball, and hit it back to where Clemente, his captain, waited, picked it up with the end of his mallet and hit it away. And then the clock ran out and the horn sounded and they had secured their place in the Finals on Sunday.

There were handshakes and hugs all around, quaint relics of a bygone era when sportsmen held more love for their game than for themselves, and as soon as he could Morgan walked Macarena from the field and unclipped his chin strap and took the helmet off and still in the saddle he leaned over her neck when they were a little off to themselves and he told her how much he loved her and how she was the best polo pony he had ever sat and how she had made him look good when he had let himself get distracted and how no other horse could have recovered the way she did and he rubbed her big neck and crooned to her until they were at the sidelines. Then he kicked out of the stirrups and rolled off and looked into her limpid eyes and realized that she knew that from Bucephalus to her, in a straight line that ran through the centuries, little had changed between horse and man. They shared a common soul.

It took him two steps before he felt the sharp pain in his knee. With the adrenaline pumping he hadn't noticed and he took a moment to adjust and take a breath and then started toward Alexis, Macarena's reins in his hand.

Alexis hugged him, crisp in a white blouse and jeans still cool from her air conditioned car against his sweaty jersey. Amado touched him on the back and the two of them exchanged looks that went beyond words. Morgan knew Amado had seen what had happened, knew what was on his mind, and he raised his chin imperceptibly, an acknowledgment, as the Mexican took the horse from him.

"What a horse." Alexis said, caressing the creature's sweaty neck as she moved away. "What a horse. You weren't bad, either."

Morgan shook his head, still not believing what the mare had done. "She's enchanted. That's the only word I can think of. When I play her, I'm sorta along for the ride. She's worth two more goals in rating."

Alexis had been to the ranch only one time before, never with the furniture in it, and when they got back Morgan poured her a glass of wine, one of the buttery chardonnays she favored, opened a Corona for himself, and they walked that way from room to room with Morgan as the tour guide. Outside the master bedroom, from their perch on the low wall of the patio, they watched the afternoon sun dapple the rocks around the pool and she got to her feet after a quiet moment and went to him and held his face in his hands and kissed him. "I missed you." She said, after a moment.

"You can stay, you know. I don't mean until Monday...I mean forever."

"I know. I will, one day."

"Just not today."

She shook her head from side to side, a slow gesture, solemn, full of words never uttered. "...not today."

"The bunkhouse...last stop on the tour." his voice pitched in imitation of an old-time circus barker. "Built, oh, about 1935, once the old farmhouse. Now home to the pool table, the television set, and various assorted guests. Someday. Come one, come all."

The moment the door opened he was conscious of the chill that enveloped him and he hoped she wouldn't notice but there was no mistaking her shiver and she hugged herself, an involuntary gesture. "C'mon..." he encouraged, "there's more." and he went ahead of her, expecting her to follow, but she stayed near the door, her face a distracted mask, her eyes darting from side to side.

At last she moved ahead until she was near the pool table and then she stopped and looked at him, her skin suddenly pale, and for a moment it was as if she would faint. "What's the matter?" he asked, his words inadequate.

"It's been a long day, Nick. You mind if I lay down for a few moments before dinner?"

"Don't be silly." He took her arm and walked her across to the main house and watched her while she lay across the bed.

He had planned to cook for her that night but it seemed to him that something had changed so they went for an early dinner instead at Jillian's, in Palm Desert, and by the time they had eaten their salads she was back to being her old self. It was after ten when they detoured past the barn on the way back to the ranch. With the headlights turned off for the last hundred yards so as not to disturb the horses, he coasted her car to a silent stop and then slipped out. Except for Buddy and Macarena, all the horses slept standing up. Those two could shake the stress of playing quicker than any of the others. Morgan moved from stall to stall, looking carefully at each one, assessing body language, and finally content that all was well, he got back in the car and drove slowly along the fields, trying not to raise too much dust.

They were at the South end of Field One when Alexis moved her hand out of his and squeezed his leg. "Stop the car." Morgan rolled the car onto the edge of the manicured grass and cut the engine. The silence was palpable, broken only by the silvery whisper of the night wind in the date palms and the occasional yipping of a coyote not far away. It was a few days past the full moon and there was a soft light over the bleachers and the clubhouse in the distance hunched quietly in the warm darkness and she opened the door, got out, went around to the trunk, and kicked her shoes off. Morgan watched with hungry eyes as she stripped off her blouse and then her bra and then pressed them to her breasts, the classic pose of a woman trying to protect her modesty. But she was deceived by the desire in her eyes. She turned her back to him then and still holding the blouse to her breasts with one hand she balanced on one leg and then the other and using her other hand she kicked out of her white slacks and threw a glance over her left shoulder, coquettish, wanton, and then she was running toward the middle of the Field, naked, laughing. He followed, his clothes a telltale trail. They made love in the middle of Field One, on the grass right in front of the venerable clubhouse, and after they came they lay together, his penis still inside her, both reluctant to break the spell.

He slept dreamlessly that night, in her arms in the massive bed with the four posters and the canopy frame covered with the gossamer linen cloth she had sent down with detailed instructions when he had first set up his furniture at the ranch. It was a little contrived, perhaps, in a Ralph Lauren kind of way, but she had gotten the cloth on a detour to Morocco during one of her trips to France and Morgan liked it more than anything else because when she was in the bed with him it felt like a nest.

7

June 1933

It was a maroon Packard and the killer had never seen that car before. He retreated out of sight along the side of the house and peered out. The black eyes of the driver seemed to find him where he hid and then he realized it was his patron at the wheel. The killer brushed crumbs of dirt from his pants and showed himself in the open.

The patron was young for someone who had amassed such a record of evil. Slicked- back, jet-black hair set off his skin, the color of mocha coffee. He wore a black suit. When he got out of the car, the killer could see the clothes the patron wore seemed cut a half-size too tight, so prominent was the bulge of his muscles and that was strange as well, the patron never seemed to lift a finger for the retainers that constantly buzzed around him like attentive handmaidens. Except now.

The killer half-ran, half-crawled, down the driveway, a grotesque kind of obsequious bug, anxious to intercept the patron, to show his fealty, to demonstrate his absolute command of the situation before the patron got out of his car, trying at the same time to conceal the brooch.

He might have saved himself the trouble. The patron waved him off like a troublesome fly. "Usted llega temprano," *the killer said, rapidly, stumbling over his words.* "Yo…"

"Ensena me." *the patron said,* "Enseña me donde los cuerpos estan."

The killer was trapped. He had to show him the bodies. He backstepped rapidly, gesturing to the path in front of him in a sweeping motion that the patron might follow. The patron quickly stepped around the killer and strode purposefully to the ranch house, taking in everything, the traces of blood on the sand, the broad swath of blood out the door and down the steps, everything. "Dos hombres?" *he said, unnecessarily. He could read the evidence as well as any man.*

"Si, pero…fue necessario."

"Ensena me." *The patron said again.*

They could hear the noise of the flies before they rounded the corner of the ranch house, and the patron walked to the grave and looked down and then sucked in his breath. "Una mujer? Mastaste una mujer?" *The killer had come to the side of the small grave and he stood silent, transfixed, a specimen bug on a pin before the patron's eyes, seeking approval and puzzled that killing one woman would anger the patron.*

"Usted que dijo no testigos." *It sounded lame, even to him.*

But the patron was enraged. "Si, y estaba nada, estupido." *With one casual motion, the patron pushed the killer forward and as he lost his balance, the patron reached out and neatly extracted the murder weapon from where it had been tucked into the man's belt. Then with the killer frantically scrambling to get out of the shallow grave the patron fired once, twice, and the killer's body jerked with the muzzle blast.* "Estupido pedazo de mierde. Y estaba nada." *he repeated.* "Mira que haces, mira." *His voice was strangely sad.*

The patron looked into the grave, looking into the face of the dead girl. Except for the flies, all was quiet. There was no one within miles.

He stared at her face for many moments. With her dark, auburn hair, her skin, she could have been his sister. When he finally noticed the brooch in the sand he brushed it off and placed it on the girl's chest but he didn't look at her face again.

Nothing ever happened here, especially when the weather was this hot. It was just as well. No one must ever know.

It was not much effort to cover the bodies. He didn't even bother to remove his coat. They didn't have to be deep because he knew that no one would come looking for them and between the warmth and the sandy soil the traces would be gone before long. The car, and the blood gave him pause until he remembered that with Ramirez as his driver, his car and the murderer's car on the property would be nothing unusual. He could drive the shithead gabacho's *car into the desert, not far off the road, back beyond Avenue 62, and walk back to the hacienda with no one the wiser. No one would ever look for it there and if they found it no one would be stupid enough to ask too many questions. This was still* la frontera, *the border, and the Gutierrez family carried enough weight in the desert so that even in private people were careful about the kind of questions they asked and what they said.*

The book. He remembered the chingado abogado *kept a notebook. He himself had seen him make notes in it and had told the gringo he didn't want any records and the* cabeza de vega *had laughed and told him not to worry, that it was his problem and he would take care of the business. Still, the patron had told the lawyer to bring his books, that he wanted to go over some things and it would be wise of him not to fail him but the more he looked, into the glove box, the trunk, under the seats, everywhere a journal could be hidden, the more he realized the gabacho had done just that. There was no notebook. Nothing. He would have to send some boys into the city to look or send a few guys from le Boyle, but that could wait. He had other business to take care of.*

The patron fancied himself prudent, ready for any eventuality.

He kept a small can of gasoline in his trunk and he got that and walked into the ranch house, splashing it around, careful of splashing on his shoes, grateful for the chance to obliterate the death smell. The patron had seen the lawyer's keys still in his ignition and he knew there was nothing more he wanted from him, not in this world anyway. In the doorway he extracted a thin twisted black cigar and then he lit a wooden match against the doorjam and ignited the cheroot and took a long drag. The matchflame barely flickered but it remained alive and the patron arced it disdainfully into the ranchhouse. The gasoline had had a chance to vaporize in the heat, and the forceful whoosh drove the patron back a couple of steps. Nothing would stop the fire. There was nothing in the desert, no policia, no firemen, nothing in the desert. Anything that burned, burned to the ground.

Without hurrying, the patron got a small water jug and a folded towel from his own car and carefully splashed water on his face and rinsed his hands and dried them before getting behind the wheel of the lawyer's roadster. The engine was loud in the silence, powerful, and he wheeled the car out of the driveway, admiring the way it handled. Once on the street, he drove west toward Jefferson, and once on Jefferson, he made a left and accelerated on to the mountains. When he looked back behind him he could see the ranch house blazing, a long, oily, black plume rising lazily into the sky.

He nodded to himself and shook his head. It was not the way he had planned it but he would make it work out. He would take care of paying Ramirez for the house and in any event the man would say nothing. A few of the boys would be glad to get into L.A. for a day or so to look for the missing notebook. Maybe he would even go himself. It would give him a chance to contact the le Boyle crowd so he could see what they were up to. He would get another lawyer, a smarter one this time. They were cheap, the abogados. *There were too many of them and they'd do anything for a few* dolares.

By the time he crossed Avenue 54, the smoke was a thick pencil line. A few blocks more and it vanished into the heavy, hot air and he smiled.

8

Morgan left the ranch early in the morning with Alexis still asleep and the big dog curled by the side of the bed near her, head between his paws, thumping his tail against the air and trying to be extra quiet and daring the man to shoo him out of the bedroom. She had promised that she would be at his game but that wouldn't be until noon and so he left her there, her face childlike in sleep, her body half-exposed, half-covered, curled up among the soft sheets that had already taken on her familiar fragrance.

By the time he got to the barn, Amado had given each horse a small flake of hay and he was filling water buckets and Morgan came over and stood next to him, blowing the steam out of his coffee mug in silence and watching the horses eat. There was something primal about this time, the morning with the horses, preparing for a game, something that hearkened back to a more ancient time when mounted men prepared to do battle with their lives and their fortunes in the balance. The horses always seemed to know somehow that it was a game day and about them at those times there pulsed a sense of anticipation, edginess, not nervousness, like pro athletes before their event.

They saddled Perla Negra and Macho and Morgan took three and Amado took three and they walked them around the four nearest fields, an effort to stretch their muscles and limber them up and settle them down. All of them, two-legged and four.

When they returned Amado brushed each horse again until its coat gleamed, and then its legs were wrapped with blue woolen bandages, and after that he tied each horse carefully in its own stall. Later, sometimes not until they reached the field, each horse would be bridled with its own bridle, bit, reins, martingale, breast collar, saddle pads. The last thing to go on would be the polo saddle, smaller than a conventional English saddle, more like an old-time cavalry saddle, flat to the sides so that there could be maximum contact between horse and rider.

Morgan fussed with his personal gear himself, his own way of putting on his game face, and then he loaded it into the truck himself, the tall polo boots, leather knee guards, helmet, polycarbonate goggles, gloves, spurs. He wigwagged a half dozen or more of the bamboo and maple mallets in the air in front of him until he found four or five that suited him and he added those to the gear that was already in the truckbed.

It was the Final tournament day of the season for Morgan's 12 Goal Division as well as for the 18 Goal Division. The packed-dirt road that ran down the middle of the club fairly hummed with unfamiliar cars filled with unfamiliar faces, drawn to the lure of a 2,000 year old sport that was ultimately more dangerous than auto racing, trying to belong, to somehow connect, wondering why this esoteric, exotic, arcane pursuit that they had heard so much about and had dressed so carefully for looked so much like a gathering of cowboys or of mounted hockey players. Some of it was that it was California, some of it the Western influence, but it didn't look like those pictures they saw of polo in Florida in TOWN AND COUNTRY. More hats, perhaps, more champagne glasses, certainly, fewer beer bottles in Florida, but the horses, the ultimate constant in the sport, were the same all over the world, and the riders as well.

They set up their camp at the side of Field One next to his other teammates, Clemente Shanahan and Ruben Mendoza, the two Argies that were the professional backbone of the team, and Tom Mardikian, the other semi-pro player who was splitting the bill for the team with Morgan. Mardikian hadn't been playing that long but he had taken a company public the year before and now he had the money to buy some good horses and spend more time playing.

Even though it was almost noon there was no sign of Alexis and the truth of it was that he wasn't all that surprised. It was a fairly common syndrome. Wives, girlfriends, significant others, if they were at the game and if they watched they usually looked the other way unless there was a crash on the field and then there would be a collective holding of breath until they could see who was involved and then there would be more breath holding until whoever was laying on the field moved. Or until the paramedics were signaled in from where they perched alongside the clubhouse like skeletons at a bacchanal, a constant reminder of the all-too-frequent price of playing the game.

Morgan's team had been through the mental pre-game exercise of matching the weaknesses and strengths of their horsepower with the team they were to play and they had spent much of the last four months playing together so there was a minimum of conversation as they each made their last minute preparations. A few of the players cantered easily along the sidelines, stretching, taking practice swings. Morgan swung up on Buddy, his stalwart first chukker horse, and ran through a few quick lead changes at the canter and then a few rollbacks. That would be enough for the horse. Buddy had been Best Playing Pony in two tournaments a few years before and even though the horse was a little older now and there was a step or two off his speed he made up for it with sheer polo experience and the indescribable quality known as heart.

They rode out on the field together, Morgan and his teammates, falling into a line abreast naturally, and Morgan threw a glance back at the tie rail where Amado remained, putting the finishing touches on the next chukker horse but there was still no sign of a red Mercedes. Then the umpire threw the ball in and everything but the game left his mind and time seemed to compress and expand simultaneously.

Morgan's team was matched play for play and by half time the score was tied. At the start of the second half, the mounted umpire threw the ball between the lined up players and Morgan, at defense, stopped it an passed it up to Mendoza who whirled his Argie-bred mare off the wrong lead and the animal tripped and Mendoza flew forward, tucking as he went. It was what saved his collar bone.

The horse hadn't been hurt but the game was delayed until another mount was brought out and everything should have been alright after that except that the Argie held back just a little and a little was all their opponents needed. Morgan was helpless as their edge slipped away and at the end they were down two goals.

There would be no tomorrow. The season was over.

By the time they made the sidelines Alexis had arrived, looking cool, together. She had stopped at L & G's market for a twelve pack of ice-cold Coronas and from some unknown place produced two icy cold bottles of Veuve and she was waiting at the tierail and when they rode in she gave Mendoza and Shanahan each a bottle of Corona that they accepted with a solemn bow. Mardikian offered a sweaty kiss she took with grace. With Morgan's bottle she threw in an extra long hug. "I know how you wanted the win. Heck, from the sound of the cheers it sounded as though everyone at the clubhouse wanted you guys to win."

Mardikian opened the champagne and they passed the bottles around from one to the other with the champagne bubbling out. "Thank you, guys," he said. "We didn't win but we deserve the champagne. Thanks for getting it, Alexis."

"I really wanted the win," Morgan said, when he and Alexis pulled away from the knot of players. "We probably were the better team going in. Sour grapes, I suppose, but I missed an easy goal, and Ruben missed two and one of them on a perfect pass from Clemente. We were outplayed in the second half but we were up by one until the fourth. Maybe that counts for something. Shit. We hung in there so long I thought we could pull it out."

He boosted Alexis up onto the tailgate of his pickup and got up after her while he held Macarena to a loose lead rope and she grazed in front of them. While he sat there cooling off Amado untacked all the horses except Macho Man and stashed the saddles and bridles in the back of Morgan's pickup and climbed on the gelding. Finally he rode over to them with the other four in tow and took Macarena's lead rope from Morgan. "*Lo siento, amigo.* I sorry you lose."

Morgan's just shook his head. "Bad day for the team to come apart. After the whole fuckin' season. You okay?"

"*Seguro, patron. Te miro mas tarde. Divierta te.*"

"*Muchisima gracias, mijo.*"

"You play good." He laughed, the sadness already gone, and threw Morgan a half-salute with a hand full of lead ropes and started off.

"He loves you, you know. And he knows you better than just about anyone." Alexis said, softly, when Amado had ridden off.

"That good or bad?" Morgan said, looking after the groom.

"Good, for the most part. You're a pretty special boss to him. Although after, what, ten years..."

"...eleven..."

"...eleven..."

"Right...the *patron-trabajador* relationship has long since gone out the window. It has to. Whatever your horses thrive on, consistency seems to be a major factor. We've got to be of one mind with the horses."

"And you are. But it's more than that." She appeared to be preoccupied. "You two ride so alike it's impossible to tell you apart from a distance."

"No one's ever said that. I never realized."

"Realize it."

"We've been lucky with the horses we've made."

"If luck means a lot of hours. Funny. You two come from such different worlds and sometimes I watch, and you and he aren't saying anything but you'll both reach for the same thing or go to do the same thing at once."

"C'mon," he said, passing it off. "Let's go up the clubhouse and watch the 18 Goal Finals and I'll buy you lunch."

"Let's go back to the ranch and I'll give you a bath."

"Wanton woman, you are. How 'bout we compromise and we watch the first half."

"And I only bathe your top half?"

"No, I bathe your top half. Follow me."

Life sometimes turns on seemingly offhanded decisions.

They took plates and went down the line at the brunch inside the Clubhouse and they went outside and pulled up chairs in the sun where the low white fence came to a corner at mid-field by the gazebo that served as the announcer's booth. It was a place where many of the professional players congregated, most still in their playing whites, now dirty, and many still with their team jerseys on, not as an affectation, but rather out of sheer convenience. Alexis and Morgan hopped the low fence and spread their feast on the ground to give them themselves a few moments alone.

Knots of players here and there, with half an eye on the game being played before them, replayed their own games to each other, their hands being first this player, then that, their gestures like nothing so much as those of fighter pilots after a sortie. Like fighter pilots, they tended to dissect on-field crashes in great detail; the more serious the crash, the longer and more detailed the discussion. The reason for the crash, particularly a bad one, ultimately had to be a mistake of the rider and if they discussed it long enough, looked at it from enough angles, they could immunize themselves from that mistake and make sure it wouldn't happen to them. In practice it never happened that way.

"You know, if memory serves me correctly, there was a lot of action right out there about mid-field last night."

"I can't imagine what you're talking about, dear boy. I think you maybe smoked some of that whoopee weed."

"Not me...I know a lot better than to light anything up around you, least of all a cigarette. But had I known in advance, I would have had someone out there with a video camera. Lordy, you were hot, hot, hot." Morgan laughed, and Alexis aimed a shot for his shoulder.

"Don't fight, you two. I was just telling someone that you guys get along so well." The voice from behind them was easy, with the merest suggestion of a drawl, more of a slur perhaps, but the inflection marked him as a native Southern Californian as distinctly as a Beach Boys tattoo.

"Burnsy. Pull up a piece of dirt." Morgan pantomimed brushing off an area as Hollister Burns slouched to the ground and stretched his legs out in front of him and moved the Nikon cameras and the long lenses that he was carrying around to his lap.

"Thanks. Don't mind if I do." He popped an Altoid and crunched down. "It's only fair, though. Your team kept me busy looking for a shot where you were all playing together."

"Smartass. You didn't get one." Morgan signaled one of the waitresses and a bottle of Corona with a lime hooked on the mouth appeared in a moment. Burns, shook his head, crunched the Altoid, touched bottles with Morgan, and tipped the beer into his mouth.

"But I got a hell of a shot of you. And it's right here." He tapped the body of the motor-drive Nikon F5 that he carried slung from his shoulder.

"I haven't seen you in a couple of weeks. You're sure shooting enough though. Sellin' any?"

"Yeah. To SIDELINES, and POLO. And I'm doing a piece for the ROBB REPORT."

"I still say you could sell some to the players. Everyone likes the pictures you take. You do seem to capture the essence of it."

"That'd be a real pain in the ass, dealing with polo players. You guys never seem to want to spend anything unless it's on your horses."

It didn't take long until Maureen Rogers, the wife of the club's marketing director, spotted Alexis and once she did she wasted no time in coming over ostensibly to say hello for in reality to pick her brain about what she had been buying for the boutique. Burns turned back to Morgan. "How's your new place?"

"Perfect. You have to see it. It's just what I was looking for."

"But…"

"What do you mean, but?"

"Sounds like there's a 'but' there."

"At this point, I'm not sure. Amado and his *compadres* think there are spooks there. As in ghosts."

Burns looked at him and nodded. "Haunted. Yeah. Right."

"Look, I know what it sounds like but I've seen a few things I can't explain. And you're talking to the guy that doesn't believe that junk."

"So why are you talking about it?"

"Don't know. I still don't."

"Try me."

"When I moved in, the guesthouse, what I call the bunkhouse, was cool. Cold." And there, in the bright sunshine, on the edge of Field One, Morgan laid out the bizarre things that had happened since he closed escrow, the poltergeist type things, the sensory things, even the offer from Delores' psychic friend, and except for an occasional "no shit", Burns listened in silence. By the time he came to the gunshots, he had Burns' complete attention. After a while Burns sat back and breathed a long "whew". And then he added: "So what are you going to do about it?"

"I don't know. Exorcism? Maybe I should buy the soundtrack. You know, TUBULAR BELLS."

"No, I mean aren't you going to look into that?"

"Yeah. I'm going to go to Harris Department Store in the morning and buy a crystal ball. And then I'm gonna get my damn head checked out."

"Everyone and everything leaves tracks. Heck, nowadays you can't even get a blow job any more without someone making a note of it, especially if you're the President. Things were a whole lot less structured then, sure, but like I said, everyone and everything leaves evidence. Tracks. It's just a matter of uncovering them." He stroked his wispy black goatee and his dark-brown eyes grew darker.

"And you just happen to know a good, cheap detective. I've got all these horse mouths to feed, don't forget."

"Well, two out of three."

"What do you mean?"

"I know a good detective. Just not cheap."

"Who?"

"Me."

"Hollister T. Burns, I've known you for at least three years and now you're going to tell me that you're a dick?"

"Please, you're insulting me. Don't put it in those terms. A private investigator. A PI. And good enough so's even you didn't know."

"True." Morgan mused. "That probably would explain all the times you seemed to drop off the face of the earth."

"Some of the times, maybe. Not all. They tell me, in fact, that I'm one of the top ten homicide investigators in the state."

"What do they do, publish a list? The Hit Parade of Private Dicks. Sorry, Private Investigators. Seriously."

"You didn't think I kept that place up in Malibu and drove a BMW selling pictures to cheap-ass polo players, did you?"

"Maybe I thought you had a trust fund. Who knows? No shit, though, licensed, and everything?"

"Well…right now my license is, let me put this delicately, invalid."

"I'll bet there's a screenplay there."

"I'll tell you about it one day. I'm still not through with it. The story, that is."

"I'll take your word." The metamorphosis in the detective's eyes brought Morgan up, conscious of having seen something deadly there, the look of a killer. He had seen that look in the man's eyes before but it made no sense and had doubted himself. Now there was no doubt. Since he had been a youngster, Morgan had studied eyes and he had developed the unconscious intensity of a horsetrainer or of a gunfighter, occupations that shared the necessity of reading intent before it changed into dangerous, often fatal action. It was a habit now and he sometimes found himself moving through groups of strangers seeing nothing but eyes. He knew it unsettled people, but it was a habit he chose not to break.

"Speaking of screenplays," Burns said, changing the subject: "your ranch might have a good story. Might be something to it."

"I didn't want to go there. But you really think you want to get involved in this thing?"

Burns patted himself down and drew a tin of Altoids out of a side pocket. It rattled quietly when he shook it and he took the one remaining mint and popped it in his mouth and immediately crunched down. "Why not? Can't dance. At least not right now, not without a license. How come you didn't think of this, you being a writer and all?" He tossed the empty tin on the table behind the railing.

"Like I said, maybe 'cause I didn't want to give it any credibility. You know how that goes…validate it by talking about it."

"Well, give it some. We've talked about this area before, the desert, I mean. This feels like something that could have happened back in the 30's and you know what went on here in the 30's. Christ, the La Quinta Hotel was built in 1926 when it took five hours to drive out here from L.A. and every movie star worth his money had a squeeze on the side that he brought out here. Word is you could get anything here. It wouldn't surprise me at all that something could have happened. You've heard all the stories about Capone and his boys bein' out here. Who knows?"

"I don't know that any of that is any more than Chamber of Commerce crap."

"Hell...it might be fun to look into anyway."

"So what would you do if you had this case handed to you? Mind you, I'm not hiring you. But I'll trade you out for a credit in the screenplay."

"Aren't you the generous son of a bitch. Okay...here's what I would do. You start by snooping around here, Indio, I mean. They've got to have a historical society or a museum or something. Every little burg has that. You're gonna turn your horses out for a vacation for a month, right, so this is a perfect time. See if there were any unsolved murders here and just fill in some local color from the 1930's or the 40's. See if it's plausible. You know, put it through the filter of 'could it have happened'."

"I'm already there. This area was the Wild West then and it's still the Wild West. About four months ago, Timoteo, Amado's cousin, was going to buy a truck and shows up flashing a wad in that badass Mexican bar we went to once on 86. Maybe two grand or so. The last anyone saw him he was going to get a drink there. Mistake. Don't flash. No one's ever seen him again. Word is someone killed him and threw his body up against the mountains. The coyotes took care of the rest." He paused. "But that's not proof and you're right, I need more solid evidence."

"Check it out and call me in the morning. I've got to get back to Malibu tonight but we can talk then. Unless I miss my guess, this is going to take some old fashioned leg work. Nobody's put this shit on computers yet and no one wants to. It's the desert man, and no one in the desert wants to look too closely at the past. Hell, if they could they'd keep records on

Magic Slate."

"Want to stop by on your way out?"

"Next week. I've got to meet with the club honchos and give them some pictures so I'll be down."

It was just after four, but already the sun was slipping behind Santa Rosa Mountain. With the growing shadows came a chill in the air as much or more from the rapidly fading weekend as the disappearing sun. When the two men rose, Alexis disengaged from Maureen and got up with them and slipped an arm around Morgan's arm and something about the way she did that and looked at him just then, wistful somehow, made him know and he said: "You're going back tonight." A statement, not a question. She nodded, relieved that he had guessed..

"Let me guess. Early meeting."

"Madison just got back in from Hong Kong and he's only going to be around for a few days and I'm..." It seemed to sound lame, even to her, but he chose to ignore the feeling.

"So I'm one-upped by the director of the store."

"Never, cowboy. No one could ever one-up you."

"And you're going to be going to New York in about ten days."

"I thought you'd forgotten. And I've got to be in San Francisco tomorrow night. Back Wednesday. I knew you'd be down here so it wouldn't matter."

"Not a chance. When are you going to quit your job and come down here full time and..."

"...let you take care of me."

"Why not? Crazier things happen between two people, you know."

"Because. I don't want anyone taking care of me. I like to make my own way. It's taken me years to get where I am and what happens if I give it up and something happens to us, or to you. Polo isn't exactly golf. Not that I don't love you with all my heart. You know I do. You're by far and away the only man in the world for me. It's just that..." she shrugged eloquently.

It was an argument that he had heard before. Many times. "Do you need to get your things from the ranch?" he asked.

Her eyes flicked in the direction of the ranch and a dark expression crossed her face as if she remembered something suddenly, something troublesome. "I packed this morning." She said with determination. "I do want to shoot for getting back to Beverly Hills by dark. But can we go see the horses before I go?

The top was down on her Mercedes and they drove down to the barn alongside the south end of the fields, Morgan riding shotgun, slouched elaborately in the seat and waving at the grooms and players he saw with a stylized regal wave. Amado had fed the horses and had poulticed the front legs of the ones that had played to cool their tendons and now the big animals were contentedly picking wisps of hay from the ground. Morgan retrieved a bag of carrots from the tackroom and gave them to Alexis and she went from one to the other, cooing to each one, rubbing a nose here, ears there. They always seemed to respond to her and even though she said it was only because she was a Taurus it was more their sense of her soul and both Morgan and Amado could see that. Horses were masters of non-verbal communication and there was no way to fool them.

He rode with her to the dirt road that was Avenue 51 and said goodbye and got out. Hands in the pockets of his whites, his hat pulled down, he watched as her car got further and further away until it was finally a red smudge on the brown road against the darkening bulk of the mountains. Then he turned and walked back to the tackroom.

In the deepening gloom he became aware of a gathering of men in front of the tackroom of Juan Carlos Ashford, four or five of them talking at once in the softly slurred Spanish that could have been Italian to the casual ear but that marked them as Argentines as surely as the yerba mate tea they passed around. Morgan started over. The yellow light that spilled out from inside the cinderblock building outlined their hands as they spoke, moving in gestures as fluid and unique as their speech, as if they had their own peculiar sign language. There were six of them, all professional players, the nucleus of the two teams that had played in the 18 Goal Finals but looking at them just then you couldn't have figured out who won. They were professionals and this was a time for the players and for the horses. The partying and the celebrating would come later at the Cantina.

Polo mallets and miscellaneous leather bridles and tack hung from nails driven in to rough wood 4 x 4's on the tackroom walls. Two saddles were draped over the porch railings on either side. The players welcomed Morgan into their circle with a few handshakes and someone put the mate in his hands and he sipped twice on the *bombilla* and watched what was going on. On the wooden tackroom porch someone had spread a smallish rough woolen brown and white striped blanket with fringes of the kind the Argies used under their saddles and lying face down on the blanket was Juan Carlos himself, still wearing the whites he had played in earlier. His boots were off and over him, straddling his back, was the small body of Ramon, the *brujo*, and he held the player's head turned sideways. When Morgan walked over Ramon looked up for a second and grinned and then looked back down at Juan Carlos. "*Listo? Listo?*" he said, and when Juan Carlos mumbled "Si." Ramon gave a sudden jerk and the sound of his neck cracking was sharp. Ramon ran his hands down the man's back, nodded with satisfaction, and stood up, the baseball cap he wore canted to the side, looking like someone's caricature of a crazed Dead End Kid. "*Bueno. Arriba. Arriba.*"

Juan Carlos got to his feet and Morgan thought he looked dazed but he shook his head and someone handed him the mate and packed in a little more *yerba* and added some lukewarm water out of the dented metal tea pot that had been warm on the hotplate and Juan Carlos took two sips from the silver *bombilla* and passed it to Morgan. "*Que tal?*" Morgan asked him.

"Okay, okay." Juan Carlos said, his tone tentative. He smiled. "I be okay."

"If you weren't before, you'll be now." Morgan agreed. He sipped on the bombilla again and passed it to Julio Castagnola. One of the other players Morgan only ever heard called 'Negro' took up his position on the blanket and Ramon got over him and ran his hand up and down his spine once or twice and moved his arm behind his back and held it a certain way, assessing the situation. Again he looked up at Morgan. "*Espera te.*" he said to him. There was another series of "*Listo? Listo?*" and this time Ramon moved the man's arm in a certain way and the player grunted. Ramon nodded, satisfied with what he had done. Then he stood up and took a pack of Camels out of his pocket that looked as crumbled and dusty as he did and put one in his mouth where it dangled and for a weird second he looked like Brando while he fumbled for a match and then lit it.

The *brujo* arose and Morgan extended his hand knowing even as he did so that shaking hands was not something the Mexicans did but it was too late to take it back and the *brujo's* hand in his was small and cold. "The woman…" Ramon said.

"You missed her…she just left."

"No, no, no. Not that woman. The woman." And he

pointed in the general direction of the ranch.

"I told you. She went back up to Beverly Hills."

Ramon shook his head as if Morgan was a backward child. "No. I no mean *su novia*. I mean *la mujer at su rancho*." Something like a chill went through Morgan right then and almost against his will he asked: "What woman at my ranch?"

"You know." Ramon said. "The painter see her. The one wit' *pelo canela*, the olive skin."

"Okay...let's say he saw a woman. Let's say...for argument's sake. I don't believe that crap, but what about her."

"She need you."

"Oh, bullshit."

Ramon held both his hands up and shrugged. "Okay. You no believe it. Okay. She go to L.A. because she need you. You'll see." And he turned back to the blanket, to where Miguel Lisioli had taken Negro's place and he crouched over him.

Once off the polo grounds Alexis felt more in control and she drove past the ranch without even looking through the gate, without even slowing down. A few moments later, when she turned north on Jefferson, she began to feel like her old self and she crossed Highway 111 and pulled into the Circle K on the corner, thinking a cold drink in the car would hit the spot while driving up to the city. She filled a cup with ice from the machine and added Diet Coke and took it to the counter.

Above the counter, rows of cigarettes were lined up like colored dominoes and she hesitated, a five dollar bill in her hand. Finally she heard herself say: "Give me a pack of Luckies." Without comprehending what she was doing, she took the cigarettes and the drink, went back to her car, and lit one.

The absurdity of the gesture made her feel ridiculous and she took a puff, suddenly self-conscious. Then she stared at the lit cigarette, tossed it into the street, and drove away.

By the time she reached the Freeway she had lit another and by the time she got off on Robertson in L.A. she had smoked three more.

Morgan dreamed again that night. This time he was not surprised by it and he almost expected it. When he awoke, or at least when he thought he awoke, it was about 4 AM and her face was there in front of him, shimmering, so that at first he wasn't sure whether it had been a dream or a ghostly apparition. It hung there in the air and then it gradually faded like the last note of a Puccini aria, so that you weren't sure exactly when it ended or if it hadn't really ended long before and all you were doing now was hearing it hang in the air or remembering it. He tried to notice details, of what she wore, of her hair, but all he thought he could see was a marcasite pin, silver, ornate, with what could have initials, maybe the letter "A" with an "S" or "E". Or maybe it was just the moonlight.

He got up and went across to the bunkhouse and sat in one of the wing back chairs that were near the back bedroom. The scent of lavender enveloped him, warm now, and then he leaned back, content, at peace.

9

Just before sunrise Morgan poured a cup of coffee and opened the front door to let the dog out and as soon as he stepped outside he heard the noises. Sonofabitch. Who the hell would be working out there this early when it was barely light. The dog was sniffing near the oleanders and he shooed him away from there with his hand, not speaking. Whoever it was, he was going to give them a piece of his goddamn mind. There was no vehicle in sight, not on the front driveway, and not back by the garage. It sounded to him like shoveling, the rhythmic harsh sound of blade going into sandy dirt followed by the thunk as the shovelful hit the ground. They must've parked their truck back there on the grass, he said half aloud, and if that's the case they don't know me too goddamn well.

The closer he came to rounding the corner of the bunkhouse, the louder the shoveling sound became, until finally he could look down the slope to the barn with the small corral where a gnarled twisted orchid tree curled around the pipe fencing.

There was nothing there. And there was only silence.

Impossible. So impossible was it for him to imagine that he continued to walk down, looking for signs of disturbed earth, tire tracks in the grass, anything, but there was nothing.

What the fuck is going on, he said to himself. He walked back and forth, pacing, the twenty or so strides up and down the slope, back and forth between the bunkhouse and the barn, and back and forth again, and then he finally walked back into the main house and dialed the phone. "Delores," he said, "This is Nick Morgan over in Indio," she sounded sleepy on the phone but he plowed on. "I'm sorry, you were asleep, but look, as long as I woke you, can you give me phone number for your psychic friend."

By noon he was sitting on the rocks in front of the bunkhouse with Amado when a vintage early 80's purple Cadillac convertible that could only belong to a psychic or a very eccentric local pulled into the gate and stopped at the turn of the driveway near the *pirul* tree. The Mexican had brought a few tacos over from el Ranchito Restaurant in La Quinta and they were in the process of finishing, watched closely by Max and almost as carefully by a slender green lizard almost a foot long that was relaxing in the heat and the sun. Morgan got to his feet and waited.

The car door swung wide and nothing happened at first and then a woman of large proportions emerged, not truly fat, but very ample. The first thing Morgan noticed was her hair — what little was left of it was scattered over her scalp in clumps, tufts that she had dyed a cheerful, incongruous carrot color. She wore purple, horn-rimmed sunglasses and from her neck swung a crucifix that was at least 10 inches long and encrusted with purple stones. She bent back inside to retrieve a knitted purple shawl and this she wrapped once around her head and then around her neck with the practiced moves of a Bedouin.

She couldn't have looked more out of place if she had put on a purple robe with moons and stars.

"I'm Rosalba but most people just call me Alma. What is it that I can do for you?" she began in a voice that sounded like too many years of three packs a day and a toddy or two after work. Morgan started to speak but she held up a silencing hand, long-fingered, bony. "Let me look around..." she said, and without another word she turned and made directly for the ancient orchid tree behind the bunkhouse. Left standing by himself, Morgan watched her as she disappeared down the slope, then he shrugged and went back to the tacos.

He shrugged again when Amado looked a question to him with an upward cast of his eyes and the two of them said nothing more and ate in silence. After a while she seemed to materialize from behind the bunkhouse and just as quickly disappear into it, then she reappeared and went behind it again, peering here and there, her head moving like some kind of curious bird, until finally, after about 20 minutes, she emerged, blinking in the sun, and stopped where Morgan sat. Again he rose.

"There's three of them, you know..." she began, without preamble.

After years in the desert Morgan had heard most of the stories about Indian graveyards and he figured that she was going to go off on something like that so he attempted a serious expression and said: "Really...right. Indians, of course."

"No...white people." And holding aloft a lone finger, she pointed in the direction of the orchid tree in back and said, in an agitated voice: "And they're buried in front of your barn beside that tree, that tree that bears flowers."

Morgan took a deep breath. Now he didn't know whether to laugh or look serious or smile or what and he settled for a noncommittal shaking of his head. "Really. What were they doing here?"

Drawing her face close to his, a distant light came to Alma's eyes and she began to speak in another softer voice, flat, almost completely devoid of expression, of emotion, mixing her tenses as confused, narrating a scene she was viewing for the first time and telling it to him years later. "It's hot," she said. "I can see two men and a woman by this house here." She pointed to the bunkhouse. "It's the only house here. One of the men was young, early thirties, perhaps, he's wearing a white shirt and a vest but he's not entirely comfortable. And a hat. Not a western hat, a dress hat, maybe a fedora. The other man looked dark, a moustache, dark skin, small. He's wearing a suit that he borrowed. The girl is beautiful, brown hair, no, dark-red hair, and so soft, so vulnerable." Alma pulled a lawn chair out and collapsed into it, seemingly exhausted, while Amado, who had been feigning indifference but straining to hear, scrambled to his feet wide-eyed.

"She's looking out of a window, over there, over by that window." She pointed to the bunkhouse kitchen window that opened onto the Jacuzzi as if she could see her now. "Her face…she's absolutely terrorized. She's watching something. Oh, God, no. She's watching the tall man. He's been shot, right here, right on this spot, right where we are. And he's going to die. Her face, she has such a look of terror. I must send a blessing to her soul." And she bowed her head and her lips moved and after a long moment she straightened up but now she was almost shaking, her face pale, her eyes reflecting a picture for which there were no words and she got to her feet, the ends of the shawl flapping like feathers. "I must go. I can't stay." She pointed toward Morgan's bedroom in the main house. "They go back and forth through there, you know."

And then quicker than Morgan ever would have thought she could move she was behind the wheel of the Cadillac and had the engine running and the car turned around.

"Can you tell me any more? Who was the tall man? Who killed him."

"The tall man is, was, a lawyer." Now her words were tumbling out in her haste, her composure lost. "He did some work for the mob and came down for his money and...and they're buried back there. All of them."

"What do you mean 'all of them'? Came down from where? And when did this happen?"

"I don't know. It feels like the 1930's. 1933. Or maybe that's the lawyers age. I can't be sure. All I know is that it's hot. He came down from Pasadena, I think, no, L.A. It's L.A." She looked like she was going to cry.

"Who was the girl? What happened to her?"

"She was never meant to be here. What happened to her, it was a mistake...the wrong place at the wrong time."

"Who was the third man?" Morgan knew he was pushing it.

"He is known as *el matador*, the killer, an evil man. And that is all I know." Now she gunned the Cadillac engine and Morgan thought for one wild second that she would run over him and he stepped out of the way and a look of relief came onto Alma's face that she wouldn't have to because in her state she might have.

"Wait just a second..."

"I've..."

"Wait. What happened to the girl? How much did she know?"

She gunned the engine, and started to roll down the driveway and Nick grabbed the doorframe as if he planned to climb on the car. "At least tell me this...how many shots were there?"

"I'm really going..."

"C'mon," he almost pleaded, "Don't you know?" he challenged.

The psychic bristled. "Of course I know." She paused, listening, watching something that only she could see, only she could hear and then she looked at him, looked intently into his eyes, her own eyes filling. There was absolute silence. She said it so softly that Morgan wasn't sure until she repeated it: "Three. There were three of them."

He peered into the storefront on the end of the one story stucco office building just off Jackson Street in the area that was known, more or less tongue-in-cheek, as downtown Indio. Like the glass in the door, the glass in the window was fly-spotted and old, but he could see clearly enough when she appeared from behind the counter. She sized him up from the inside, looking intently over the top of her gold-rimmed granny glasses and peering birdlike first this way, then that, a benign crone whose very skin echoed the coloration of the building, of the street, a dusty, faded gray-beige. Her blue-tipped gray hair was cut smartly around her face and he imagined she was wearing a hairnet. Apparently reassured by what she saw, she unlocked the door and opened it a few inches. "We don't open for twenty minutes," she said through the crack, "right at ten o'clock." Her head nodded like a bobble-head doll in self-validation.

It had seemed real clear when he and Burns had spoken on the phone after Alma left, Burns would check out the old Bar Association records while Morgan would see what the local historical society knew. Clear, maybe, at the ranch, with Alma's heavy perfume still in the air, but here in the light of reality, this was another story.

He tried a different tack. "You can see the crowds gathered outside," he needled. "Everyone wants to come in."

Her laugh was genuine. "I'm sorry. Didn't mean to be cross. We don't get many visitors."

"Any?"

"Damn few. Kids from civics class once or twice a year. One of the DESERT SUN reporters once in a blue moon. What can I do for you?" The door opened wider and she beckoned Morgan inside with a conspiratorial movement of her head. The room smelled like an old motel in Palm Springs, in the section that Tom Ford and the WOMEN'S WEAR DAILY crowd hadn't rediscovered yet, an amalgamation of stale cigarette smoke, disinfectant, old age, and old sage.

"Looking for some local color."

"Try the Mexican swapmeet on Wednesday night. 48th and Jackson."

"Not that kind of color. History kind of color...what Indio is, was really like."

"You one of those development types?"

"Heck no. Not hardly. Although there's been a lot of 'em around lately."

"Yeah, and if you are, you can keep on goin'. Can't imagine what they all want with poor little Indio."

"Money would be my guess. All the cheap land back toward Palm Springs is gone and they've already messed up La Quinta...it's our turn now. No, I'm a writer. I'm trying to find out what this town was like back in the 1920's and the '30's. What was here. Who lived here. Things like that."

"That's when I came here."

"You're not that old..."

"You're kind. And you're right. But I have been here for about 45 years."

She had come to the valley as a schoolteacher in the 50's

and soon after that she had fallen in love with and married a local Mexican boy and had spent the rest of her life with a foot in both communities. When she retired, taking over the small historical society was the natural thing to do. She had already taught the majority of city council members when they had been in 7th and 8th grades. Before long, charmed by Morgan and his dry sense of humor, she found herself escorting him from one to the other of the old black and white pictures on the walls, pictures that showed large empty lots and wide streets and solemn-faced families in stiff poses.

"So what was it like then? I mean, to live here."

"Wasn't much. Date Palms, citrus. Army Corps of Engineers brought in the Date Palms, you know, and then tried to figure out what to do with this area. Even brought in some camels. I guess you could've called it a frontier town then. Hard to believe, in California and all that and only 60-some years ago, but it was sorta the land the travel brochures conveniently forgot about, particularly once the interstate came through. Like now. To the east and south, Mexicans, to the west, toward La Quinta, whites. Off in the mountains to the south, what was left of the Indians. Not many blacks. Mostly desert, but some agriculture. And of course, the Date Palms."

He hesitated for a moment, and then plunged in: "Do you think it's possible for someone to have been killed here and for no one to have ever found out?"

She looked at him, eyes narrowed. "Why are you asking?"

"Curiosity. It's a writer thing. It's called looking into deep background."

The answer seemed to satisfy her. "Mister, there are bodies buried all over this end of the valley. Most of 'em aren't in the graveyard, either." She gave him a studied look. "When in particular?"

"The '30's. Early 30's."

"Oh, I thought you were talking about last week. The '30's, heck, a piece of cake. Like I said, it was a frontier town. You could have blown up an atom bomb at 111 and Monroe and no one would have even noticed. Where are you figuring?"

"Around 50th, near Jefferson."

"That area wasn't even a part of Indio until recently."

"So the police…"

"What police? Sheriff's Department was the only law for these communities back then. And they were spread so thin they didn't get to some things for days. Weeks." She looked at him over the tops of her glasses. "Just who're you thinking was murdered?"

"I'm not sure."

"You don't know who was murdered. Who are you thinking did the killing?"

"I don't know that either. Like I said, I'm not sure what I'm looking for...deep background, that's all." He tried to put indifference into his voice. It would have been just as easy to kill someone in L.A. in the 30's. So why would the mob from L.A. have bothered to kill someone from L.A. down here? Unless. Unless it wasn't someone from L.A. who did the killing. "Tell me about the gangsters around here then, the bad guys, the men who ran this area."

"Most of them are still around. Not them, actually, but their gangs, *bandas* they're called in Spanish. You wouldn't notice, being an *anglo*, and all, but there's the Mexican Mafia. They call them the *emme*, or *la familia*. But it's still the Mafia. And they still have a lot of influence."

"I thought that was mostly an invention of the media."

"Some, maybe. But it's real enough. They have been here since the beginning of the century, some offshoots of Mexican mob families. Now they're deep underground, deep in the subculture but for a long time they were up front, as in the open as Capone and the Chicago mobs, and they controlled the trafficking in drugs and people. Some say they still do." Involuntarily she looked around. "Then again, who cares? As long as you're not involved. They don't bother me."

While she spoke, Morgan continued to prowl along the rows of pictures on the walls. If what Alma the psychic said was true, the man that was murdered was a lawyer. Not that it was a great loss, but there were only a few reasons for murdering a lawyer apart from good taste, a desire to clean up the world, and an innate revulsion for the profession — money and knowledge. And Alma hadn't said anything about any reason. So what did he know? Not very much more.

"What would have been big enough to kill for then?"

"Who?"

"Like a lawyer." And he laughed. "Of course now they kill you if they don't like your bandanna. Maybe those days were more civilized. But were there any big turf wars?"

"Not really. Money, of course, drugs. And smuggling people. Some things never change."

"I think it might have been bigger than that. Call it a hunch."

She looked up at the ceiling and walked around behind the counter. "Water. That's the only other thing."

"What do you mean"

"You think there was a scandal in L.A. with Mulholland and the Owens Lake thing? Well out here it was completely wild, maybe because this was even further out of the scrutiny of the press and they figured no one would ever find out. The biggest thing to happen to this area was the construction of the All American Canal in the 1930's. Same as the L.A. Aqueduct, if you would have known where the canal was going and could have tied up the land cheap, it would have been like hitting the lottery."

"Who knew?"

"A few of the surveyors, some of the engineers, some of the politicians. Some of them were honest. But some of them, they kept it pretty much to themselves and made a pretty penny. But..."

"...the mob knew."

"Of course. They always know everything. It was a real free-for-all then. A lot of what they called floaters in the canal in the old days. Bodies, you know. The Wild West. And a lot of whispers. A lot of the people nowadays that look like they always had money made it then."

After a while, he thanked her and went outside. The air was already heating up in the unrelenting sun and it was clear that Spring, what little they ever had, was over. Across the street and closer to Indio Boulevard, Theresa's Restaurant was preparing for dinner, the sweetish smell of frying *manteca* already in the air. Down a little further, the old Indio Hotel where Patton had headquartered in the 1940's loomed, its façade shadowed in the strong sunshine. Little had changed about the hotel in almost 50 years, the railings still iron wrought into curlicues, the paint only a little more faded. Morgan took refuge in the shade of a Jacaranda, its branches heavy with bunches of purple-blue florets, and dialed Burns up on his cell phone and then punched "send" two more times when the first two calls dropped. The detective answered the phone with a cautious voice as if on a surreptitious assignment and not wanting to divulge who, exactly, he was. "'lo?" the voice said.

"It's Nicholas." Morgan said, his voice a broad imitation.

"Bro. Where the hell you been? I tried your cell phone at least ten times."

"It's the desert. Reception sucks. Listen up. I just walked

out of the historical society and I found out enough to make me want to look further. Apparently this place really was the Streets of Laredo. I'm not sure what was behind my murders but it certainly wasn't Leave It To Beaver down here. Besides the usual, money, there was this thing about water rights."

"The California curse."

"None other. You come up with anything?"

Burns had pulled a marker from a friend who worked in the L.A. County Bar Association and had gained access to their archives. "Yeah. There were exactly 16 lawyers who disappeared from 1930 to 1935, dropped off the rolls for non-payment or whatever, six in 1933. They didn't die, because they apparently noted those."

"Gee, is that all?"

"Can't be lucky all the time. Could've been 50 you know. There were a lot of stray dogs in those days might have killed a few for sport."

"I always thought dogs were more discriminating. I guess not."

"We should start with 1933 since that's what your weird lady said. Sutton's Law, you know. Check out the addresses and all that."

"What, no computer?"

"Easy, son. It won't do everything. Besides, you learn a lot just looking around. And anyway, I had someone check on a few of the names already so we're down to three."

"You along?" Morgan asked.

"Hell, yes." Burns snorted. "Got to keep my hand in the L.A. dirt or I might as well be a dick in Des Moines."

"It's almost eleven. I'll leave Max the Dog with Amado and be up there by three and I can go check 'em with you."

"You ever hear of the Coyote Flat murders?"

"No. Why?"

Burns' voice was softer. "I've been thinking of that ever since you called yesterday. It seems there was this 21 year old guy took his 17 year old girlfriend deer hunting back in 1928 up in Eureka. He was shot in the back and his girlfriend was found shot dead two weeks later. Shot twice. Once in the head, once in the throat. It was all over the papers. They wound up putting a guy named Ryan in prison for 25 years. He was let out on parole and it wasn't until about '91 that they discovered he had been framed. Tough shit. By a crooked D.A., of all things."

"Like the P.R. says 'L.A.'s the place'. The more I find out, the more I'm convinced L.A. was not very different from the desert."

"And stayed that way, too, maybe right up through today. Who knows. If you had enough scratch you could get away with anything. They ever figure out why the guy was murdered?"

"Bootlegging, they thought. Money. What else is there? The girl was simply in the wrong place at the wrong time. That's what struck me. When you told me that Alma had put it in those words…"

Morgan took his hat off and ran a hand through his hair, sweaty in the rising heat. "Yeah, well, they had bodies. We have ectoplasm. Big difference."

"Details. Oh, yeah…one other thing."

"Chain of title?"

"Hey, if you even want to quit writing, I'll hire you on."

"I had an idea that might be interesting. I'm going to stop off at the Hall of Records."

"No, no, no, brother. This is a 21st century thang." He needled. "This is a job for the Pentium processor. I can pull all that shit up for you from the County Assessor's office on my computer. You be up here and I'll meet you with the info. The

411 as they say in the 'hood."

"What can't you get on that thing?"

"Flavor. But basically what I can't get, you don't need. I'll see you at 3:30. Meet me in Glendale, Arden near Brand. It's just off the 210. I'll keep my cellphone on."

"Why there?"

"Rush hour, my desert friend. Trust me."

"My grandpa always told me never trust a man who says 'trust me'."

"And…"

"I never listened. I'll see you there."

10

Tendrils of smog or fog were oozing over the top of the Banning Pass by the time Morgan left the valley and by the time he crossed into San Bernardino the sunshine had given way to a leaden, gray sky. When he hit the 210 heading west at the San Dimas curve, the temperature had already begun to drop and the mountains to the north of Pasadena, the San Gabriels, had disappeared. The traffic going East was already bumper to bumper.

Burns was asleep in the front seat of his car in the parking lot of the Mobil station on the corner of Arden and Brand in Glendale and Morgan passed over a thought about waking him and instead went inside for a Coke. When he emerged he started to tap on Burns' windshield but the detective opened one eye slowly and grinned. "Gotcha."

"Bullshit. You were asleep."

"You went inside for something. Watched you the whole time."

"You looked like you were sleeping."

"Cover, my friend, cover. Don't forget I'm a professional."

He moved his hands from under a sweater on his lap and Morgan caught a glimpse of the .38 Colt Detective Special and his eyebrows raised. "Never can tell, my brother, but I'd hate to sit here and say 'oh, shit'. That's my motto: Try never to say 'oh, shit'."

"I'm impressed. What now?"

The detective offered Morgan an Altoid and crunched on one himself before answering. "Okay…we check out this area and then hit Boyle Heights next before the traffic is too heavy, and double back to Hollywood against the stream. We'll leave your car here and pick it up later."

"Bogart didn't have to deal with traffic."

"I'm not Bogart."

"You can say that again."

"Lissen, sweetheart…" Burns lisped, in a dead-on Bogart imitation. "I'm much better. Get in. We're burnin' daylight."

They drove around the corner, down Burchett and past a row of classic old Craftsman cottages that looked much as they had when they were built in the early 1920's, quiet porches and real wooden stoops, relics of a bygone era. It could have been the 20's until you looked up at the tall office buildings that had come to surround the area. The address they wanted was nearer Arden in a nondescript office building that looked to be the same vintage. There was a rickety elevator that took them to the third floor and when the elevator stopped, Morgan slid the metal accordion-style door open. "Lead on, MacDuff." He waved Burns ahead of him.

The sign on the door read "Samuel LaMont, Attorney at Law" and it looked at least 60 years old. Burns pushed on the door and it opened in. The woman behind the desk was easily about 10 pounds too big for her outfit, the merest shade past voluptuous, but she oozed over the top of the blouse in a way that made them pause. The very short skirt of her dark suit stopped just at barely prudent and when she walked, the rustle of stocking against stocking between her thighs sounded loud against the background hum of the air conditioner in the window. She wasn't chewing gum, but should have been to complete the image. "Can I help you?" she smiled, leaning over the desk toward them, displaying the tops of her breasts.

Burns tried to cover a leer. "We're looking for Mr. LaMont."

"Wait here. Oh, yeah, who shall I say would like to see him."

Morgan looked at Burns. "My name is Nicholas Morgan. Tell him I'm a writer and I'm doing some research."

She left and reappeared with a man in his late 20's and Morgan and Burns shot a glance at the sign on the still-open door.

"Oh, no. I'm not that Mr. LaMont. I'm his grandson. That Mr. LaMont passed away in the 1970's. I keep his sign up there just for old time's sake."

"Was he the attorney?"

"Reluctantly. But he never liked it, hated the lawyers as a matter of fact. He quit practicing years before that and went into real estate investment. He raised me and that's what I do."

"What happened to him? The Bar Association shows that he just dropped off the rolls. Why would he have just disappeared?"

The man laughed. "You didn't know my grandpa. He had a big feud with the Bar Association and just quit. Except he didn't let them know. He let them write him for years. He drove everyone nuts until he died. A real character, he was. But no, he didn't disappear. Everyone knew where he was until he died."

❖❖❖

By 1 PM Alexis had managed two vendor interviews, a short staff meeting, an inquiry from the bean counters at corporate in Santa Monica, a complaint from Sharon Stone's stylist, and had split a sandwich from Il Fornaio with Jerome Sorvino, the Director of the Boutique. Pamela, the Boutique Manager, stuck her head in just as Alexis was gathering the last of her papers from the desk and trying to cram them into her black leather attaché. "Save it, if you can." Alexis said, holding up her hand. "Sorry…I'm only going to be gone for two days. I haven't packed yet and I'm on the 6:30. Of course, that's United, so there's no telling when we'll take off."

"Sure." Pamela smiled. "It'll wait. Safe trip, now, okay?"

Alexis bailed out the back door onto the parking lot that flowed onto the wide back alley that ran between Rodeo and Camden Way. But for the world-renowned names on the backs of the nondescript doors, Gucci, Zegna, Hermes, it could have been a parking lot and back alley anywhere, dumpsters overflowing with cardboard boxes, papers blowing in the occasional breezes. She stashed the attaché in the trunk of her Mercedes and continued on foot up the alley to Brighton. She had managed to snag an appointment with Peter, her colorist, and she was running late.

The hair salon, Esthetica, presented a narrow profile to the street, wedged as it was between two other buildings but once inside it opened up into a two story space filled with pounding rhythms and svelte bodies covered mostly in black, more a club than a salon. Peter had the chair at the top of the stairs and from his vantage point he watched as she swept in, admiring how she looked and how she carried herself, and her body, even though she was almost ten years older. "Hi, beautiful." He hailed. She tossed a wave up to him in reply.

Alexis emerged from the changing closet in a rayon smock, exchanged air-kisses with Peter, and melted into his chair with a deep sigh. "The usual?" he asked, and then, without waiting for an answer. "I'll be right back."

She put a hand on his arm as he went by. "Wait a sec. Talk to me. I want you to change my color."

"Sure," he said, "I've been thinking that you could go a little lighter."

"No. Darker."

"Really? How dark?"

"Auburn."

The address in Boyle Heights was just off the 5 Freeway south of the East L.A. interchange, hard by the park in the center of the area where the Mariachis played on Sundays when they were looking for new gigs. Now it was empty except for groups of kids, boys mostly, in their early teens, heads shaved, tattoos on their arms and necks, bared chests showing elaborate jewelry. Here and there a street vendor had dresses or colorful cloths arranged on wooden chairs and makeshift clotheslines. As Morgan and Burns cruised slowly by, the cholos wigwagged each other with elaborate hand signals and strutted like banty roosters.

Morgan shook his head. "Tell me, Burnsy, what country are we in?"

"Shit if I know. Maybe Guatemala, maybe el Salvador, maybe even Mexico. I don't know. What I do know is we just keep moving and ignore. We'll figure it out later."

Burns rolled his BMW to a stop in front of an old, two story office building. Built of tan stucco, it had a small porch of dark wood that ran around three sides of the second floor. Morgan went for the handle of the car door and Burns stopped him with a hand on his arm. "One sec," and he flipped open the Detective Special, checked the cylinder, and closed the action with one hand and then he tucked it in a belt holster behind his right hip. "We'll be alright. They can smell serious a mile away. As long as we don't bother them, they won't bother us."

"Do I look worried?"

The corridor of the building was dark with little of the day's waning light finding its way inside. The whole building smelled of urine and vaguely of burned toast or fat. They looked at one closed door after another and finally found signs of life in the back on the first floor where a sign read "Julio Sanchez Ibanez, M.D." They pushed open the door. A few women occupied the metal chairs in the waiting room and the receptionist, or nurse, or whatever she was, sat behind what was obviously a bulletproof lucite shield. Burns bent to the small opening. "Hi." He said, flashing his best smile. "We're looking for someone who had an office in this building. A lawyer named Morris Rabinowitz. You ever hear of him?"

"No." she said, drawing it out with the peculiar singsong East L.A. accent. She shook her head for emphasis, a motion that went all the way to her toes, and followed it with a wagging finger. "As long as I work here, three years, maybe, we the only office open in the building. If you wait, I ask the doctor."

After a while during which the women in the waiting area tried not to look at them and they tried to look casual the doctor came to the only other door to the waiting area, dark-eyed, an Omar Sharif look-alike. As soon as he was satisfied that Burns and Morgan weren't *la migra*, and weren't going to get his patients into trouble his demeanor opened and he took them into his inner office, a small room overwhelmed by the clutter of unread journals, unread lab reports, and undictated charts. He had taken over the office on a deal from the City of Los Angeles in 1995, he said, and he occupied it rent free on some sort of grant, but the building had been completely empty when he had moved in and no one ever came around.

And no, the kids outside never bothered him.

"You know this area was the Jewish center in those days." He offered. "Someone named Morris Rabinowitz would have fit right in. I didn't live here then, obviously, but there was a famous clothing store across the street run by this Jewish guy. It only closed a few years ago. And you know Cesar Chavez Boulevard...it was called Brooklyn Avenue then. Times change."

"And not always for the better."

When they walked out, the cholos hadn't moved but their strutting around had intensified and Morgan and Burns wasted no time getting into their car. "I can't believe anyone named Rabinowitz would have been involved." Morgan offered. "I mean...Morris Rabinowitz...please."

"You can never tell. The Jews made some of the toughest hoods. It's one of the first things I learned in this business. I'm keeping his name on the possible list." Burns slid behind the steering wheel and inserted the key in the ignition while Morgan buckled in and after a few seconds, when nothing happened, Morgan looked over. Burns was gripping the steering wheel with white knuckles white and staring off somewhere ahead. "I'm the one that found him."

Morgan stopped himself before he could ask who Burns was talking about. It was as if the detective was watching something intently, there, but not there. "It was four months ago. We were supposed to meet for a drink at the Palm, on Santa Monica, our Friday routine. I got there early and when he didn't show I tried to call him and finally went over to his place near the Greek Theatre. I let myself in with my key." Burns was breathing quicker, short breaths.

"Brooks was dead," he said, and Morgan realized then that he was talking about his old partner, Bob Brooks. "There was blood all over the place, more blood than I ever knew a body had. Shit. I couldn't do shit." In the silence that followed, Morgan chanced to say: "You ever figure out who did it?"

"Idea? Hellfuckinyes, I have more than an idea. Brooks was doing some freelance work for the LAPD. Being a scout, he called it. He was trying to find a connection between the *emme*, the Mexican mob in prison, and the cholos on the street, those boys over there, or others like them. The kingpins in prison control what goes down on the street, even though they're nowhere near it. They want someone erased, he gets erased."

"Just like that?"

"Just like that. He had obviously gotten too close. We shared an office and he showed me some of his field notes about a week before. It would have broken it up big time. Since then, I've wanted to kill all these motherfuckers." He said, indicating the *cholos* and the neighborhood with one lift of his head. "I knew some of the names on his notes and I finally caught up with one third level asshole about a week after his funeral. I wasn't sure he'd had anything to do with it but I sent him to sleep with the fishes anyway. I was crazed. They pulled my ticket."

"And the mob?"

"Never came after me. Probably never realized we were in the same office. Since then I've been layin' real low…shootin' pictures and makin' believe I'm retired. Probably am, if the truth be told."

"Sucks."

"Don't it. He had a 14 year old son and a girlfriend that was crazy for him." Burns was quiet, clenching and unclenching his hands on the wheel. "Last thing they did, they cut off his dick and stuck it in his mouth." he said finally.

Morgan exhaled sharply. After a while Burns turned the engine over and pulled the Beemer away from the curb.

"Where to?" Morgan asked.

"Hollywood Hills. Off Sunset. Old Hollywood Hills."

They somehow made it past the East L.A. interchange before the traffic closed down and picked up the 5 and then the 101 going slower as it got later. They took the Sunset offramp by the Fox studios and from there they went west, through the Asian neighborhoods and west along where it went somewhere close to Hancock Park and then it was the Strip that hadn't changed that much since the 1930's, certainly not since the '60's. Traffic slowed to a crawl at La Cienega, the volume and the out-of-sync traffic signals too much for even the Strip to bear. The man on the Marlboro billboard squinted into the sun not yet behind the coastal ridge and the club scene was beginning to throb even at this early hour as the detective turned his car past the Tower Records on the corner of Horn where Wolfgang had opened the original Spago.

The address was across the street from the House of Blues and they both looked over at it and breathed "oh, shit" simultaneously because right where the address said that the lawyer's office had been was a Starbuck's. "Starbuck's." Burns said. "How much more fucking mundane can you get?"

"Like being run over by a garbage truck."

They drove around the block in vain, looking for an open space. After their second turn around the block Burns slipped the car into the almost-empty House of Blues lot and told Morgan to give the attendant a twenty and after that they crossed Sunset and walked up the block. Further down on the street, between some apartments that had once been grand in the way that architects once thought grand should or would be, a cluster of old Hollywood bungalows sat, unrestored, unrecognized, empresses of a bygone civilization. Morgan was running out of patience. "C'mon, we won't find anything here. Let's get the fuck out."

"Not yet. Patience is a precious virtue in my business. Let's snoop around a bit."

They walked across the Strip and back behind the Hyatt and down toward where the hills began. One lot off Sunset they passed a venerable duplex that looked as though it hadn't been touched since the 1920's. It was all but invisible from the Strip. Equally hard to spot was a small sign swinging from a white-painted hanger, the lettering faded and hard to read. "Bob Jamison, Attorney at Law," the sign said. Burns spotted it first. "Bingo."

"What's a boring game for old people?"

"Very funny. Check that out. Let's see if anyone answers the bell. I mean, a lawyer is a lawyer, right? Isn't there some kind of code among those guys?"

When Burns pressed the doorbell the USC fight song, rendered on electronic chimes, filled the office. "Bizarre. Do you even believe this shit?" Morgan said, mostly to himself. "What is it when the line starts to blur between real life and fiction? When the whole goddamn world starts to look like something out of Dashiell Hammett or an old episode of Dragnet?"

"Or a Bogie movie...I don't know...California? L.A.? Maybe we've all just accepted that kind of weirdness as normal or maybe it just thrives in the smog. Maybe we've all driven to work past too many movies being made on too many streetcorners and we've come to think that maybe that's normal."

The door was open, with only a brown wooden screen door ornate with Victorian turns blocking the entrance. When no one appeared Burns walked up and peered through the screen. There was nothing to see but a couch covered in some kind of flowery chintz, and a desk that was mostly clean. He shrugged and rang the bell a second time and had to listen to

'Conquest' again and this time a man shuffled out of the back room and came to the door and looked up at them through the screen as if they might be the prize patrol from Publisher's Clearing House. "Help you?" he finally said. When he spoke his poorly fitted dentures clacked and he shifted his lips elaborately. He had a cardinal and gold cap tilted slightly off to one side and wore thick horn rims.

Morgan let Burns do the talking this time and listened while the detective ran through the story they had contrived. They were doing some research for the Los Angeles TIMES, they told him, and wondered how long he had had an office there. "Mister," he said, "I'm 87 years old and I opened up this office when I passed the bar back in 1933." Did he by any chance remember a lawyer who had practiced locally back in the 1930's and that he had lost track of? Maybe even more specifically, one who had disappeared? "Listen, I was 25 years old then and I had just two things on my mind—making some money and getting laid. The order varied depending upon what I was getting more of. So can't say as I do. You got a name?"

Morgan shrugged at Burns and finally gave him the last name on the short list: "Scott Carruthers." And then he found himself holding his breath waiting for the man's answer.

"Nope. Don't mean a thing to me. Except there was one guy, kind of a sharpie who just dropped out of sight right after I opened. Can't remember his name, though. But I do think I remember he went to UCLA. This guy go to UCLA?"

Burns shrugged. "Don't know…"

"Flashy guy, as I recall. Drove an Auburn. When he didn't come around, no one really looked for him."

"You have any idea what kind of law he did? Maybe that would explain why he would have disappeared?"

He moved his mouth thoughtfully and seemed to shift his denture plate again. "Nope. Sorry."

Morgan and Burns thanked him and started for the door. "What did you say the address was?" he called after them.

They told him and again he repeated "Nope."

"It's where the Starbuck's is now. If that's any help." The old man shook his head.

Morgan had his hand on the screen door when the man spoke up again. "There's one thing...you might check your address, but when I started practice there was a little office across the street where I think this guy might have practiced. But then right after he stopped coming around there was a big fire burned up the building. Maybe it was the same one. That address you gave me, ya know, maybe it was his building caught fire. They changed the addresses right after that."

"What now?" Morgan said when they got back to the BMW.

"Not bad...one possible out of three. Now you get to buy me dinner. Part of my comp work. And I want to check out some of the LA TIMES files. See if they have anything about a lawyer who disappeared in 1933."

"That definitely seems like something out of an old movie. You sure we can't find out what we need through some of that internet stuff? Or how about local files."

"Not that easy. Next time have your guys killed after 1945. Before 1935 or so they haven't transferred any of that information to computers. It's all on microfiche. Which is easier to handle than old newsprint. But harder on your eyes. We're following a very cold trail, bro, and any tracks we find on the side of the road can only help."

"So when do we go over there."

"No, no, no, my friend. This ain't the movies. They don't let anybody into the files."

"Damn."

"At least not during normal business hours. But despair not. You're not hangin' around with just any old dick, you know. I know a man who works up there and he just happens to owe me a favor. That's the good news. The bad news is that it won't be until after 10...tonight. The rest of the bad news is that you're takin' me to Lola's. It'll be alright...the maitre d' does some surveillance for me sometimes."

It was almost full dark by the time they rolled down Fairfax, past the changes, the evidence of the endless transformations the neighborhood had gone through. Canter's Deli was on the left, brightly lit, impervious to the calendar, and when they crossed Melrose Avenue, Burns began to slow. The building on the right was dark, the address barely identifiable, and the name, if indeed a name was displayed at all, was invisible. A small low sign on a metal stand said something about valet parking for five bucks and Burns swung the Beemer to the curb. It reminded Morgan of the 70's, during the heyday of Ma Maison, when L.A.'s seminal restaurant was signless and its telephone number unlisted. Patrick Terrell had the quirky habit of answering the phone with a non-committal "Allo..." in his French accent and if you didn't know better you might have thought you had the wrong number.

Lola's had been open for three years and it managed to combine martini bar, hangout for models and young movie industry types, and a more-than-credible restaurant all at the same time. At one time in his life, Morgan would have been there at least a half dozen times by now but his life had moved on and even now when something brought the change to his attention it surprised him in a faintly disorienting way.

It was dim inside, what little ambient light there was absorbed by the dark paint on the walls and pointed up by the stained glass only slightly more visible on some of the windows. Even at 7:30 the crowd was there, dressed in dark pants, dark skirts, dark shoes, dark tops, designer sunglasses, greeting each other enthusiastically yet hardly knowing each other's names. The faces were the only things that changed from night to night. Even then the faces, most of them, had the same absent look, the look that enabled them to appear to listen to their dinner partner or drink partner or escort while they looked beyond them to see who else they'd like to be with. It was a perfect conversation. No one paid attention.

Many of the men, young mostly, had wispy goatees. Some of the women, the ones that were voluptuous, drop-dead gorgeous, went through the charade of concealing their beauty, others frankly marketed their attributes. In all, it was a less sophisticated version of the bar at the old Eclipse, less of a scene than the Mondrian, smaller, more intimate.

Burns and Morgan walked through the front and on into the back bar where it was easier to get a drink but where there was a lot less happening and they ordered two Coronas from a very tall, overly buff bartender. They waved off the glasses that were offered and the bartender handed them the bottles with a wedge of lime in each one. Burns squeezed his into the neck of the bottle and rubbed it around the rim and Morgan extracted his and pitched it into the bar sink.

"Nick," he heard from behind him and he hunched his shoulders in a reflex reaction and tried to ignore whoever said it and looked around for an easy escape route at the same time. "Nicholas Morgan." But there would be no ignoring whoever it was and he turned slowly. The man who had called his name waved as if flagging down a cab. He was perched at one of the small tables with another man and Morgan recognized the face and knew that he knew him from the polo club but he drew an absolute blank on the name. The man held out his hand. "Gerry Williamson."

"Sure. Good to see you. I missed you at the club this season."

"You know how it goes. I had a few shows in development and thought I'd better stay up here."

Morgan remembered him, just not his name. He was one of the players that came into the sport for a season or two, made a big splash, and dropped a bundle of money, and then bailed when he realized it took more than bucks to be good.

"By the way, this is Trent Daniels." Morgan vaguely recognized the other man at the table from something or other on television, maybe one of the soaps, and nodded in his direction. "Did I miss much at Eldorado this season?" Williamson asked.

Morgan was going to ask him what had become of his horses, thought better of it, and was mercifully saved from what he realized could become an awkward situation when Burns came over with another man in tow. "This is Greg Carlson, the Manager."

A few moments of conversation and Morgan and Burns peeled themselves away and followed Carlson into the dining room to one of the prime tables Carlson always kept aside. "I'll be back." the maitre d' said, already smiling in another direction.

"Who was that?" Burns asked, indicating the man in the bar.

"Television director…Gerry Williamson. Had two or three big sitcoms up until last year, then…" he shrugged, "who the fuck knows what happens. His life went into the shitter and he had to sell his horses. I don't think he knows that I knew or he wouldn't have called to me.

"What is it about that sport? Not that I'd like to try it, or anything, but it seems you guys would sell your souls to play."

"It's only a shame that souls aren't worth what they once

were…more players would sell 'em. Someone once said that you only quit polo when you die or when you run out of money. I don't suppose there's a difference. Normal people would call it an addiction."

"Yet you managed to hang on to your horses through some lean times."

"Priorities, Burnsy. They were always my number one priority. They would have been the last things to go. I'm glad now." He took a swallow of his Corona. "So how are we going to handle this TIMES thing? What do we look for?"

"Leads, pointers, ideas, hunches, inspiration. You said that psychic lady…"

"Alma."

"Yeah, you said she said it was warm. It starts to get warm in the desert in June so let's start with June. You take one 'fiche, I take another, and we'll page through the first section like that. We can get through three or four months before they kick us out. If we find nothing, we go buy a Ouija Board, I guess."

"And if we find something…"

"We check it out in the morning. Don't look at me like that. We PI's don't need sleep. And I know your cowboy ass can make do on two hours."

"How about this 'kick us out' thing?"

"We're basically trespassing. For you, a slap on the wrist. For me, a little longer before I get my license back. Maybe a lot longer. Either way, we don't want to get caught."

Carlson showed up just then, a young waiter in tow bearing two appetizers of macaroni and cheese and two martinis in frosted glasses. "Compliments of the house, guys." He said.

Burns took a sip of his martini. "Wait'll you have this, Nick." He gestured at the macaroni and cheese. "It definitely ain't like Momma used to make."

11

They strolled casually into the lobby of the TIMES about 10:15, two chameleons looking respectable enough to relax the security guard with a smile. Burns' contact was a skinny little man who looked like he wore a white shirt and tie every day including days off and holidays. He spotted them from where he was waiting near the security desk, fluttering like a nervous butterfly, with badges that identified Burns and Morgan as visiting journalists and then he hovered over them while they put the badges on just so and then escorted them onto one of the elevators. At the fifth floor, the elevator door hissed open and they walked down the corridor, their footsteps a hollow echo in the empty hall. The building was silent at this time of night, at least this end of it, except for the distant whirring noise of a buffing machine or a vacuum cleaner, too far away to tell.

Bruce was almost beside himself with anxiety, and he ushered them into a large room lined with racks and files and installed them in the back at a long table where there were two microfiche machines and a cart on which perched a couple of cardboard fileboxes marked "1933". They watched impatiently as the man showed them in meticulous detail how to work the machine, going over each point as if they were poised to defuse a bomb. When he was satisfied they wouldn't break anything, he told them he'd be working up front. "Uh, I don't mean to be pushy, Mr. Burns, but how long you going to be?"

"Well, I don't know now…when do you go home?" Burns asked, grinning.

"Six AM. But you're not staying that long, are you?" he asked, panicked.

"If we have to."

"Look, Mister Burns, you said…"

Burns held up his hand. "But I don't think so." The man fell silent and looked around one more time. "Please…" he mumbled, "don't do this to me…" and limped off.

"Let's get crackin'." Burns said, when they were alone. "Don't get bogged down in minutia, either, we're lookin' for a story about a lawyer who disappeared. Don't be reading the stories like it's the morning paper."

"What would I do without you?"

They started in May, 1933, and divided the month in half, Morgan taking the first half and Burns the second and after an hour they broke and scouted up a Coke machine and waited while the cooler disgorged the cans amid much clanking and clashing, the noise of it loud in the late hour. "Well? What'd you find out?" Burns asked.

"A lot more about L.A. than I ever wanted to know. I think that what we'll find will be on the second or third page. Much past there it becomes a real small-town paper and page one looks like it's strictly national news. Kind of a revelation, though, looking at an old newspaper. You really get a feel for a city."

"You're learnin' country boy. The TIMES hasn't changed much, has it?"

"I think it was better then…although they were always pushing a point of view, even back then."

"No sign of any fire?"

"No, that's Boston."

"Boston?"

"You notice how different cities seem to concentrate on different things? I was in Boston years ago. It was fires. L.A. is murders. I think it was always that way here. Well maybe not exactly all murders, only the lurid ones, but definitely not fires. How far did you get?"

"Almost finished with my two weeks. Problem is, you're right. You start reading this thing and it's a lot more interesting than today's paper." They divided up the June files and went back to their screens. When they stopped again it was almost 1:30 and Morgan found himself running out of steam. They prowled around and found some instant coffee in a room off the back and tapped some hot water from the red spout on the cooler into paper cups.

"Sheeit, bro. If I didn't need glasses before I started, I sure as shit need 'em now. I'm beginning to think this wasn't one of my best ideas. A lot of time, no money."

"Just send me the bill. Well, on second thought, don't. I haven't found a fucking thing either. But I'm not ready to quit. Not yet."

"You done with June?"

"Got another two days. Let's split July. That way we can keep working."

It was just before 2 AM when Morgan went back to his screen. June 29, 1933, page one, world news, nothing local except for some pressure on the Mayor's office to authorize another investigation of the LAPD and he looked back at the date again and sniffed. Page two, a lot of local stuff like the upcoming celebration of the 25th anniversary of the Malibu Pier.

He rubbed his eyes and brought up page three and scanned the page the way he had perfected in the last three hours or so. Quadrant, quadrant, quadrant, quadrant. Nothing. The rest of the first section. Nothing. Okay, June 30, 1933. Page one, U.S. Government becoming involved in disagreement between California and Arizona on Colorado River water. Page two, local stuff. Page Three. He heard the click and whir of the machine Burns was using and he heard a fire door slam shut at the far end of the deserted corridor outside and then silence again. And then the air seemed to go out of the room and he could suddenly hear the beating of his heart and a vertiginous throbbing started in his head. The only thing that he could see was the picture in the lower right-hand corner of page three and it seemed to expand like a telephoto image in reverse until it filled his field of vision.

The face was unmistakable. It was the face he had dreamed about back at the ranch and he stared at it, into it, not wanting to believe.

"Burns." he whispered hoarsely. And then louder. "Burns." The detective took one look at him and scraped his chair back and walked over to where Morgan was staring at the screen. "Jesus H. J. Fuckin' Christ." Morgan was saying, over and over, softly. "It's her."

"Her?"

"It's her."

"Her? What her?"

"The girl in the bunkhouse. The murdered girl. My spirit."

"Are you sure?"

"Sure I'm sure."

The caption might have been written to him. "Have You

Seen This Woman?" it said. "That's her. That's the one I dreamed about."

"She's beautiful, I'll give you that…but…you sure? C'mon, it's a pretty face and all, but it could be anyone."

"I'm sure. It's black and white, of course, and grainy, but I'd recognize those cheekbones anywhere and those lips. My God." They enlarged it, and printed it up, and suddenly Morgan was holding her face in his hands. Now that it was in front of him he was not at all sure that he had ever wanted to find it, to have it all made real.

The two of them read through it aloud, standing together leaning over the table, like a solemn Greek chorus chanting. April Sawyer, the article read, had reportedly left for a drive with a friend, a local attorney, on a Friday the week before. She had not been seen since and her parents had reported her missing to the police two days before the article appeared in the paper. That would have been the 28th. LAPD was seeking the attorney, one Scott Carruthers, for questioning but thus far there was no sign of him or of his car.

"Holy fuckin' shit." Burns breathed after a moment. "You know what the odds are against finding that?"

"Eighteen million to one. Fuck, I don't know. I think I have a pretty good idea that I would never have noticed the picture if it hadn't have been for the dream…keep reading."

April Sawyer had been 26 years old and had been employed as a secretary in a lawyer's office. She lived with her parents and a younger sister in Bellflower, and they gave the address. Carruthers, the article went on to say, was a recent graduate of UCLA and was in solo practice in the Hollywood Hills.

Morgan and Burns straightened up.

"I say again…holy fucking shit. Even if you didn't recognize the face, everything else hangs together. And you're sure you saw this face before."

"Look...the other morning when I opened my eyes, or when I think I opened my eyes, this is the face that was hovering in front of me."

"You didn't tell me."

"Didn't think it was anything."

"What was her expression?"

"Dreamlike, certainly not terrorized, or anything. Nothing like the expression here. This could be a yearbook photo or something. But I'm sure."

"And you're the guy who doesn't believe in any of this stuff."

"I still don't and I still believe there's got to be a rational explanation for that."

"Yeah, I'll give you a rational explanation. The spirit of a girl who's been dead for 66 years knew you were going to come up to L.A. and go through the morgue at the TIMES and she wanted to be sure that you wouldn't miss her picture."

"C'mon. I'll give you that I don't have a rational explanation but one's coming."

"Mind if I don't hold my breath."

"You'll turn blue. Tell Bruce over there that we're gone, outta here so he can relax. He's been as nervous as a cat trying to bury his shit in a marble room. If we hustle we can get a few hours of sleep and head over to the last known address first thing in the morning."

They spent what was left of the night at Alexis' place with her out of town. Morgan took the bed and Burns the couch but Morgan was wide awake two hours later. He showered and dressed quietly, made a cup of instant coffee, and went outside, coffee cup in hand. It was the time of false dawn, if night ever comes in the city, and the marine layer still hung in the sky and the air smelled that peculiar smell of jasmine flowers and smog. The first time he had ever smelled that smell was the first time he had ever set foot in L.A., when he had bummed a ride to the city aboard an old DC3 from the Pentagon where they had stuck him when he came back from Central America. He walked, lost in thoughts of what his life had been like back then, walked down Charleville, up Rodeo, back over on Wilshire, and then it came to him and he spun suddenly and half-ran back to the apartment. Burns was awake, still in his skivvies, perched on one of the two barstools that Alexis always kept next to the cooking island in the middle of her kitchen. His laptop computer was open and his face was a study in concentration. He waved a hand in the general direction of Morgan and Morgan walked over and peered at the screen covered with stock quotations and charts.

"I've got it."

"Got what?" Burns was looking at the computer screen, tapping, looking, and talking at the same time. Outside a car alarm sounded, but only for a second.

"The girl I dreamed about was wearing a marcasite pin."

"What's a marcasite pin? Hey, look. AOL's down three and I just bought a hundred shares of that piece of crap yesterday."

"I'm not sure…it looks like it's made of silver with rhinestones. Costume. From the '30's. My mother had one. Everyone's mother had one. I'm sure yours did. Anyway, she had one."

"Who."

"Pay attention, will you. The girl in my dream. The girl in the picture."

"Ya, so."

"This one had initials. And I think the initials might have been 'A. S.'"

"Burns stopped in mid-keystroke. No shit." he looked at Morgan for the first time. "You're serious."

"Pretty damn certain. The letters were script, so I can't be sure. It could have been a G. But I would swear by the A."

"April Sawyer. Imagine that

"I'm trying to."

"This is weird. Man I wish I had paid more attention in Paranormal 101. You're convinced that this really is the girl who has been visiting you in your dreams, or in a dream state, right?"

"I don't know. I'm not saying anything. It's probably my imagination. But if it's coincidence, it's a helluva coincidence. The picture in the paper looks like the girl in the bunkhouse, for sure. The initials on the brooch are close. Who knows? Maybe I'm spending too much time in the desert and I'm turning in to one of those kooks. Too much heat on the brain, maybe. I wish I knew. Or wish I hadn't ever started with this."

"Well it's too late to turn back so we're gonna damn sure find out. Let's get this show on the go."

By 8:00, with Morgan's car stashed in Beverly Hills, they headed down La Brea for the 10 Freeway. Morgan, more impatient than he cared to admit, had taken over for Burns behind the wheel. "Where you goin'?" Burns drawled when he saw where the car was headed.

"Bellflower."

"What are you, a barbarian? Not at this hour, bro. This isn't the old days. We're gonna do this in a civilized manner and stop at Campanile." Burns announced. "Your treat." Morgan gave him a look so Burns added: "C'mon, you cheap bastard. Don't forget you're getting my services at fire sale prices."

A trendy eatery by night, morning at Campanile turned it into a kind of entertainment industry chuckwagon, a not-too-distant relative of the lunchwagons that rolled onto construction sites all over the city every day. If you were in the know, you parked in the lot to the south of the building and walked in through the front or through La Brea Bakery and ordered your breakfast and coffee at the bar from bartenders who appeared vaguely familiar and who seemed somehow to know what you were going to order before you opened your mouth. Waiters took note of which one of the smallish tables you chose and when your order was up it was quietly delivered and you could sit there for hours undisturbed, with scripts and manuscripts and newspapers among the latte cups and croissants or scones and schmooze. Or hope for a deal. Or if you were that kind, you could hope to be recognized.

It was a familiar drill to Morgan, and Burns, ever the chameleon, blended in without effort. Morgan took the check with a great flourish and they positioned themselves where they could keep an eye on two blondes, dancers from the way they dressed and the way their legs filled out the black tight retro pedal pusher pants they wore. Both of them wore their hair gathered into pony tails and both had on clingy cotton t-shirts that stopped just under their breasts and left almost nothing to the imagination. They were in their early 20's and beautiful in lipstick alone. "It's a crime against humanity to ignore women like that. If you do, God takes away your sight." Burns mused, and Morgan nodded his agreement and sipped his coffee.

"You ever been married?" Burns asked.

"You grilling me, now, detective?"

"No. Just a habit. You know how a detective's mind works. It's automatic. You sit down with a cup of coffee and the mental tape recorder starts. Didn't mean to pry."

"I was just givin' you shit...I don't mind. The answer is "yes". To someone just like that." Morgan indicated the taller of the dancers. "Didn't work. I found out too late that she was the type who would talk about herself and then say 'enough about me, let's talk about you. What do you think of me?' But that was later. I was young and she was a knockout and we used to fuck each other's brains out."

"Kids?"

"No."

"Where's she now?"

"Don't know. With some producer for a while…then, who knows?"

"And now?"

"I'm with Alexis. And we have an agreement of sorts."

"So you have a commitment."

"Who said that?"

"You did. Maybe not in so many words."

"Alexis is deep in the career of a lifetime. And I'm not willing to give up what I have in the desert and move back to the city. But we're both veterans of the bad relationship wars. Maybe it is commitment. Married or not, we're trying to see if this is the relationship that works. You don't know until it's over. You're not supposed to know. That's why God made the world round."

"So you can't see too far ahead…heavy shit for early in the morning."

"Anyway, like the man said, maybe life isn't like a river."

"Sounds like a punch line."

"It is. A man spends his entire life seeking the meaning of his existence, spends his fortune, turns his back on his family, and finally finds himself at the top of a mountain in Tibet with a holy man who answers his question about the meaning of life by saying 'Life is like a river.' The man protests, asks him if that was that, that was what he sacrificed his life to find out. And the holy man says…"

"So maybe life isn't like a river."

"Should never give the punch line first. But you asked."

"Not funny. It's true."

"And you, my private detective friend?"

"Five years ago, when I was 29. We had a kid, a little girl. It's the only good thing we did together. The work I do scared her. We're friends, now, but I wasn't happy about it then. Or now. I take care of the girl. It's the usual California story. And I might get married again. My job is not exactly risk free, but that's an excuse, I know."

"And for now, there're too many hotties running around Malibu."

"Well put," he grinned.

Morgan drained his coffee and checked his watch. "Enough folderol, Burnsy. We're burnin' daylight. Let's go."

The address was off Rosecrans, between the 605 and the 710 and they drove east on the broad street with the post-rush hour traffic beginning to thin. The area looked tired, drained, as if the very stones had been worn down by the waves of Californians who had come west, lived in the Bellflowers and the Downeys and the Lakewoods, the walled cities that were the common architectural denominator of the city-state that was Los Angeles, and had moved on, each taking another piece of the life force of the area. Nineteen million people lived now in what was loosely termed the basin, and most of them had come at first seeking open space, room enough to dream. Now all that they had was ever-lengthening commutes on the ever-more congested freeways.

Morgan made a left off Rosecrans onto Sage, then a right onto Sycamore and Burns called off the numbers as they drove. The house at 40825 was on the south side of the street, a tan, one story bungalow. There was a side arch that once was an architectural statement, and a brown fence that went from the house to the neighbor's fence on one side and to a small garage on the other. When Burns got out of the car a dog of nondescript lineage poked his head underneath the fence and tried to bite his way out, growling and barking. Morgan climbed out the other side and muttered something to the dog who retreated.

"What'd you say?"

"I told him he wasn't intimidating anyone."

"No, really."

"Really."

"That all?"

"No. Told him to be quiet. But he knew I meant it."

"Damn cowboy. How do you do that?"

When they reached the porch, the name on the mailbox said " Gloria Rodriguez" and they exchanged glances and Morgan mouthed "shit" through clenched teeth. His knock on the solid door was answered by a hollow silence. He knocked again, and this time they heard steps, deliberate, firm steps, and the door opened, but just a crack, secured by a chain. The lined face of a very old woman peered out. "Can I help you?"

"I sure hope so." Morgan answered. "We're trying to get some information on a family that used to live here. Their name was Sawyer. Did you ever hear of them?"

"Why? Who are you?"

"My name is Nicholas Morgan. I'm a writer. In fact, here's my card." He took his wallet out and handed over his business card. The old woman was not impressed and then, on a sudden inspiration, he produced his WGA card and his driver's license. "This handsome young man with me is Hollister T. Burns. He's my photographer and..."

"...research assistant."

"Right...research assistant."

She stared at the information and looked between the license and Morgan's face several times and finally nodded, closed the door, and undid the security chain. There was a rattling while she took the keys out of the deadbolt and then she opened the door and stepped outside and locked the door from the outside. She was wearing a blue cardigan sweater and she carefully put the keys in the right hand pocket and patted the pocket. "You can't be too careful, you know."

"You're absolutely right, ma'am. I know."

"You didn't answer my question, young man. Why?"

"My information says that a Sawyer family used to live here. I'm doing some legwork and coming over here is a good way to start. But if you don't know anything…" He began to turn away.

"Didn't say that. I just want to know why you want to know."

"I'm writing something about some women who disappeared in the 1930's. One of them was April Sawyer. Matter of fact…" On a sudden inspiration, Morgan reached into the folder he had and extracted the picture they had copied the night before. "You ever see this lady?"

"Oh, my. Oh, my." She paled and steadied herself on the stoop railing.

"You okay?"

The women shrugged his concern off. "Oh, my…that's a picture of my sister. Rodriguez is my married name. But I'm a Sawyer." Her face morphed into a mask of sadness.

Morgan looked closely at the woman. There was something about her green eyes still clear despite her years, the way she held her head and jutted her chin that made him feel protective and he hesitated, trying to decide what to say. Burns, however, had no such compunction. "Do you know where she is?" he blurted out.

"No," she sighed. "She disappeared. Disappeared 60 some years ago. Without a trace."

"I'm sorry. Do you mind if I ask you some questions?"

She shook her head, no. "I suppose it doesn't matter now.

Sure."

"Could you tell us something about her?"

The old woman moved to the edge of the small porch and sat on the stoop, gathered her legs under her, and gestured to Morgan and Burns to join her. They sat. "No one has asked me about April in years." she began. "You can never really know someone, or just when you think you do, something happens and you find out you didn't after all. I was only 16 when she disappeared but I do know that she was a nice girl. Not wild, or anything. There were a lot of rumors in the neighborhood when she disappeared but as far as I know they were only rumors. I can't believe she was bad in any way." She paused. "Let me show you something."

She excused herself for a moment and unlocked the front door and let herself in. "I hope you don't mind. I won't let strangers in the house and, you know…"

"I agree. You can't be too careful." Burns reassured her.

She came back out again with some framed pictures and handed them to Morgan before turning back to the lock and going through the drill again. They were graduation pictures and a few stiff, formal family pictures. "April went to high school in Downey, and then she took college classes in Long Beach until she became a legal secretary. That was about two years before she disappeared. Before then, she worked as a sales clerk in Woolworth in Long Beach, but she always had this idea that if she worked hard, no matter what her job, she would make a success. I remember when she started in the law office, I don't remember the lawyer's name now, but…"

"Was it Carruthers?"

"No, no. Carruthers was Scott. Scotty. That was the man she went off with." Burns glanced at Morgan. "She told me that one day he just showed up in the office to see one of the lawyers and they started to talk and he asked her to lunch.

They knew each other for about six months before she went out with him on a real date. We used to talk about those things, even though I was younger. She was nervous about going out with him because he was in his mid-30's and she was only 25 at the time and that was sort of a big deal in those days."

"Did they date much?"

"Casually. Lunches and things. Like I said, she wasn't wild, or anything. He was a smoker, I remember. I didn't like that, even then. She picked up the habit from him."

"When you saw her last, what was that like?"

"I don't know if I said it was a Friday, in the morning. You get older, you forget sometimes what you said, you know. Anyway, school was out for the summer and I was going to the beach. I remember I was surprised that she was home so early. She had some things in a small bag and I remember that I asked her where she was going. She didn't want to tell me at first because, old as she was, my father wouldn't have allowed it. But you know how sisters are and after a while she told me that she and Scotty were going off for a weekend together.

"Do you have any idea about where they went?"

"No, not at all."

"Do you have any idea now about what happened?"

"No. My father asked me and I told him I hadn't been home when she left and I never changed my story. I was too afraid. And all I really know is that when she didn't come back by Monday, he went to the police. I was sick inside, because I blamed myself. Maybe if I would have said something earlier…"

"Is there a chance that Scott and your sister ran away? Eloped?"

"I don't think so. She would have contacted me at some point. Especially after our father died."

"Is there any reason to suspect that Scott might have

harmed her and become a fugitive?"

"I don't think so. Scotty really liked her. Of course, I could be wrong. I know that he took us both out for sodas once, and to a movie once. It sounds corny nowadays. Both times I really sensed that he liked her. She was very pretty, as you can see from the pictures. Vivacious. Charming. She had a great figure and she was smart and she looked you in the eye when she talked and when you talked she listened. Even to her sister. Everyone liked her, especially Scott."

"Did you like Scott?"

"Liked him, yes. But there was something about him, an undercurrent of worry, perhaps, that I didn't trust. Even in my young mind then he might have been insincere sometimes and I wasn't happy that April was dating him. But he always treated her well and she seemed to like him and I guess that's all that mattered. She looked happy that last Friday, the last day I saw her. Bubbly, like she was going on a great adventure." Gloria gathered herself, as if to get up. "I've spent too much time on ancient history already, Mister Morgan. If you don't mind, I've got some things to do today. I hope I've been some help." and she turned suddenly, the interview concluded. She reached a hand out and grasped the doorknob and almost reflexively Morgan put his hand over hers. He felt her cringe and immediately withdrew it. "Wait, please…there's more I have to tell you." he said.

"What else could there possibly be?"

"I may have an idea about what happened to your sister." The woman turned and seemed to sink down onto the stoop, never taking her eyes from Morgan's face as he unfolded what he knew for her. She listened quietly, somber, tears filling her eyes several times and in a bizarre way he found himself speaking of the dead woman as if he had known her, as if they were linked somehow, and he knew now that they were.

"Maybe I watch too much television," she said, when he paused, "but you know how on "Unsolved Mysteries" they sometimes find siblings who have been lost for years? And even though she would be in her late 80's now, maybe I never stopped hoping." She questioned him carefully about the chances of finding clues if they dug in the area and he responded, telling her what kind of soil existed in the desert, and what would be left after all those years of sandy soil and dampness and heat. She was silent and looked away as if she could see over the vista of decades. Finally she looked at Morgan, deeply, the way she had when they first met, and shook her head, as if making her mind up. "Come with me."

She walked down the two small steps of the porch and began to walk briskly around the corner of the house, Morgan and Burns following behind like baby ducklings, to where a narrow garage sat, its door closed like a huge somnolent eye against the sunny morning. She tapped a few numbers out on a keypad and the door swung upward. A blue Buick, at least 15 years old, rested in the middle of the garage and she walked down one side and pointed up to an open overhead storage area where a small grip could be seen, brown leather trimming a tapestry covering. "Could you please reach that for me?"

Morgan swung the grip down and laid it on the ground, and the three of them bent over it and when Gloria opened the suitcase the scent of lavender filled the air and Morgan took his breath in sharply. There were a few dresses, carefully folded, that occupied most of the suitcase. On top, separated from the clothing by crinkly white paper, rested a yearbook and a photo album. "I haven't looked at these things in years." Gloria mused, "Maybe 20 years. Would you like to see them?" she asked quietly. "I guess that's a silly question."

Morgan found himself holding his breath, afraid even to speak for fear that she would change her mind, and a nod was all he could muster. Gloria took out the album and knelt down, and with Morgan at her side and Burns hovering over them she carefully turned page after page. In small three by three inch black and white pictures, printed on paper with deliberately ragged edges and fixed in the album with small black paper triangles, the life of the girl played out. She went before his eyes from a solemn-eyed child to a long-legged teenager, to a serious face under a graduation cap. After that there were some pictures of April at the beach, managing to make a one piece bathing suit look painted on. And then dressed up for some kind of dance in a long, flowy white thing.

There were pictures of her alone and pictures of her with girl friends and in one sequence she posed with a two wheeled bicycle in front of the house, her head inclined in a coquettish pose. In one picture taken with an old girlfriend, she held a small dog to her face. There were only a few family pictures and Morgan looked closely at them, unaware for a moment of what he was seeing. Then he realized. "You were blond."

"I was."

"And your Mom was blond."

"Almost a natural."

"And in this picture where your Dad didn't have a hat on, he looks blond."

"Actually he was light brown."

"But April had dark hair."

"Reddish, actually. Her friends used to tease her about being left by gypsies, although she hated that. She wanted to be blond in the worst way. What about it?"

"Nothing…unusual is all."

"And that's it for family shots."

"That's it. My father didn't like to take pictures. He had a drinking…was an alcoholic. Nowadays it's no big thing. You admit it, get treatment for it, and it's no shame. But all those years ago…my mother would have died of embarrassment. So instead she almost died from all the beatings Father gave her and if he hadn't died a few years after April disappeared, she would have died for real. He kept us all under his thumb, watched everything we did, and tried to keep us at home as long as possible. When April was gone, he used it as an excuse to keep me home." She began to cry. "Now it all seems so stupid, with all of them passed on."

Quiet, unable to find anything to say just then, Morgan put a hand on her shoulder while she wiped her nose. "So if what you tell me is true, Mister Morgan, this is the girl that's haunting you. My sister. How about that. I'd go down to your ranch, but to be honest with you, I'd just as soon leave it alone. I've done all my mourning and all my missing and being near her spirit isn't what I think I want to do. I've put it all away. I'll see her soon enough. I believe that, you know."

Morgan didn't know what to believe at this point so he just nodded. "Thanks. I didn't know how to tell you at first. I did know that I really didn't want to upset you. Now I'm afraid I've done just that."

"No. I knew somehow I'd find out what happened one day."

"Thanks again. We'll be off." He rose and jerked his head at Burns who was trying as hard as possible to look patient.

"Wait." Gloria reached back into the suitcase and came out with a slim, small package wrapped in a paper bag and secured with a very old rubber band. "That day Scotty left these with me and told me to put them somewhere where no one would find them until he came back. He was very serious and told me not to show them to anyone." She unwrapped the package and took out what looked like two small journals and studied them in silence for a moment. "I put them in this bag under the back steps. The police asked a lot of questions later, asked me everything but they never asked about any books or journals so I never told them. I don't know why except that I didn't want them to find out anything bad about April and so I told them I hadn't even been home that day. You see, I suppose after all something told me Scotty wasn't the best guy in the world. I wrapped them like this all those years ago and haven't touched them since. Anyway…" And she held them toward Morgan. "Do you want 'em?"

The two journals had thick black covers and pages of a light greenish tint, numbered but not dated, edged in faded red. 'Scott Carruthers, Esq.' was written inside the front cover, and 'July, 1932' under the name. "I have no use for them and they won't do anyone else any good now."

Burns took one from Morgan and quickly scanned the pages filled with numbers and entries in small handwriting. He closed it just as quickly and tapped it against his leg, an impatient gesture.. "Let's go." he urged Morgan. "Thank you Ma'am. I'll meet you at the car." he spun and started down the driveway to where the BMW was parked, trying not to run, not even concerned with maintaining the pretense of civility.

Morgan hung back. "Here's my phone number." he said, handing her another card, reluctant to leave. "Call me if you think of anything else. I'm not sure what's going to happen…but I'll let you know what comes of this."

Gloria extended her hand palm forward, as if bestowing a benediction, shook her head and all but pushed the card back at him. "You have everything. There won't be anything else. Goodbye."

12

By the time Morgan got back to the car Burns was already hunkered down in the passenger seat flipping the pages of one of the journals front to back to front, his brow drawn in deep concentration. The car door was open and Morgan leaned in, one arm on the roof. "You damn near broke your leg getting out of there." he needled.

"This is some kinda hot stuff, pard."

"Like how hot?"

"It's not all numbers. This guy's written some shit, too. Want to know what I think we got here?" He nodded to himself and continued to flip pages. "Yup…I'd be willin' to bet on it. Ya wanna know…okay…I'll tell ya. What we got here belonged to a dead lawyer, and I bet it's your dead lawyer. Everything hangs together right. Thing is, I'd be willin' to bet that you could get a lot more for these if you showed 'em to the right people. I mean more than you could get selling them on the Antique Roadshow."

"How's that?"

"Look…one is an address book." Burns riffled the pages

and as he did a yellow piece of newspaper fell out and did a lazy pirouette to the ground and Morgan dove for it and smoothed it out.

"Don't know what this has to do with anything." Morgan said. It's a story about some Indians being murdered in the desert.

"What's the date on it?"

"The date looks like it was torn off. The question is why did he keep it?"

"Good question. This other ledger is a journal, and unless I'm off, it's the one with the hot stuff. Let's go find a place where we can look this over and I'll show you." Morgan made a motion to take the ledgers and Burns gave him a look. "You drive. These ain't gettin' outta my hands."

Morgan turned the BMW back onto Rosecrans and headed back to the 710. There was a Norm's Restaurant right before the onramp on the right and Morgan swung the car into an empty space near the front. Only with the engine off, and Morgan standing outside his car door, did Burns reluctantly close the journal but he kept his place with his index finger. They walked into the restaurant like that and headed straight for the back booth. The vaguely familiar 50's sign, the slightly rancid odor of bacon frying, the décor, all of it, echoed the era when all things seemed possible and Morgan couldn't help smiling at the anachronistic establishment all the while looking around furtively. Ridiculous, he thought. Even if anyone knew, why would anyone possibly care that he had a matched set of 60 year old address books, or day books, or whatever they were?

Two waitresses were sitting behind the low counter and they looked up, resenting the intrusion. The larger one who looked as though she was the restaurant's best customer pulled herself to her feet with what seemed some effort and came over slowly, two menus in hand. Morgan waved the menus aside and motioned at the upside-down coffee cups while Burns ordered a cinnamon bun. The waitress started away but Burns called her back.

"Changed my mind...can I get an English muffin? Dry?"

"Sure, honey." She said, and started away as slowly as she had come.

"You trying to get healthy?" Morgan asked when the waitress was out of earshot. He moved around to Burns' side of the booth and they opened the first journal together.

"Not a chance. I got a look at her from behind and that was enough. I knew someone like that once...you asked her to haul ass she had to make two trips."

They opened the first journal together. Inside the cover, in a firm handwriting, was written: "Scott Carruthers, Esq." and below the name was the office address and the telephone number. On the top of the right hand page, in the same hand, was written: January 1, 1933. Names and addresses followed. There was nothing else.

The second journal was not laid out like a day book, with pages assigned to certain days, but the lawyer had used it as such, drawing a line at the end of one day and writing the date of the next day below that. It was in chronological order but there were days that were left out, the typical schedule of a beginning lawyer, busy one day, twiddling his thumbs the next. They paged through the first few weeks without finding anything other than notations of meetings with a succession of seemingly unrelated names, none of them Hispanic, and an occasional place where he had written "will", or "lease review" and the billable hours.

About mid-February 1933, they began to notice more and more entries marked "Riverside Court House" and one or two Latino names. The entries had begun in January. The names changed but the remarks were always the same—"papers filed" or "party served". Most of them had a small notation, the initials "R.G." circled and there were occasional references to a meeting with someone designated "R.G.". In the address book there was only one name that matched those initials— Rolando Gutierrez. The name and phone number had been carefully printed.

They paged back and found Carruther's first meeting with "R.G." that had taken place the end of January, at lunch at the Roost Café on Temple, a legendary joint in those days, a roadhouse kind of place less than 15 minutes from downtown. A meeting followed every month, sometimes every three weeks, at the Roost or at the Ambassador on Wilshire. Twice they even met at the Brown Derby. After each meeting was a number and the letter "G". "Could be dollars…" Burns said, "like two thousand, five thousand."

"Yeah, and it could be that it came from Gutierrez. Doesn't matter right now."

The trips to Riverside began shortly after, sometimes once a week, sometimes skipping a week, until April, 1933, when the entries suddenly stopped and there was no mention of the Riverside Courthouse or meetings with R.G. until Friday, June 23, 1933. All the note said then was "R.G.", 2 PM, Ramirez Ranch.

There were even more cryptic references throughout to transfers of money to initials, written as 5G to "P" for R.G., sometimes it would be to "C". Occasionally he would meet these individuals at Musso & Frank's Grill, or Philippe, or the Farmer's Market, sometimes at the an address on Fairfax or on Olympic or even back at the Roost.

There was a separate section almost two-thirds of the way through the journal that Burns missed on his first pass but they came across it this time through and studied it in silence.

Every name against which something had been filed or served was listed, along with a legal description of the property. From what Morgan could see, the properties were all in the Coachella Valley east of the railhead in Indio. "I hate to say this, partner, but I have a feeling." Morgan mumbled.

"That's a switch."

"That's why I can hardly stand to say it. But I can't help but wonder that if we put these property descriptions on a map, they wouldn't be damn close to where the All-American Canal runs."

"What's an All-American Canal?

"It's a canal that brings water into the desert from the Colorado for the farmers. It was built in the 30's and designed so as to run in the U.S. territory exclusively so the Mexicans wouldn't be able to shut it down if they got pissed at us. The first canal that ran part way through Mexico and that worried some politicians."

"What about it?"

"I don't know. I'm trying to find a motive. That lady at the Indio Historical Society told me yesterday that knowing the location of the All-American Canal in advance would have been hot stuff in the '30's. Like winning the lottery. Hot enough to kill someone for. Or about. There's damn little else worth killing for in the desert. Family honor. Money. To our knowledge, Carruthers had no family there."

"And he was a lawyer so..."

"...that takes care of the honor part. So what do you make of it?" Morgan interrupted.

"I've seen enough things like this to figure that the lawyer was getting cash from this Gutierrez guy for something he wanted kept secret. Our boy probably was the middle-man, the bag man, the go-between, paying people off for him."

"Sounds logical. All that good government money was

being spent on buying the right of way. Big, easy, tempting money. Gutierrez could have hired the lawyer to do his dirty work for him and to be a bagman, too. And he could have used the information he got to tie up land on the canal right-of-way."

"And at some point the lawyer could have tried to shake him down."

"Or Gutierrez just got tired of working with him."

"And the girl…"

"Old story…'wrong place, wrong time.'"

"So who was the third guy? You know, didn't she say there were three of them?"

"Beats the shit out of me"

"And what's the clipping have to do with it. And what's it all mean 60-plus years later?"

Morgan shook his head. "Not jack shit. Half, hell most of L.A. was built by graft and swindling and mobs and extortion. I've heard stories about Mulholland and the boys that lined their pockets while the city was appropriating water from the Owens Valley."

"So for all that, Owens Lake is a dustbowl now and they've all got their pictures up in City Hall. And not on Wanted posters either. What're you gonna do with your own particular treasure trove of information now to make things right?"

"Meaning what?"

"You gonna go home and sit down and tell the spirits you found out what happened? Or you gonna get someone to exorcise the spirits?"

Morgan was quiet for a moment. "I don't know. It would make a great story but I don't know enough about this water stuff right now. As soon as I get back down in the desert you can bet your sweet ass I'm going to go into Palm Springs and look some of it up. As for my spooks, they don't bother me that much although it's a little weirder thinking I know who two of the people were." Morgan exhaled. "What am I talking about? A week ago I would've laughed me out of town."

"I wish I knew more about this Mexican familia. I'm gonna run down some leads up here. There's something about these motherfuckers that brings to mind the dickheads that offed Brooks. I need to go back and check on some names." He paged through the daybook once again and stopped near the middle. "There's one entry that doesn't make sense to me."

"Where."

"Here." Burns said, turning the journal so Morgan could see. It doesn't read like any of the other entries. In code, or something. Maybe a report from someone about an investigation, the way it's notated, PIREP, and maybe an address. 52804 S in D. And then this is scribbled, but it looks like RGSIB or something."

"Makes no friggin' sense to me."

"Maybe the spirits'll tell you."

"If they do, smartass, I'm not tellin'."

"Anyway, for now I'll drop you back in Beverly Hills so's you can pick up your car. There's a new candidate for the next Mrs. Burns I met last week up in the Colony and I think I'll call her tonight and see if she wants to cook dinner for me. No sense in depriving myself, right? Why don't you come up and stay at my place? It's about 15 degrees cooler on the water and when you wake up tomorrow morning you can sit on my porch and ogle the starlet wannabes on the beach."

"Generous offer, Mister Burns, but I'm back to God's country. Well, maybe it's not exactly God's country but it'll do for now. I'll pick Max up when I get back and take a horse and go up into the mountains in the morning and ride down a coyote or two and listen to absolutely nothing and sort all of this out."

"Still think better on horseback?"

"Old habits…"

"My life's kind of quiet workwise right now. Except for an assignment for POLO I'm finishing. So let me know when you find out more about the canal and if you make any more sense of some of these entries." He tapped the cover of the journals, a gesture full of meaning. "Copy these," he said, and then he slid them across the table to Morgan who picked them up and tucked them under his arm.

"I plan to."

Burns looked him in the eyes. "ASAP. It's important. Copy them."

Burns drove this time, and Morgan leaned his head back on the seatback and closed his eyes. "You ever stop and think about coincidence?" he said, after they had gotten on the 710.

"What do you mean?"

"I mean coincidence. You're walking out of your house and the phone rings. You stop to answer it and it's the wrong number and you get in your car and when you get to the corner there's a badass accident and if you wouldn't have answered the phone you'd be hamburger. Or you don't answer the phone and the person who's calling you goes out earlier than he would have and gets hit by a car. Or nailed in a drive-by."

"I suppose so, but that's the road to craziness, thinking about all those possibilities."

Morgan studied the car alongside without seeing it. "Craziness, or do you get a new appreciation for the bizarre tapestry of our lives? What's fate and what's free will? That's Kaballah stuff. It comes up so many times in so many philosophies—Sufi, Hasidism, Zen. That our lives are the sum total of a million small decisions that we make every moment and when it works out or doesn't we bless God or curse our stupidity. Here's one for you…" He turned to Burns. "A few years ago this guy I knew was going skiing in Aspen and invited me along in his private plane along with some other people. He sent his pilot off on vacation on his yacht and he was going to fly it himself."

"Nice life…you didn't go."

"No."

"Why?"

"I had just started to date Alexis and she was working the weekend and I thought at the time it was more important to stay around. They were due back in San Francisco on Monday morning so he took off out of Aspen just as they were shutting the airport down because of weather and stacked it into the last mountain before the airport at Brian Head. They were just 20 feet short of the top when his wing de-icers failed."

"They were…"

"All killed. I heard the flight data recorder conversations before they went in. Not fun."

"If you'd have gone…"

"I'd be dead."

"Where're you going with that?"

"Nowhere, except to wonder if there is any kind of a grand plan or is it all some kind of cosmic crapshoot? I happened to drive down 50th two hours after the sign advertising the ranch for sale was put up. So I'm the one that owns it. And I'm the one with the connections to get the story out and with a PI who just happens to have the time because he shitcanned his license. With a different family life, April might have gotten married and not have gone to work for a lawyer and most probably she wouldn't have met our dear dead lawyer. And then if she refused to go to the desert she would have grown old with her sister."

"Maybe. If her father left her alone. Maybe she would have become the Black Dahlia. Who knows?"

"Who, indeed."

Burns pulled the BMW up alongside the Mercedes where it rested in the underground parking space of Alexis' place and Morgan opened it up, put the journal in the trunk, and waved at Burns. "Copy those." Burns said, pointing to the journals. "Don't forget."

13

The onramp of the 10 headed east at Robertson was in a seedy, rundown area of Los Angeles where the pavement was potholed and the cement on the freeway overpass was crumbling and the traffic was always bad and you couldn't help but check to make sure all your car doors were locked even if it was broad daylight. A fitting place to bid goodbye to the City of Angels, especially if you were having noir thoughts. The buildings were old and the signs old and the trucks that belonged to the butcher supply company that wryly boasted 'you can't beat our meat' were old, just like on Delancey Street in Brooklyn where the delivery trucks double-parked and dared you to blow your horn in protest. It was just before 2PM and already the traffic was building. Years ago the rush hour was just that, or maybe two, but now the crest of the wave of traffic no sooner broke in one direction than it began in the other so that there was never a lull.

The Mercedes was stopped by every one of the convoluted traffic lights under the freeway but Morgan eventually made it on to the 10 headed east and as soon as he had a feel for the traffic he phoned Amado. It took three tries of dropped calls but at last the Mexican's *"hola?"* crackled over the cell phone. *"Que onda ese?"* Morgan asked.

Amado laughed at the slang. "Not much. When you be back?"

"Four thirty, five. How's Max? How's the rancho?"

"Tranquilo. Todo esta bien. You like to ride?" After the tournament they had turned the horses out, two at the pasture on the ranch, and more at a pasture by Donegal Farms. They had kept the two newest made horses, Negra and Guerrero, as well as the two greenest ponies, Nino and Groovy, at the club for pleasure riding and casual stick and ball practice now that the season was over. They planned to work on them during the summer, turning them from barely rideable animals into horses that would get you through a chukker of polo by time the season began in late November. Morgan checked where the sun was and figured in the traffic. "Not today...but in the morning. You have Max with you?"

"Seguro."

"I'll meet you. Buy you dinner at el Ranchito. You got a date?"

"Usted." he laughed.

"Funny, *maricon*. But let's do something different in the morning and take the horses out into the mountains. They could use the change, and so could I."

By 3:30 he had topped the Banning Pass and started the long descent into the valley. The sun at his back threw the mountains into sharp relief and they rose up on either side and embraced him although still ten miles or so away to the north and south. From there they marched on to the eastern horizon and beyond in coves and inlets and islands of granite rising from the sand floor that was all that was left of the prehistoric sea. If you squinted your eyes and looked into the distance just so you could imagine what it had been like in those days, when dinosaurs lived and the area looked like endless giant fjords before the water retreated and sought refuge in the massive underground aquifers that made all of the golf courses possible. The lower he descended, the higher the outside temperature became and with it the growing otherworldly quiet that he sensed rather than heard, and he could feel himself being drawn back, sucked back into the arms of the desert like a long-anticipated lover who would henceforth be even more jealously guarded.

At the corner of Jefferson and Highway 111, about 20 or so young people clustered, college age, perhaps, or younger. They were casually dressed and the typical California amalgam of anglo and latino and black. When Morgan slowed down to look them over they held up signs and clapped and cheered and when they noticed him they waved and he waved back, half-heartedly. The signs protested a plan to open a major gambling casino on the east side of town near where Indio bordered on Coachella. It was something that had escaped Morgan's attention and he made a mental note to get a local paper.

El Ranchito occupied a small, one story building on a side street in the village of La Quinta, the next town over from Indio and a mile or so from the polo club and closer in to the Santa Rosa mountains. Except for the La Quinta Hotel that had morphed into a resort in the 1980's, the village had remained an economic backwater, more or less the way it had been since before the war, dusty streets, half-empty storefronts, no streetlights, no curbs, no gutters, no sidewalks. It could have been a typical western town but for the fact that it was California. It was there, in a far different time, and in a far different incarnation, that the great Garbo had rendezvoused with Brian Heath for long quiet morning breakfasts, Garbo driving in from the Ingleside Inn in Palm Springs while Heath would drive in from his place deep in the valley.

Morgan and Amado took one of the outside tables on the small covered patio set off with potted plants and little sections of white picket fences stuck this way and that in terra cotta pots. Even though it was barely six, the sun had already dipped behind Santa Rosa and the sky was still bright overhead, the way it would remain for another hour or so. Strings of small Christmas lights were suspended in the *pirul* tree that grew on the side of the building and they winked a weak white in the flat light. Except for a fitful stream of cars that pulled up before the liquor store on the corner near the bank, little traffic moved. Already the restaurant's tables were filling up with vaguely familiar faces, cowboys, a few horse wranglers, and one or two golfing types from the resort or from some of the more expensive housing tracts that clustered not far away.

Maria, the waitress, was a fixture in the place and they smiled a greeting to her while she brought over two ice-cold Coronas opened and sat them on the table without asking. She followed that with a wooden bowl of pico de gallo and a small dish of a fiery hot, red sauce and chips and waited while they looked at the menu without seeing and ordered what they always ordered, the plate of fajitas with flour tortillas.

When their food came, they ate quietly, and talked about the horses and how the two green ones were coming but Morgan could see that there was something on the Mexican's mind and when he asked him if the ranch had been quiet, Amado looked him in the eye and then looked away. "I go in yesterday, and a big piece of cactus outside the bedroom is on the ground." Amado showed him with his hands that it was at least a foot long. "I want to throw it out so I pick it up an' put it on the long table inside. But I forget. So I go back this morning, an' the piece of cactus, it's back by the plant."

"You must have made a mistake."

"No, I no make mistake." He was adamant that no one else had been there and that he hadn't forgotten to set the alarm when he left.

"You're sure."

"Nikko. I sure. No one else get in there."

"You afraid?"

"Of what? *Espiritus?* No." The Mexican shook his head vigorously for emphasis. "No. I not afraid. I just want to know one thing."

"What's that, pardner?"

"What go on there?"

"When?"

"You know when…with the *espiritus.*"

"I don't know, for sure. You heard the *bruja*, Alma. Maybe two murders. Maybe three. *Quien sabe?* I just spent some time in L.A. with my friend who's a detective. We have an idea, but that's all."

"One of the dead guys *es Mexicano, si?*"

"Again, *no sabes*. I have no *pinche* idea. Why?"

"I no sure. You tol' me she say he name is *el matador.*"

"So it's a nickname. Bullfighter. Who knows."

"Maybe he the guy my *abuelo* tell me about. The one he tell me not be like. How you find out?"

"Beats the shit outta me. What are you gonna do when you find out? If you find out…"

Amado was quiet, pondering the idea. "Don't know. Excep' that my grandpa say it very dangerous to me."

"C'mon, *amigo*. How could your grandpa in Mexico know anything about this when he never was here? No…I wouldn't worry about that." Morgan paused. "I've got something for you, though."

"*Sí.*"

"You ever hear of *la emme*, the Mexican mafia?"

Amado looked around suddenly and it seemed to grow quiet on the street and the kitchen noise and the noise from the diners grew quiet. He leaned close to Morgan. "*No hablo cerca esta cosa aqui.*" He repeated himself in English. "Don't talk about that here."

"Morgan made a short, mirthless sound that might have been a laugh. "C'mon. Is there really such a thing still today?"

"No...I mean it. You don' know who listens." And he bent his head suddenly engrossed in what was left of his dinner and his white straw Stetson shielded his eyes and Morgan realized the conversation, at least that part of it, was over.

It was full dark when Morgan dropped Amado off at his car back at the polo club but the moon and the still almost-full moon cast a pale light over the misty green-gray tamarisks that lined the road and the tall oleanders. "Tell me about *la emme*." he said finally when he shut off his engine.

"I don' know nothing. *Nada.*" Again he shook himself.

"C'mon, *amigo*. Don't bullshit me."

"*No le busques.*"

"Tell me what you know about the mafia. Just between you and me. And I'm not looking for trouble. I'm doing a little background for something I'm writing."

"You *loco, amigo. La emme* run everything. You talk about them, they get you. *Drogas, putas, migra, pentamos...todos.* They no like you to talk about it. They *muy peligroso*. Better you forget you hear about *la emme*."

"Okay, okay." he lied. "Just one thing." Amado watched him in the light from the dash like he would watch a snake. "What's the name of the *emme*, the family?"

Amado was almost sweating with anxiety. He shook his

head in a movement that began somewhere in his midportion and wound up somewhere by his eyes. "No se."

"It wouldn't be Gutierrez? Would it?"

The expression on the Mexican's face froze and his eyes narrowed and he looked at Morgan as though he were looking at a dead man. "Nikko, you forget about this. *Voy a su casa con su pero e olvida lo.* I see you in *la manana* and by that time, you forget everything.

"It's Gutierrez, isn't it?"

"How you know that?"

"Just say the *spiritus* told me. Actually, what happened was that…" But Amado was holding up a brown hand. "I no want to know. I no know, I no lie." And he opened up the car door and almost sprinted for the ancient Camaro that was his car *du jour*. Max had been asleep on the back seat of the Mercedes and sat up at the commotion. "Okay, old man. Here's a little hors d'ouevre for you." And he opened up the small bag he had brought out of the restaurant and slipped the dog a small piece of chicken that Max inhaled. "Now let's go home and I'll fix your dinner."

The sun had barely been up an hour but the air was already warm by the time Morgan got to the barn. The clear cerulean sky promised an even warmer day. Amado's truck was parked off to the side with the eight horse trailer hitched and the horses saddled and tacked and loaded inside and Morgan ducked into the tackroom to retrieve his chaps and his deerskin gloves and came face to face with Cindy who was inside in front of the small mirror, fixing her ponytail. She was one of the endless string of female admirers the Mexican perpetually seemed to have around but she was an old friend of Morgan's as well and a credible polo player in the bargain and he was genuinely glad to see her even though he suspected Amado had asked her along to deflect any more questions.

With Morgan driving, they stopped first for coffee at L&G Desert Store and then headed south along Monroe, sitting three abreast in the cab of the truck, quiet, sipping from their steaming cups, each in their own heads. As the desert emerged from the covering of civilization the small houses and occasional shacks and dategroves became fewer and further apart and the fields grew more wide open and wild, covered with ranging scrub and tumbleweed. The road went from striped blacktop to a lane and a half asphalt strip, and after about 20 minutes of driving and a few turns they came to where the road ended. A mountain loomed ahead and in the barren landscape and the sandy soil the nopal and ocotillo climbed steadily upward to the south. "You know where we are?" he asked."

"No se."

"I was hoping you'd know." the girl answered.

"Nope. But I'm tired of riding the old trail and I've been meaning to come here and thought this would be as good a time as any. You game?"

"Sure."

"Compadre?"

"Seguro."

Morgan secured his worn trail canteen to his saddle, buckled his chaps, and swung into the saddle and they took off from there single file with the Mexican in the lead, following a depression in the sandy soil that could have been the site of an old rivulet or a dry creekbed. The morning sun etched their shadows onto the sand that the wind had shaped into waves and they floated there upon the sand like liquid silhouettes, part of the sunlight, part of the land

As they gained elevation, the mountains to the east slid

away like ancient sentinels, now red, now brown, and black rocks and gray promontories became visible and then shifted shapes and faded into the background as the sun rose higher. Soon the entire landscape came to resemble a burned-out caldera from the inside of a volcano older than man, older than time.

There was silence except for the crunching sound of hooves on sand and the sometime chink of metal horseshoe on rock as they moved up and except for an occasional comment or an occasional acknowledgement of an animal track in the sand, they spoke hardly at all. When they did it was in half-whispers as if not to disturb the cathedral-like quiet of the land. Once they rode up on a coyote, a female, with two pups in tow and she nipped them off when they stopped to wonder at the sight of the strange creatures, men on horseback. Red tail hawks played on the wind currents that swooped around the rocks and when two turkey buzzards swooped low to check them out, the effect was surreal.

The trail all but disappeared. The winds had been exceptionally heavy since March and the shifting sands had obliterated almost everything. After more than an hour of riding, they pulled up where there could have been a narrow trail on the north side of the mountain and from there they could see to the distant Indio Hills and the valley stretched out between. Nothing moved and there was no sound; it could have been any time since the dawn of the world.

They rode that way for a while longer and then Morgan took the point going down, and when they were almost close enough to see the truck he swung off toward the east, hunting a whim, for no good reason. A cluster of rocks made a natural promontory and Morgan kept them on his left, planning to come at the truck from a different way and from there they followed the curving trail. The sun, now almost directly overhead, glinted off rocks, then on a long curved piece of dull red metal. They seemed to notice it all at the same time and the horses watched as they rode up on it, as if they expected it to jump up out of the desert sand at them. A strip of rusty chrome was visible along the length of it and as they approached they could see a peculiar chrome device that appeared to be sticking out of the sand.

"What is it?" Cindy asked.

"Don't know." Morgan said, resetting his cowboy hat. "I guess you can find just about anything up here. You see that couch back up the trail a ways?" They rode closer still, leery of what they might find, what it might be, Morgan's mare snorting in ill-concealed alarm.

Amado rode protectively around Morgan and then went close to it and then he turned. "*Mira. Es un pedazo de carro. Un carro viejo.*"

"Now where in God's earth did that come from?" Cindy said. "I've been all around near here before, and never saw nothin' like that."

"Looks like maybe all that wind we've been having moved the sand away." Morgan swung off Negra and walked slowly forward, her reins in his hand as she shied and snorted and blew and made as if she wanted to go off in the opposite direction, but he spoke softly to her and she calmed down as she always did. When he got to the shape he cleared a little more of the sand and as he did so, what looked like the long hood of a car emerged magically beneath his hands, like he was some kind of sculptor working in metal.

"*Que tipo, patron? Tu sabes?*"

Morgan had most of the hood uncovered now and Amado had dismounted and handed Geurrero's reins to Cindy and was busy clearing sand along with him. "Not yet. Wait a second." Morgan pried the hood and it opened with a long squeaking noise, metal protesting on metal. The engine compartment was remarkably clear of sand and he looked along the top of the engine block until he saw a narrow black and silver plate. "It says here 'Auburn Motor Car Company, Dearborn, Michigan.' I'll be damned. I don't think they made a car like this in maybe 50 or 60 years. Sonofabitch."

"*Es muy caro?*"

"I don't think these were that rare, but maybe if it was cherried out, it would be. But it's not worth anything here, and I can't imagine that it would pay to move it. Strange, I wonder how it got here."

"Does it matter?" Cindy called over.

"Not really, except that there are too many weird things going on right now and my curiosity is aroused. Just say I've become fascinated by coincidences."

"Well as far as I'm concerned you can chalk it up to another desert mystery. Certainly enough of 'em." Cindy had joined them on the ground now and was around the front bumper, clearing sand with a branch and looking for a license and she finally uncovered the frame and it gaped at them, empty. "Figures." She huffed. "Hold on...weren't you supposed to keep the registration on the steering column in those days? I think I remember that from 'The Maltese Falcon' or 'The Big Sleep', where someone wants to find out who's inside a house and checks the registration on the steering column."

"Can't imagine anyone taking a license plate off and keeping a tag on the column, but let's see." They cleared more sand and gradually the form of a roadster took shape, the top open or long-since eaten by rodents. Amado was shifting sand quietly in the back of the car and when Morgan looked over, he marveled at the boattail shape that was emerging but when they got to the steering column it was free of any identification.

"Last chance is the serial number on the engine block. Got a pencil or something to write with?" The girl fumbled in all her pockets without finding anything, then bent to retrieve a small black stone while Morgan dove under the hood again and paused for a moment to let his eyes become accustomed to the darkness of the shadow of the hood. He read the numbers off the plate while Cindy wrote them on her shirttail with the black stone. "Always knew you were a friend. You'd give me the shirt off your back." he said, straightening up.

"Not a chance, cowboy." She laughed. "You can copy them off when we get back to the barn. Which it's not a bad idea to do now. It's getting warm and I want to get some water for my mare."

They unsaddled the horses and loaded them into the trailer and then drove back in silence, passing the last of the water back and forth between them in the truckcab. Back at the barn, Amado and Morgan bathed each of the horses and gave each of them a flake of hay. "*Montar esta tarde?*"

"I don't think so. I'm gonna go into Palm Springs and dig out some more information."

"*Que informacion.*"

"Don't know. I want to check some dates and things like that. Maybe find out who owned that car. It's too hot to leave Max in the car so I'm not going to take him and maybe you can check on him before you go home."

"*Seguro.* Maybe I want to take him home with me. If he no home when you get home, call me."

Morgan went toward his car and stopped when Amado called out. "Wait, *amigo. Un cosa mas. El matador*, you know, the guy?"

"What about it?"

"In English, that mean 'the killer'.

❖ ❖ ❖

On the way back to the ranch, Morgan dialed Burns from his cell phone, went through the usual series of dropped calls and innumerable squeaks and pops, and finally heard: "What's up, bro? You copy that sucker yet?"

"Burnsy, this is the desert. We're disadvantaged. I have to drive 20 minutes to find a Kinko's."

"You have it in a safe place?"

"My trunk. I've got a hunch I'm going to check out with that old lady at the historical society in the morning and then I'll head into the library in Palm Springs. I want to find out some more about this canal business. I'll do it then. On my way back."

"So what's up?"

"Found a car."

"I didn't know you were looking for one."

"I wasn't. Not that I realized anyway. This is one we found back up against the mountains that probably has been sitting there for years. Maybe 60 years. Engine block says its an Auburn. It's an unusual body type. Looks like a boattail, of all things."

"As long as you were lookin' at the engine block, you get any numbers?"

"Sheeit, you betchum, Kemo Sabe."

"See, I knew you were a detective deep down inside." Burns listened while Morgan read them off. "If they used the same system then, that makes it a 1932 model whatever. If, that is."

"Good year, '32. This place is beginning to sound like it was Broadway and 42nd back in the '30's. You think you can trace the numbers?"

"Who the fuck knows. I'll give it a shot. DMV will take days but I'll pull some connections out of my closet and see who I can come up with. There's always someone somewhere. Hey, I'm good. That's why they pay me the big bucks."

"When you have a license."

"Details." Burns sniffed. "This car you found was an Auburn, right? Let me guess...what are you thinking?"

"This car is a real flashy number. Not your run of the mill Chivvy or Ford you find dumped in the desert."

"And..."

"So I'm thinking that if I was a young lawyer...back in the 30's...with a lot of cash around..."

"...that this'd be the exact car you'd buy."

"Why the hell not?"

14

At the Historical Society in Indio the woman greeted him as if he had been an old friend. "Been thinking about you." she offered, looking up from the newspaper she had been reading.

"I'm flattered." Morgan smiled, and she seemed to melt.

"So what brings you?"

"I'm looking for more information. And I wanted to see if you were as beautiful as I remembered."

The old lady blushed and grinned back. "Strange…but I was thinking about our conversation after you left. I remembered that I had met someone in Palm Springs a few years back. An unusual old man who worked on the canal project. We talked about that, like any two old people, and he seemed to know a lot. I took his card…don't know why. But I'll bet that if anyone knows anything about the canal and all that water stuff, this probably is the man. I wondered if you were still interested."

"More than ever."

"Good. You wait right there and let me make a phone call for you." She went into the back room and he could hear her voice over the drone of the air conditioner. When she emerged she handed him a name and address that she had written on a yellow Post-It note in her careful schoolteacher's hand. "He was busy so I left word with his housekeeper."

"You're a real champ. Thanks."

He headed the truck down Highway 111 and tried Alma's number. There was some New Age-y music and then a message and he left one of his own and hung up. The traffic on the road was light and at the intersection with Jefferson, where he had to decide whether to use the freeway or Highway 111 he decided against the freeway and two stoplights later he regretted it. He had hoped that this late in the season most of the Snowbirds had cleared out, gone back to Oregon or Washington or wherever it was they came from when they descended on the desert every Christmas. Every year it was the same, a virtual infestation of blue-haired, white shoed retirees driving brand-new, big Cadillacs or Lincolns and overloading the roads and everything else between then and Memorial Day. In the last few years the summer population had been growing as well, and with it the charm of the place, the essence of that which had attracted him at first, was diminishing proportionately. Ah, for the days when you could fire a good sized cannon down Palm Canyon Drive in July without hitting anyone.

In years past, the Annenbergs had always left like clockwork on the first of May, shipping themselves and their art work off to some museum back east regardless of the weather. Most everyone else left then as well although they had long since forgotten the reason, if indeed they had ever known in the first place. Even the Annenberg name was unknown to most of the desert's inhabitants now although the former ambassador to the Court of St. James, occasional host to the polo-playing Prince of the royal family, still frequented the area from December through April. The Annenbergs were perhaps the last arbiters of the valley's social world, a world that once ran the gamut from former presidents to celebs like Sinatra and Astaire and Chaplin and Hope.

It was already straight-up noon and the temperature on the front of PFF Bank in Rancho Mirage read 105 degrees. With the heat came an intensification of the layer of alkali that eventually covered everything in the desert, and it gave the colors of the buildings, of the signs, even of the palm trees, a muted, subdued hue, a desert sand color that would remain with only subtle changes until the first rains sometime late in the summer. It was a subtle pallet, of few colors but with infinite variations and shades. A Zen tapestry.

The mountains came closer after Rancho Mirage and the die-straight road began to turn and curve in response. Bighorn sheep still prowled the higher reaches, secure even this close to civilization in their magical ability to elude anything that tried to catch them on the vertical surfaces they inhabited. By the time he crossed Frank Sinatra Drive the slopes, brown and rocky with sparse vegetation, began to sprout houses, but spaced far apart, cantilevered out with high flying roofs and expanses of glass to afford them views of the valley in either direction. These were the houses that had been designed by the disciples of Frank Lloyd Wright, architects like Richard Neutra and Albert Frey and Stewart Williams who had set the tone of the fledgling city of Palm Springs in the 40's and 50's.

Palm Springs and the valley to the east of the city had begun the early years of the century as a cowboy town, complete with its own Indians, and even though the local Indians were the completely assimilated Cahuilla band of Aqua Calientes, they passed for Indians when the Los Angeles matrons came for their dude ranch experience and to dance with real cowboys. When Hollywood discovered the area the celebrities knew they had found a place where they could escape the gaze of the studios and the scrutiny of the media that had not yet mastered the art of total obnoxiousness. A Movie Colony of sorts grew up around the Racquet Club that had been built in the 1930's and it attracted stars like Gable and Powell and Tracy and Rooney and Lombard and Flynn and Bogart.

Even in those days, Palm Springs had the reputation. A place, everyone said, where people came to drink, lie in the sun, and fuck each other crazy. There had always been wackiness about the place, a feeling that anything was permitted, but those days took it over the edge. Yet, looking back, it had been a unique, innocent time. Sometime in the 50's, Frank Bogert, a former mayor, had the brilliant idea of building a golf club and within a few short years the number of holes exceeded the number of permanent residents and even the weather had become affected, the humidity increasing each year from of the sheer acreage of green grass.

By the 70's, the epicenter of what was happening began to move further east, Down Valley, as they said, to Rancho Mirage and Palm Desert. It was in Palm Desert where a side street named El Paseo had transformed itself into a more intense, concentrated Rodeo Drive. The old houses and the flying wedge gas stations and the kitsch that made Palm Springs the greatest collection of modernist architecture in the country fell out of fashion. In old Palm Springs where Martinis and rare beef never went out of style the Movie Colony slumbered, and even though, to the casual eye, parts of the city came to resemble a rejected dowager, its heart continued to beat.

Something began to happen in the mid 80's and the trendy people, the Tom Fords and the Brad Dunnings and the movie directors and the actors from both coasts rediscovered the area and all of a sudden magazines like VANITY FAIR and LOS ANGELES were noting that the desert was hot again although of course they didn't mean the temperature. Crowds of people returned to see and be seen in places like Muriel's Supper Club and the Left Bank but the influx of beautiful people was beginning to kill the city's wonderful quirkiness, destroying it in the same way that SoHo had become commercialized and destroyed, and Laguna Beach, and TriBeCa almost like a scientific experiment was changed by the very presence of the observer.

It was ironic to him. The dead lawyer had been there, witness to the rise of the area, on the face of the wave as it were, and all those years later, Morgan was riding the backside of it, scrambling to stay out of the soup. Already there were tract homes within a few miles of the ranch and a supermarket planned for the corner and even though he could still go outside at night and hear the coyotes, he sensed that they were already anachronisms, the man and the beasts, and that their days of wildness were well and truly numbered. More was the pity.

He made another call to Alma and again the message machine picked up but this time he didn't leave a message. After a while he rounded the base of the mountain and began to cruise through Cathedral City — Cat City, the locals called it — and he noticed a sign for San Pablo Street and wondered why it sounded familiar to him until he realized that he remembered it as being the street Alma lived on. He wished for a second he had held on to her card, and realized a moment later that he had stashed it inside the sweatband of his hat when she had visited the ranch and he took it out now and checked it and made a right turn. The address was a two-story condominium building two steps removed from better days. There were no parking spaces up front and he was idling the truck along the back of the units looking for her number when he spotted the purple Caddy, backed into a space. Still six or so car lengths away he slowed and then stopped. The motor was running in the car and Alma appeared in a few moments, carrying a white hanging bag with a Saks logo and a soft bag that looked like a carpetbag covered in a red and gold tapestry of sorts and she threw them into the trunk and slammed the lid and got behind the wheel. Morgan rolled his truck so that it almost blocked her and when she saw him she jammed on her brakes. "Get out of my way!" she shouted, wild-eyed, grasping her purple cross.

"Can I just ask you one question?" Morgan got out of the truck and held his hands up in a placating gesture.

She flew out of the car and stood in front of it, defiant. "I know what you want. Spirit said you'd be back, that you would come here. I thought I could get away before that." When she said 'spirit', she flicked her eyes over his shoulder as if someone was there and he looked but of course they were alone. He opened his mouth but before he could speak she held up a hand. "Spirit tells me it was a car, but for all the world it looks to me to be a boat, or part of a boat. It's a two seater, like one of those runabout Chris-Crafts with a canvas top. But metal, not wood. And it's red. Actually, a dark red. More of an auburn."

He felt the hair on his neck prickle. "Was it his?"

The psychic stood absolutely quiet. "Yes."

He looked at her then, into her eyes, as if to see if she was playing with him, and when she showed no sign of doing anything but reciting all he could think to do was nod "Thanks."

"I don't have to say this but...you don't have to go any further with this. Take my advice. Leave it alone."

"I'm not sure I can at this point."

"Why?"

"Because I feel a commitment to something. Or someone."

"Bad. I see great sadness, great loss if you don't leave it alone. Are you prepared for that? Prepared to pay the price? Think about that."

And before Morgan could respond she was back in the car and driving around him, leaving him standing there in the driveway like a jilted lover.

From there the highway became a strange amalgam of car dealerships, pseudo-exclusive shopping malls, and roadhouse restaurants. And unsynchronized traffic lights. Ancient, small, decaying motels littered the roadside. Somehow it fit, and it all looked right, the t-shirt shops and the Mexican restaurants and the cookie stores and the discos jammed together.

It all looked right, the southwestern architecture juxtaposed against someone's idea of what a Byzantine minaret looked like and that next to some modernist building that had fortuitously escaped the redeveloper's wrecking ball. It was a desert version of Miami Beach. Probably closer to South Beach. He drove past Desert Hospital where the old El Mirador had been in the 30's, and turned off Palm Canyon in Palm Springs, down Tahquitz Canyon, named for the ancient Indian shaman whose spirit, it was said, still lived in the mountains that surrounded the city. From there he headed south to where the road ended at the base of the mountain, a sentimental detour to where the Willows perched against the mountain. It was here that he had met Alexis, at a party years before, when she and a small horde of people had come down to celebrate the launch of a new Hong Kong designer named Barney Chang.

Bougainvillea cascaded down between the iron railings and trees and gates. Hidden waterfalls and rock gardens and colorful birds clamored for attention making the old stone and stucco house appear to be infolded against itself like some piece of architectural origami. The house was one of the original Palm Springs treasures, built by a prosperous New York lawyer in the 1930's, and the new owners had spent a year and several railroadcars full of money to recreate the details of it and turn it in to the premier bed and breakfast in the area. He had met the new owners at a polo match a few years before and discovered that they had friends in common and he had come out every so often and had always come away with an idea or two that he filed away for the day he would have his own place. He still had designs on those ideas but since he had moved in all he had had time for was to run around chasing spirits. Not what he'd imagined.

The ornate iron gate was closed and locked, a sure sign the season was over. Mixed in among the flowers he saw that they had added queen palms and here and there an aloe or succulent, the effect lush, tropical, out-of-place in the desert, yet oddly appropriate somehow. On the corner of Palm Canyon, not far away, a Starbuck's had set up sidewalk tables and overhead jets of water misted, cooling the patrons like so many tropical plants. He made a left on Indian, and continued that way until he reached Vista Chino and then he turned west. It was a neighborhood of tawdry consignment shops and antique shops, one story cream-colored sandstone buildings; many of them empty dark spaces, but a long block up Chino the surroundings abruptly changed. Large houses lay sequestered beneath old growth eucalyptus and pine, and concealed themselves behind walls that had been built long ago to look like old adobe, capped with terra cotta tile. So long ago that at last they looked as though they belonged there.

This had been the heart of the Movie Colony, Hollywood's home away from home. Jack Benny had lived on Chino, and Bob Hope at one time, and countless others. Morgan slowed the truck, savoring the quietness of it, the darkness created by the giant trees even in the midst of the sunny day.

At the address, the large flat rock in front of the wall said Casa Posada Manana, and Morgan pulled to the side of the street in the shade of an olive tree and cut the engine. Emerging from behind the wheel he closed the door softly, reluctant to disturb the silence. There was no traffic and no sound except for a fountain that burbled from behind the high stone wall. There was a bellrope that protruded from the wooden gate that sounded incongruous distant chimes when he pulled it and after a few long moments, the slow shuffle of ancient feet and a small port that he had not noticed opened in the rough wood. "Whaddaya want?" The voice was metallic and the effect was so unexpected that it took Morgan a moment to realize that what he was hearing was an electronic larynx, a device used after surgery for throat cancer. It worked by picking up and amplifying the vibrations from the throat. The effect was all the more startling because all he could see through the port was his eyes, pale blue, rheumy, covered with thick glasses. "Whaddaya want?"

"Mister Barton?"

"Who the fuck did you expect?"

Morgan exhaled and struggled with his composure and finally said: "I'm Nicholas Morgan." and he offered his card that had nothing on it but his name and the name he had given his ranch, Spirit Ranch, and his phone number. "Lucy Candelaria over at the historical society in Indio was supposed to have called ahead for me. Can I ask you a few questions?"

The eyes stared, piercing, and the man said nothing at first and then he said: "Gimme the fuckin' card."

"She spoke to a woman...perhaps your housekeeper."

"Damn bitch. She didn't tell me jack shit. She never tells me jack shit." Barton examined the card and after a while, reached down and unlocked the door and then opened it a crack. Morgan could see that he was dressed in cotton shorts with a Tommy Bahama shirt and a pair of Birkenstocks on his feet. Barton turned and shuffled back toward the house while Morgan watched until Barton turned and crooked his finger at him. That was all the encouragement he needed.

The house looked to have been built in the late 40's, with concrete walls that rose like slabs from concrete walkways. The landscaping was lush, dark, overgrown with banana plants and greater birds of paradise and ferns. When they went around the corner of the house he was startled to see a large swimming pool and sliding glass doors and furniture that looked like it had been laminated out of light wood in a color once called blond mahogany. It was a home that could have been designed by David Frey, or influenced by him. A large white cockatiel strutted back and forth on his perch and whistled and when Morgan looked over, the bird fanned his yellow crest in a threatening manner.

The old man stopped at the sliding glass doors. "So? Whadda ya want?"

"Lucy Candelaria over at the Historical Society in Indio. She gave me your name. She said you were the man to see about what went on with the water in the 1920's and 1930's. Her exact words were that you knew where the bodies had been buried.

"What's it to you?"

"I'm not entirely sure. I bought a ranch down in Indio not long ago. And then I found out that it was...I found out some things that have gotten me interested in the history of the area."

"Not much history. Mexicans, mostly. Place is becoming another Tijuana if you ask me. Or Mexicali."

"Actually I found that there's a lot went on there. That

lady at the Historical Society, Lucy, she said that water rights were one of the things that drove the development of the area…"

"So what's it to ya. What're you gonna do with the information? If I had any, that is." Barton could also make himself understood by a peculiar method of swallowing air and letting it go through what was left of his throat. It wasn't as clear but the man used a combination of that and the electronic device, switching just when Morgan least expected it.

"I'm a writer." Morgan answered, trying to conceal his growing impatience.

Barton wrinkled his nose and turned away. "Damn tabloid hacks. Always lookin' to dig in the dirt."

Morgan had enough. "I don't write for tabloids. I'm doing some research for a book on the area." It was the first time he had verbalized the thought to anyone, and he was surprised at how good the idea suddenly sounded. "I'm just doing research now. Background. Deep background. I may do something with this information, maybe not. I won't know until I get it. If you want, I'll be glad to let you know if I use it."

"You'll let me know…"

`"I'll let you know."

"And if I say don't use it…"

"I won't use it."

"If that's the case, you'll be the first sonofabitch writer to keep his word. Made up my mind never to talk to another one." Barton turned his back and began to shuffle away. "Let yourself out."

"Thanks for friggin' nothing." Morgan mumbled. "I'll go to the fuckin' library." Morgan found himself talking to back of the old man's Hawaiian shirt again and he exhaled his frustration and made his way back to the puerto. He got behind the wheel of the pickup and left the door open while the air conditioner cranked up and he was about to close it and pull away when there was a tapping on the glass on the passenger's window. Morgan looked over. The old man was peevishly trying to move the glass down. Morgan leaned over and opened the door.

"The library doesn't have jack shit. You want to know what really happened? What the goddamn truth is? I can tell you better'n any friggin library. Now get outta that goddamn truck and c'mon in. And how come you don't have a car?"

This time Barton guided him though the sliding glass doors and into the house and sat him down in an aluminum chair covered with some kind of nubby, cream-colored fabric at a long glass diningroom table.

"Now tell me...who sent you? Was it those goddamn San Diego motherfuckers? Them bastards are still pissed about signin' away some of their rights to Colorado River water."

"Not a chance. No one sent me. I'm here on my own."

"So why do you give a shit?"

"I said I'm a writer. It's background. I'm just digging for ideas for a novel or a screenplay maybe. I have an idea that there are some stories that need to be told...so...that people can appreciate this area. People seem to think you know more than anyone."

Barton straightened up and thought for a moment. "Wait right here." He padded out of the room and Morgan watched the minutes tick by on a clock mounted in the wall, its numerals crafted out of what looked like brushed aluminum, of a kind that could only be found now in the consignment shops on Palm Canyon.

When the old man reappeared he was carrying a cardboard carton that could have been designed for legal documents or storage, black and white with a matching cover, and when he took the cover off the musty smell infused the room. "Only reason I'm doin' this," Barton growled, "s'because I haven't shown this shit to anyone in 50 years. Figure mebbe it's time 'fore I die and some know-nothing asshole throws it all away. And mebbe it's about time they know."

Like a magician, Barton reached in to the cardboard box and began to extract papers, maps, pictures, one after another and these he spread over the glass table moving them around in a montage of sorts until he was satisfied with the arrangement. Morgan watched in silence broken once or twice by the old man's deep, rasping coughs until at last a notebook emerged and Barton finally straightened up and spread his arms over the table like an ancient priest bestowing a benediction of some sort and took a breath. "I was a surveyor," he began, "assistant to Joe Chiriaco. *The* assistant. They named a mountain after him, mebbe you heard of it. Patton trained his tank troops there for the invasion of North Africa. They had more mountains in those days than they had names and Chiriaco was one of the better ones. The others…well, the others just got all the money. Chiriaco, he didn't get jack shit, not that I know of. Me, I got nuthin'. "

Morgan thought about getting his tape recorder out of the car and then thought better of it, reluctant to break the spell.

"This was a desert. A real, fuckin' desert in the 1920's. Palm Springs, well Palm Springs had about five, mebbe ten thousand people, and most of 'em was Indians seems like. We knew there was plenty of water then, but it was underground and it was too hard and too expensive to get up to where it could be used for anything more than wells. I don't mean used for Los Angeles, either. I mean used for the farms. We knew even back then that the Imperial Valley and the Coachella

Valley could become the richest area in the state if they had water. But there was the Colorado River. We knew there was a way to get it to the farms. By canals. There was one canal that brought it in from the Colorado back down Yuma way but the canal ran through Mexico and there was all kinda talk that it gave the Mexicans a hold over us and there was big movement to get a canal set in the U.S. An all-American canal, they wanted, and that's what they called it even before it was laid out."

He unfolded a yellowed, stiff map, spread it out, and traced the route with a bony finger.

"The concept was approved in 1928, and Joe did most of the surveying. I came on board not long afterwards. I was a kid, 19, and I told him I knew more than I did and he knew I was lyin' but he needed someone dumb enough to run around the desert with him so he hired me. They decided on the exact route in 1931 and Parker approved it. They named a dam for him. I didn't know too much about him but I did know the route was supposed to remain confidential. Thing is, if you knew the route, you could turn a quick buck by buyin' up the right of way. Same exact thing happened with Mulholland. Them bastards made plenty of money.

"The small landowners and the small family farms didn't have a chance. Lotta big bucks changed hands then. There was some kinda law that you couldn't hold over a couple of hundred acres so a lot of these boys got these here shadow landowners to hold it for them."

"You ever hear of a Gutierrez family?"

"Mebbe. I'm not sure. All them Mexican names sound alike to me. There was talk about the Mexican mob, and there was one guy, I saw him ever once in a while talkin' to Parker, tough lookin' character, built like a weightlifter. I remember to this day sayin' to myself I wouldn't want to fuck with him. But

I don't remember a name."

"You think anyone was ever killed over this."

"Be serious. More than a few, I'd guess, but who the fuck knows. Or cares, now. A guy wouldn't show up one day, and no one ever looked for him. It was hot, hard work and guys got weird out here. I'm not talkin' about them *braceros* now, I'm talking about some of the front office guys. Weird. No one ever looked for them. But it was the desert, kid, and it was the frontier, and that kinda shit happened. You learned not to ask too many questions. Look it over." He said, suddenly. "It's time for my nap. Call me if you want anything. And don't get any ideas 'cause my girl'l be watch'n ya to see ya don't take nothin'."

When the door closed at the end of the hall, the house grew even quieter. Morgan went through the yellowed clippings making notes. A dozen or so faded black and white photos showed men in dark suits standing in front of stark rock formations but not one of the men was identified. In one picture, a small burro stood patiently, looking at the camera, his back piled with what looked like a surveyor's tripod. A fly buzzed in the corner.

After a while, a dumpy woman in her 40's appeared and asked him if he wanted a drink.

"I was just leaving."

"You sure…it's hot out there."

"I'm sure."

He let himself out and then pulled over to the curb as soon as he was out of sight of the house and dialed Burns. "I've got it."

"Got what?"

"The whole fuckin' shootin' match. Well, maybe a theory of a whole fuckin' shootin' match. More to the point, a working hypothesis. I met some guy named Anthony Barton.

He was there, in the 1930's and showed me some interesting things."

"I can look him up. Got his social security number?"

"Sure. And his I.Q. And his dick size. Give me a break."

"So what's your theory?"

"It's the 1930's. Gutierrez is a small potatoes Mexican mobster, or maybe he's bigger than that. It's prohibition, maybe he's running booze across the border, or drugs, or *mojados*."

"*Mojados?*"

"Wets. Wetbacks. Anyway, he gets wind of something bigger going on...who knows how...a canal to bring in water from the Colorado River. And he knows he can get a piece of the action, but not with muscle. So he goes up to L.A. and hires himself a greedy, young lawyer fresh out of law school to intimidate the small farmers so he can get control of the right-of-way for the new All-American Canal. And while he's at it, he buys up as many of the small ranches as he can and consolidates and consolidates until he's got control of huge tracts.

"And maybe offs a few of the local Indians in the process."

"Which could be why the lawyer kept the clipping."

"Anyways, the lawyer is happy to have the money. He buys a bitchin' car, is able to pay off his bills, lots of chicks. And then one day our lawyer friend says the wrong thing, or maybe tries to up his ante, or maybe tries to shake down the patron, and Gutierrez just has him rubbed out."

"Like they used to say in the old Edward G. Robinson movies." Burns chuckled.

"Exactly. Like they used to say in the old Edward G. Robinson movies. It's the desert, it's the 30's, he's the patron, what he says gets done. One lawyer more or less, who's gonna care?"

"Some things never change. So who's the chick?"

"She had nothing to do with it. Just a girlfriend. You said it...wrong place, wrong time."

"Question is: who's the third guy?"

"Here's my theory. It's a lawyer and Gutierrez is maybe a little unsure of the ramifications of that so he figures he's gotta do it carefully. He sends a killer to the ranch, and then he has the murderer killed."

"And buried on the ranch? I don't know...it's a stretch. But it would put one step between him and the murders."

"Makes sense to me."

"What about the car?"

"Oh, yeah. I caught up with Alma, my psychic. That's another story. From her description, the Auburn could have been his car."

"You oughtta ask her..."

"Good trick asking her anything else. I caught her as she was makin' tracks outta there. From what she said, she doesn't want to see me again."

"Something you said?"

"Yeah, right."

"Hell, it's all moot anyway. All of those people are probably dead."

"She said to be careful. That somebody could get hurt."

"By who? It's probably something that those kind of chicks say to everyone."

"She sounded serious."

"No worries, man. So what you gonna do now?"

"I don't know. Barton asked me and I said I wanted to turn it into a book. It made sense then. I think I might run up a treatment of it and see if it's got legs. Oh, one more thing...any ideas about that bizarre notation in the middle?"

"I've been thinking."

"Do you remember how? I mean, all those LA chicks been fuckin' your brains out."

"There's something left. And no, I got no new ideas. But copy the notebook."

"Right. I'll talk to you."

"Copy the fucking notebook. Today, man."

But when Morgan went past Kinko's in Palm Desert on the way back to the club he was talking to Nikki at the Boutique where he had called looking for Alexis and by the time he realized that he was almost at the Grand Champions' Resort it was too late and so he promised himself that he would copy it in the morning. For absolutely sure.

15

There was a soft haze in the air when he turned for home. Off to the south, near the top of Santa Rosa, three or four dusty white clouds had gathered, close in to the dark shape of the mountain as if they had somehow become attached while scuttling by. Way off in the far distance, so far away it could have been happening on another planet, one of the clouds turned darker and a bolt or two of lightning flashed.

He opened the glove box and found the tape with the Maria Callas arias and when he loaded it into the player the truck cab was filled with the diva's otherworldly voice. What Alma said still troubled him but it was Barton's revelations that gave everything a little more validity. He might indeed be barking up the wrong tree but at least the 'coon had been there once. Morgan's experiences tended to make him believe in empiric theories—the same laws that mandated a drop of liquid will assume the most efficient shape usually mandated the simplest explanation to be the right one.

And what he had blurted out to Barton, that he was researching a book, had come from a place within him that was pushing him to do just such a thing. What the hell. He could knock out a plot summary in a matter of days, maybe if he was inspired, in a morning, and it would give him something to stand back and look at. One thing he'd envied about artists, they could always step back and look at the totality of what they'd done, but writers, well hell, writing was like trying to paint the Mona Lisa using a magnifying glass and painting a centimeter at a time and then trying to remember how and if that centimeter fit into everything else. He'd run the treatment by Burns and if it looked to the detective to be plausible and to ring true, he'd take it to Charlie and let him try to talk him out of it. If the agent bit, well…

It had been two days since he had spoken to Alexis but then again she had been in San Francisco at the Gift Show and they usually didn't talk much when she was out of town. But this was Thursday, and she'd said something about being back by then if everything went well. He retrieved the cell phone from under the pile of papers on the passenger seat, flipped the cover of it and dialed her up. When her phone didn't pick up he made the rounds of her haunts by phone, her apartment, where he left a message on her machine, her office, where they hadn't heard from her yet, and the Boutique, where they said they expected her that afternoon. Nothing. Like radar beamed into the dark of an empty night, not a ping back. He drove on, rewinding the highway like a videotape, trying to fast forward to the good parts. Making the calls and coming up empty had broken his peaceful mood and on top of that an oversize Fleetwood Cadillac camped in the left lane in front of him and refused to break 40 miles an hour. In his frustration Morgan weaved through the right turn lane at the intersection and when he went by he resisted the urge to give the driver the finger. All he did instead was nod when the old dude looked over.

The cell phone ringer interrupted his thoughts. "Hi, darlin'." Alexis said, her voice bright. "I just walked into the Boutique and they said you called. I've been trying your cell phone since my plane landed and I finally left a message for you at the ranch. I've been on the ground almost two hours and it took all this time to get to Beverly Hills. Didn't you get my message?"

"Not yet...I've been on the road since about eight or nine myself. Am I gonna luck out and see you tomorrow?"

Alexis hesitated. "You remember I told you about the new fragrance they're going to launch in September? Well all of the brass is coming into town and there's a big meeting tomorrow afternoon."

"And then you're expected to sit around and have a few drinks while they tell each other how bitchin' they are."

"You've got the drill down pat, that's for sure ."

"I have."

"But you're invited. All of those guys know you, or know of you, and they're always flattered when you show up, a real Hollywood writer, and all that. And if you drive up I just might ravage your body."

"That's a hell of an offer. Worth at least a two hour drive."

"Don't be a smartass. I don't make that offer to anyone. C'mon...I'll follow you back down on Saturday."

"Okay. Sure. I'll be up."

"You okay?" she said, hearing something in his voice just then. "What's on your mind?"

He wondered again at the finely tuned radar she seemed to have and the ability to read him that she possessed that bordered on the amazing. "Nothing. Well, that's not true. I've got a story idea percolating in my head and you know how I get. I'm not going to be much good to the world until I get it down on paper."

"Well you just go percolate, cowboy. I'll call you when I get out tonight."

He examined the cell phone carefully when they broke the connection as if on its black face some answers would appear. This certainly wasn't what he had envisioned when they had started to go together and she had talked about opening her own Boutique in the desert and moving down. Right after that it seemed that she shifted over to the fast track in the company and before he knew it she was traveling a week or two every month and working harder when she was around. And even though he had the ranch and his horses and Max the Dog and Amado and the whole polo infrastructure to fall back on, the truth of it was that he missed her when she wasn't there, like a piece of him was missing, and most of the time he wasn't comfortable with the feeling. He had a fervent belief that you made your own fate and that you were ultimately and completely responsible for whatever happened to and around you, but that didn't insulate him from frustration.

Back when he had first met her, at that party at the Willows, it had seemed easy. One moment he had been asking the bartender for another cold Corona and the next she was at his side. The first thing she said to him was: "I've been watching you and you need to try one of these." and she proffered a pinkish drink in his direction, frosty and cold in a Martini glass.

"Do I, now?"

"Absolutely." She sipped the drink and looked at him over the rim of the glass, clearly appraising him, from the cowboy boots that protruded from beneath his jeans to the cream colored t-shirt under his leather jacket. "Well, maybe on second thought, you need a straight tequila."

"Now, not so fast. Maybe you're right. Except it doesn't look like anything I've ever seen." Morgan was vamping for time until he could take her all in at close range. He had noticed her when she first walked in to the patio around the pool. She was wearing a white suit with slim cut pants and a longish jacket of some kind of soft material that clung to all of her curves. The jacket was either buttoned over her bare breasts or she was wearing the merest wisp of a blouse and the way it pressed against her accented her cleavage. This close he could see that her eyes were a greenish-grey and she looked at him directly, her gaze a challenge and an invitation. Her blond hair cut softly around her face and she looked an older version of the all-American girl cheerleader she had almost certainly once been.

"It's a cosmo. A cosmopolitan. It's all the rage in New York."

"Explains why I don't know what it is. Is that where you're from?"

"Not a chance. I go back there on business half a dozen times a year. I was back there last week, in fact."

The bartender reappeared with Morgan's beer and he took her elbow and steered her over to where two empty chairs were positioned by a small, glass table. "The tequila suggestion was closer to home than your first choice."

"I know that now. You aren't the cosmo type. I just had a hunch."

"And are your hunches right most of the time?"

"No...I'm probably batting in the low 600's. But I keep trying."

"Do you have any more?"

"I have a hunch you're not in the rag business."

"'bout as far away from that as you can get."

"So..."

"What am I doing here tonight?"

"Something like that."

"Friend of the owners of this place. They thought I'd like the party. And I'm afraid they were completely wrong. That is, until you tried to sell me on your Cosmo."

"I'm Alexis." She smiled and held out her hand. "You're…"

"Nicholas. Morgan." Her handshake was firm and they held it longer than necessary. "Oh…now I remember." Alexis said, after a moment. "You're the writer they told me about. I was expecting some little old man."

"He couldn't make it tonight. I came instead."

"And aren't I glad."

The rest of the evening became a pattern for the way they would spend countless evenings after that, heads close together, talking softly, intent on each other, as if the rest of the world didn't exist. Sometime later, the bartender came by and asked if she wanted a refill and Alexis nodded but Morgan shook his head.

"I'm playing tomorrow. Two beers are just fine, thanks."

"Playing…"

"Polo…out at Eldorado."

"I don't know anything about that. Tell me." He began three or four different times and he finally wound up talking about the horses that were the heart and soul of the game and about his horses and what they meant to him. While they spoke people had been leaving, one or two stopping by to say goodnight, and before long it was just the two of them at the pool. At last he got up and stretched. "Walk you to your room?"

She shook her head. "I'll walk you to your car."

The winding path to the street below was lighted on the edges with tiny twinkle lights and tentatively holding hands they moved slowly to where his Mercedes was parked at the bottom of the driveway. When he straightened up from unlocking the door she was there in his arms and her lips were warm and softer than he had imagined and she stayed that way in his arms for a long time and they stood there kissing like two kids until she finally said: "I don't want you losing tomorrow because of me." All he could do was nod, having been completely captivated, and drove off in a bit of a fog and it wasn't until he had cleared Cathedral City going east that he realized that he hadn't even asked her last name.

She materialized at the side of the field when he came in after the fourth chukker that next day, Amado already under her spell and the two of them thick as thieves. She kissed him full on the lips when he dismounted and out of the corner of his eye he saw the Mexican smile and look the other way. He was renting a condominium at Indian Palms that season and she spent the night and from then on they were together as much as possible, an instant item for the polo community and the fashion industry of Rodeo Drive as well, he a moderately successful writer but a very private man and she the epitome of fashion and chic, the last person anyone expected would take up with a cowboy, even a civilized one.

So much had happened since then.

He got off 111 as soon as he was around the point at La Quinta and headed down Washington and over 50th and smiled at the change in cars around him from out of state Cadillacs and Lincolns to the rough around the edges pickups and low slung sedans. The drivers metamorphosed as well, from the blue-haired polyester crowd to the Mexicans and the true desert rats that he felt more at home among and by the time he unlocked his gate and pushed it open and drove inside he was ready to fire up the word processor and retreat into his notes and maybe make some sense of it all.

But in front of the computer he sat there turning the story over in his head, coming at it one way, changing his mind, and going back at it another way. He looked at the other box, the one that held the hard copy of THE BOOK he started to write about his father so many years ago that he hated to think about it. He had gotten just so far on that, too, and it seemed to dry up the closer he got to the truth of it. After a while he pushed back, whistled up the dog, and went outside.

The afternoon air was still and the heat rose in waves off the roughstone pavers around the pool and not far off the Coral Reef Mountains shimmered like a madman's mirage. But it was cool when he walked inside the bunkhouse, and dark, and he made his way over to the window in the back, the one that looked out over the small barn and the tree they were supposed to have been buried under. After all this time, would they really be able to find anything or was it true what he had said to the dead girl's sister, that there would be nothing but sand? And when all was said and done did he really want to find out? The dog padded in after him and curled up in front of the cold fireplace on the woven rug that had once been a Navajo saddle blanket. Morgan stretched out on the couch in front of the dark television set in the den and propped a cushion under his head where he could see the dog and the dog could see him and thump his tail whenever it pleased him.

Outside by the Jacuzzi a roadrunner clicked, intent on a bug or maybe stalking a small toad, and inside the silence hung, the only sound the rhythmic ticking of the old schoolhouse clock.

The first few months had been idyllic for them. Alexis would come down to the desert after work on Friday and they would open a bottle of champagne and talk, stretched out on the couch in each other's arms, and later, slowly, languorously, make love. Morgan and Amado taught her to ride and she discovered a natural affinity for the horses and before long she was riding along with them when they took the horses out for their exercise walks, on the long loop that went from the exercise track out into the desert and around the grapefruit groves and back. He was back and forth to Los Angeles frequently then, weekly script conferences, meetings, and it was natural that he stay at her small place on Charleville and just as natural that when the polo season was over and he turned his horses out that he move in with her and so he did, giving up the tiny old house he had rented forever near the Greek Theatre.

But about a year and a half into their relationship, when she began to think of him as permanent and he began to think of her as irreplaceable, the Boutique was sold to a large conglomerate and in short order she was promoted and promoted again and her rare short trips out of town became months in Europe and frequent excursions to New York and Las Vegas and Washington. Even though they were as close as ever when they were together, perhaps even more so, the occasions when he looked around for her and she wasn't there began to outnumber the times she was. He had spent a lifetime on his own and even when he was married he kept most of himself to himself and he knew he could do that by heart if he had to but this time it was different. Perhaps it was an unwillingness to tinker with something that was working but neither of them thought or sought to make it permanent and so it went on.

He wasn't sure that he had slept or even that he wasn't still sleeping when he became aware of the familiar scent of lavender, so soft and so faint at first that he was not aware of when it had begun but it wrapped around him, intimate, intruding, possessive. It stayed around him, a dreamy cloud or hypnotic fog, so that when her by-now-familiar face appeared above him, close to his face, it was almost natural and he studied her from that perspective.

This was not dreaming.

Her skin seemed to glow a light cinnamon and her eyes radiated a luminescent aqua. From its place on her shoulder, the brooch gleamed and he could clearly see now that the initials were "A.S." The face moved closer and closer still until it was right before him and he could almost feel the warmth of her and there was an instant, a nanosecond, when he knew she would kiss him and he wanted to kiss her more than anything in the world and just then he knew he would. And then she was gone, the faintest scent of lavender hanging in the air and he sat up, still not quite believing what had just happened yet unable to deny it or explain it away.

The ringing of the telephone intruded on his reverie and he ignored the first two rings and tried to ignore the third but by the forth he gave up and picked up the cordless. The male voice on the other end was cultured, with the merest trace of the affected lisp that marked the Beverly Hills cum West side affectation, and Morgan recognized the Director of Alexis' Boutique instantly. "Jerome." Morgan said, "How are you?"

"Fabulous." It was Jerome's stock answer unless he was dying. "*FABulous.*"

"I haven't seen you in a coon's age. They've been keeping me in the closet down here."

"Well let me know when you're ready to come out..." he laughed.

"Relax, Jerome. Not yet. How're things in San Fran?"

"It's been a good show. All we have to do now is sell all the stuff that Alexis bought for the Boutique."

"How's she doing?"

Jerome's voice became serious. "Actually, that's why I called. What's up with her?"

"What do you mean?"

"I thought you'd know."

"C'mon, Jerome. Know what? Don't be coy."

"When did you last see her?"

"Last weekend. She was down here. What's up? Is she okay?"

"Physically, I'm sure she's okay. But when she showed up at the airport she had changed her look completely. I mean her hair, her dress, *everything*. *Real retro*, you know. Her hair is this *auburn* color…in a pageboy. *Twenties*, or something. And she's wearing all black. More than usual."

"I had no idea. Has she said anything?"

"She changes the subject when I bring it up. I mean, she still looks smashing, you know. But *different*. Like someone else."

"Who else?" The hair was beginning to rise on Morgan's neck.

"I don't know. Somebody vampy, maybe. Theda Bara, sort of. And did she ever smoke?"

"Smoke? I've never seen her smoke. Heck I don't think she ever even smoked a joint."

"Because she used to give me a hard time about smoking. And now she's matching me puff for puff."

"Jerome, I don't know what to say."

"I wanted you to be ready. I'm *worried*, frankly."

"Thanks. I'm supposed to see her in the next few days. I'll let you know."

"Thanks, Nicholas. Well, bye *bye*."

The dead girl's picture was on the counter of the cooking island in the kitchen and he stared at it for a long time with Jerome's words echoing. The dead girl's hair was short although Morgan didn't know a page boy from the yellow pages, and her sister had said that her hair had been auburn. Or had she? And he had seen a picture of the dead woman with a cigarette in her hand. It was disorienting, all of it coming down so quickly. Morgan tried Alexis on her cell phone, the surest way to get her when she was out of town, but the ringing went on and on before shifting over to the canned message.

The lawyer's journals were still in the trunk of the Mercedes where Morgan had left them tucked on the side beneath the trunkmat. He got them from the garage, put them on his desk, and opened the one the looked like a diary. In the light from his gooseneck lamp the pages seemed to glow a yellow color and he studied the entries leisurely this time. Most were made in ink, now fading; on each page there were one or two in pencil. The lawyer's entries were sparse until the Gutierrez name began to appear. After that it appeared he became busier. There were a few references to someone named C. Crawford that looked as though Carruthers might have set up a meeting between Gutierrez and Crawford but the name meant nothing to Morgan. Not long after, the trips to the Riverside Courthouse began and Morgan was about to go past that part when he came to the name of Frank Shaw and he remembered, from something he had read long ago, about the quintessential crooked Los Angeles Mayor from the 1930's. The dates were crossindexed to the names in the second notebook and in the last section, the names were finally linked to the properties. Under the properties, Carruthers had carefully written the eventual disposition of each one, whether sold or transferred. Gutierrez' name was absent from these sales, the majority of the properties going only to something called Southwest Growers. Other properties were sold to something called Erin Holding Group.

Burns had been enthralled with the journals but for Morgan, it was the girl. It had always been her. The third man, who he was, remained an enigma. On some level he believed that if he solved that riddle, everything else would fall into place. Then there was the notation. Why did it bother him so. The numbers…if it was an address, what did it mean? Why had the girl, April, become involved? She was an innocent…or was she? How had he met her? Did Carruthers bring her down to spend a weekend screwing or was there another reason? And then there was the setting of it, the allure of gothic mystery that lurked just under the surface of the desert and that had persisted from those times to the present. In front of his computer in the quiet office in the front of the main house time passed unnoticed.

The shadows of the mesquite and the dalbergia trees lengthened across the corral and the droning of the ceiling fan blocked out the sounds of the traffic. He didn't see the tan pickup drive in the gate and didn't hear it when it coasted to a stop in front of the door but Max, who had been sleeping next to his chair, was more alert, and he jumped up with a deep barking growl that startled Morgan. There was a soft tapping on the door. And then it repeated.

From where the front door was situated he couldn't see who was knocking. All he could see was the back end of a brown pickup that he didn't recognize so when he opened the door he opened it just the merest crack to keep the still growling dog inside.

"Hey, Nick. Thought I'd stop by to see what was goin' on."

"Vic." Morgan said. Max was still growling and Morgan said a few words to the dog and opened the door. Vic took a step backward but the dog came no closer and laid down on the lawn a few steps away where he could keep a growling eye on things.

"Just stopped by to see how them bugs were." the man answered, holding out a hand to shake. "This time of year, you know, they start breedin' like crazy. Warm weather. Everythin' okay here?"

"Nice and quiet. Just the usual scorpions."

Vic grinned. "Didn't mean to distract you."

"It's okay…I was ready for a break. You like a beer?"

"If it's no trouble, I don't mind if I do. I'm on my way home."

Morgan fished a couple of Coronas out of the bottom of the refrigerator and they headed for the stone patio by the pool where there was shade from the last rays of the sun under a massive gingko. Vic had come with the place, in a manner of speaking, had been managing the rodents and pests while the place was vacant, and when Morgan moved in the two of them discovered they had been in the service at the same time and had both been Rangers in Central America.

It was a time that Morgan would have rather forgotten and when he came back he made a supreme effort to do just that. He went back to Montana, dropped his gear at the tiny house in Dillon where his mother and his sister lived, and headed back up into the mountains, this time north of Charlo near the Flathead Indian Reservation West of the Mission Range and went back to cowboyin' for the use of a horse and his meals on a ranch that belonged to the father of an old friend. He stayed up there, riding the herd himself or at times with a young Indian boy during the day and writing during the night. When he stopped having the dreams he came back. A year and a hard winter had gone by.

He and Vic watched the sun drop behind San Gorgonio, tipped back in the white lawn chairs, feet up on one of the rocks. Once they discovered their common background they became comfortable with each other although the subject never came up again. Vic's only concession to the past was a miniature Airborne Ranger pin he attached to the front of the pith helmet he wore most of the time. Morgan kept a silver cigarette box on his dresser with the flash of his unit worked in cloisonné, inscribed Nicholas R. Morgan, LT, USAR.

The beers gone, Vic stood up and looked around for the trash, hefting the empty in his hand. "Hold on a sec before you go, Vic. What do you know about the Gutierrez family?" Morgan asked.

Vic's answer was quick but his eyes seemed to cloud over. "Not much. Hey, where's your garbage."

Morgan held out his hand. "I'll take it." And then he added. "Seriously. Who or what is Gutierrez family?"

"Them's the kinda questions gonna get you in trouble, my friend. What's the big fuckin' deal. Why do you have to know?"

Morgan was hardly surprised at Vic's reaction and he thought for a second and then said: "Come with me."

They went into Morgan's office in the main house and Morgan snapped on the lamp and turned the journal so Vic could read it. "Look at this. These are notes some lawyer kept 60 some years ago. I've just begun to study it, but it looks to me as though he had some meetings with a guy named Gutierrez who probably lived out here somewhere and it looks like he was passing money for the guy. That he was a bag man of sorts."

As if against his will Vic looked and quickly looked away. "So?"

"There's more. It looks like he did some legal things for Gutierrez that wound up with people losing their houses and their ranches."

"What's that have to do with me?"

"You've lived here all your life. I've heard there is a Gutierrez family that's behind the loansharking that goes on, that may even be into selling drugs and bringing the wets across. But it's whispers. What do you know?"

"Beats the shit outta me. What's it to ya. You're no cop.

Why you wanna get involved with this shit? Take my advice and take that journal and get it as far away from you as you can. Where'd you get it anyway?"

Morgan shrugged. "What's the difference. Who said I wanted to get involved? I just want to find out. If that's right, these are the guys that are tight with the Indian tribe that's trying to start that Indian gambling parlor that everyone seems up in arms about. I don't care about that, but I'm sure if the gaming commission boys ever made a connection between this group of solid citizens and the group that swindled all of those people out of their farms in the 30's, they'd have a fuckin' field day with it."

Vic was looking down and shaking his head in disbelief.

"What I'm going to do with it though is that I'm going to write something about this journal. Maybe make it into a murder mystery. Shit, I'm a writer, it's what I do."

Vic was pale. "Well my advice to you is toss it. Have some fun on the polo field."

"Okay. What aren't you telling me?"

"Let's say just for argument's sake that these guys are the same family. Do you think for one minute that they're gonna like that you're writin' about this shit?"

"I've already got three or four hours into it."

"Call it a wash. Forget it. Chalk it up to an investment in your health. If there is anything in common, you're fuckin' with some very bad boys. Look, put it away. Forget about it. It's not any of your fuckin' business." He looked at his wristwatch and moved toward the door. "I really gotta go." And almost before Morgan realized it, Vic had his pickup backed down the circular drive and out the gate.

So far, bringing up the Gutierrez name was proving to be a sure-fire way to get rid of people. Morgan thought about that while he whistled up the dog and walked down to the barn, put a flake of hay for each of the two horses in the wheelbarrow, tossed them over the pasture fence, filled their water trough, and stood there watching as they began to nuzzle the hay. A roadrunner chose that exact time to come out of the oleanders and Max tried to run it down but the ungainly bird managed to stay just far enough in front and lift over the fence at the last minute. "Dope." He laughed at the dog with great affection. "You've never caught one yet. And you're still trying. Maybe we really are related."

Only about a half hour had gone by since Morgan had been outside but already the red light on the message machine was blinking and he tapped the play button, his mind miles away.

"Nicholas, this is Victor. The exterminator. I just left, I know, but look…I got a mission for you. Can you meet me at that bar down on Grapefruit Avenue in Coachella? Like in about an hour…say 7:30? It's called El Coyote Azul. I've got something you need to see."

16

Something about Vic's message bothered him. He replayed it and listened to it again, and then a third time, trying to read between the breaths, trying to decipher the inflections, trying to figure out if it was his imagination or if it really was more than it seemed. Vic would never call anything a mission, not anymore, he was pretty certain of that. The man was still a renegade and the term was too regular army for him. Morgan dialed his number but after four rings the answering machine picked up and Morgan left a short message. "It's Morgan. Call me." He knew he could always ignore Vic's call but he had never stood up a friend and he wasn't about to start now. One trip to El Coyote Azul couldn't hurt. He'd be back in an hour at the most.

Morgan gathered the journals and hefted them in his hands. There was no time to copy them now and he opened the locking drawer in his desk and put the journals in, then took them out just as quickly and carried them into the bedroom. His bureau was too obvious, the nightstand, under the bed, the same. Finally he brought them into the bunkhouse.

The massive fieldstone fireplace in the center of the far wall was flanked by a door on either side, each opening to a short hall that lead to a bedroom. In the hall to the right, a floor-to-ceiling cupboard had been constructed in the wall nearest the fireplace, perhaps as a place to store wood or to warm blankets. It was closed by a wooden door of tongue-in-groove pine that blended into the rest of the wall so well that the surface appeared unbroken except for a small antique black metal hasp. He opened it and reached inside, back toward the fireplace. At the extreme end of where his arm could reach was a loose rock that gave way to an opening the size of a large shoe box. It had taken Morgan a half-dozen tries when the realtor had told him about it but he finally mastered it. You couldn't see it, or see into it, but if you knew it was there it was obvious. He placed the journals in the cache and secured the rock closure. Then he stood up and secured the wooden door with the strap and went outside. "There," he murmured, locking the bunkhouse door, "let the bastards find that."

The last thing he did was take the 9 mm pistol from his nightstand.

The house alarm system was state of the art with a digital display and Morgan watched as the touchpad accepted his four digit code and beeped and as he made for the door the dog wagged his goodbye from his vantage point on the Persian rug in the living room in front of the fireplace.

It was the hour between sunset and moonrise and in the way of the almost-tropics, darkness descended quickly. The date groves that hugged 50th seemed even darker and here and there yellow lights began to glow from the diminutive houses that he knew were tucked in there. He tried Burns back in Malibu and struck out on the detective's cell phone but got his message machine and left a brief word about where he was going even though he knew it might be morning by time the detective heard it. At Jackson Street he turned right and went south down towards 51st. The *brujo*, Ramon, lived somewhere along there.

Not far in front of him a man stepped into the street and he was about to swerve and go around him when the man held up his hand and when he got closer Morgan saw it was the *brujo*. Morgan slowed to a stop. Behind him, he could see his house, set back about 20 yards from the street, a small, old, one story that looked as though it might have originally been constructed out of adobe and then added onto by brick and concrete block. There were no numbers, no street lights, and no curbs. "*Buenos noches.*" Ramon said, his voice calm, as if he had been expecting him. "*Donde va?*".

"You seem to have been expecting me...why don't you tell me where I'm going."

He could see the *brujo* grin, his white teeth stained with nicotine. "I not know everyt'ing. It is important," the Mexican said, and he repeated: "*Donde va?*"

"El Coyote Azul, in Coachella."

"*El Coyote Azul es pinche mal lugar...entiende?*"

"I know it's a bad place, but I have to meet someone."

"You take one of the boys. Maybe Pepe, or Angel?" He gestured toward the house with his head.

"*Es no necesario, amigo. Muchisimas gracias.*"

Morgan started to move the truck forward but Ramon put an arm through the open window and onto his and stopped him with a strong grip. "You be careful. *Tenga cuidado.* You finding out some things that are very dangerous. *Muy peligroso.* Even the spirits cannot help you too much in this. I tell you again. *Tenga mucho cuidado.* No go there."

"Thanks for your thoughts." Morgan said, shaking him off.

But I'm going to be late."

"Wait. Amado, you know, he t'ink that one of the dead, *un espirito*, is *primo* to him, you know, a cousin, or maybe *un tio*, an uncle."

"What? Come on. Be serious."

"No." Ramon began to nod his head up and down, an emphatic movement. He at the ranch a lot a lot of time when you gone. He think the spirit is who his *abuelo* tell him about. Not the *abogado*, not the *mujer*. The third one. Amado, he think he know the reason his *abuelo* tell him not to come. He think the spirit make him to die."

"Why the hell hasn't he told me?"

"Because you his patron. He no want you to see him afraid."

"*Gracias por decirme.* I'll talk to him tomorrow. I can't believe he wouldn't say anything."

"*Lo creo.* Believe it." The *brujo* let Morgan's arm go and this time when Morgan began to roll the pickup forward, Ramon stepped back.

He made a left at 52nd and drove until he hit the highway in Coachella and then he turned right toward Mecca and the Salton Sea. The lights in the mini-mall that outlined Pollo Dieta and Todo Moda Market seemed even more garish in contrast to the dark and he wondered again whether coming out here was the best idea. Particularly alone. This was too far out of his element. Still, Vic sounded as though he had something good and there was no way to intercept him and change his mind anyway. Morgan had placed the Glock under his seat and he took it out now, chambered a round, and laid it on the passenger's seat, sliding it under the copy of the Indio POST he had picked up out of his driveway earlier.

The bar was beyond the Rancho Grande Market, beyond where the rows of packing houses lay dark. He had been there once with Amado, but it was during the afternoon on a Monday. Now the red neon sign glowed dimly and the script that read El Coyote Azul was barely discernible but he had remembered it right and thought he remembered the pothole that he immediately bounced through. There goes my alignment, he thought, and he looked around for Vic's truck and didn't see it and finally pulled to a stop with his front bumper up against the stuccoed cinder block building. The parking lot was mostly empty, a Chevy el Camino in one corner, and a low-rider Pontiac next to it. On the other side, away from the street, a champagne colored Infinity was parked facing out, across three spaces.

The ranchero music that spilled out of the doorway was loud enough and raucous enough for a big party but inside there were just two Mexican cowboys sitting at the bar, older, skinny, in jeans and cheap patterned shirts and straw cowboy hats perched on their heads over bad haircuts. There were some people at a booth in the back. The woman behind the bar was no more than five feet one or two, fortyish and a little plump, dressed in a full red skirt and red blouse that made her look like an aging Carmen but Morgan knew her to be the owner and he returned her smile and touched the brim of his hat.

"*Corona, por favor.*"

"*No tengo. Gusta Budweiser?*"

"*Si, gracias.*" Morgan watched as the woman went to a narrow pass-through window in the barback, said something to the man inside, and waited while the beer was passed out. It was clear that nothing was kept in the bar, certainly not any money, that it was more to give the patrons a place to lean on than anything else. No one else came in, and Morgan tried to see the men at the booth in the back but it was dark and he wasn't even sure how many were there.

He waited like that for a while and checked his watch a time or two and finished his Bud and placed it back on the bar and played with the ring of dampness it made and watched it get to be almost eight. The woman in the red dress asked him if he wanted another and he shook his head and was about to leave when one of the people who had been at the back booth walked over to him. The man was on the short side with a weightlifter's build, clean-shaven with dark hair smoothed back, and he wore dark slacks and a light-colored shirt buttoned at the neck and dark glasses that were narrow, like something you'd buy in a surf shop. He walked right up to Morgan slowly, but without hesitation. "Señor Morgan." It wasn't a question. The man knew who he was and Morgan was somehow not surprised.

"And if I'm not?"

The man ignored his answer, and continued. "*Mi patron*, he want to talk wit' you." And he inclined his head in the direction of the booth in back and gave it a beckoning motion.

"Here I am. Tell him to come on over."

The man smiled, a grin without humor, showing a row of yellowed teeth and gums with what looked like end-stage gum disease. "You no understand, mister. My patron, he say to come over there. Is better for you to go there and have him buy you a beer. When a man such as my patron want to buy you a beer, it is very impolite to refuse." He went on slowly, as though addressing a slow child. "He want to buy you a beer and he want to say you something. *Muy importante*."

Morgan looked around the bar and it seemed to have grown darker. The two skinny old cowboys had disappeared like smoke and the bartender had gone into the back and he and the messenger and the three men he could now see at the booth were all that were left inside. The ranchero music had stopped, and suddenly it seemed to be very quiet. A car went by on Highway 86 with music blaring, the bass drowning out the sound of the engine, and he shrugged, got off the barstool, and walked over to the booth. Two of the men, younger, wearing loose white guayabera shirts and with identical sunglasses as the messenger, got up without changing expression and stood a few feet away, just out of earshot. The messenger moved to the door and posted himself there.

The man who remained sitting wore a dark suit jacket over a white shirt that was buttoned at the neck with no tie. His hair was thick, wavy, and it was cut full. He sported a thin black moustache that looked as though it needed some more time or a dose of fertilizer. Morgan guessed his age at late forties. He studied Morgan with dark eyes for a minute and it was Morgan that finally broke the silence.

"I'm not interested in buying any sunglasses, if that's what you're sellin'."

"You *gabachos*." he sniffed, without concealing his contempt. "Everything is the joke to you."

"You're the one tellin' the joke, pard. I came in here to meet a friend. He hasn't shown up and I'm about to leave and John Belushi over there tells me you want to tell me something *muy importante*. Now unless I've developed acute brain fade, I've never met you and unless you decide to tell me something very quickly, I'm out that door in one *pinche* second."

"*Sienta te, amigo*." The man pursed his thin lips. "Sit...I buy you *una cerveza*."

"*Gracias, pero no me gusta*. I buy my own *cervezas*."

"Please. It is my mistake to talk espanish. I talk English only with you. Now sit, please."

Morgan looked around and the men standing a few feet away were out of earshot or pretending they were. He pushed back the brim of his hat and pulled over a bentwood chair that had been against the wall, turned it backwards to the table on the edge that faced the wall and threw a leg over it so that he could see the door. The Mexican continued. "Things, you know mister, are not always how they seem. I have a great grandfather, he ride with Pancho Villa. He look like, how you say it, a peasant and yet he is a very important man."

Morgan nodded, his senses on full alert.

"For example, maybe I look like a stupid Mexican *mal hombre*, I am sorry, a bad guy."

"Actually, I thought you were a clergyman."

The man went on as if he hadn't heard. "I am really a collector of old things, rare things, you say antiques. I live here in this valley a long time. Maybe longer, even, than you, but I no know how long you here. I have many friends. Someone tell me that you maybe have a book, a rare book, a journal that you would like to sell."

Morgan stiffened, suddenly getting it. How stupid of him not to have paid more attention while it was going down. Ah well, he thought, here goes. Grab your socks and leggo your cocks, as his D.I. used to say. "Now who could have told you that?" he said, flatly.

"What does it matter? You have friends, you hear things, who knows? It is very important to have friends." He leaned forward. "I know you have this book, this rare book. It is not valuable to you. For you it will only bring trouble. Sadness. It is only valuable to me so I am prepared to pay you. You look like a smart man and I tell you this is a smart thing. How much do you want for this book?"

Morgan took a deep breath and looked him in the eye. "I'm not sure I know what you're talkin' about, my friend. I don't have any book that would interest you, and if I did, well I'd want to find out how much it was worth first."

"This is an old book, two books, notebooks, with leather covers. They say that one time they belong to a lawyer, *un abogado.* Look around you house. If you find you have such a book, you call me here at El Coyote Azul and leave a message for Julio. I will pay you $5,000 if you have this book. Make very sure you do not have this book because if you do and you no sell and something happen, well..." he shrugged and raised his hands, palms outward. "...I am not responsible."

For a second Morgan thought about how nice five thousand in cash would be and then he got out of the chair and stood up. It was impossible to tell how tall the Mexican was but although Morgan seemed to tower over him he remained sitting, impassive, unblinking. Finally Morgan said: "I wish I knew what you were talking about, *Señor*..."

"*Señor* Julio."

"*Señor* Julio what?"

"Julio. That is all you need to know."

"I'll tell you what, *Señor* Julio. If I find your books I'll call you. First thing." He resettled his hat on his head and threw Julio a half salute. The two men who had been sitting with Julio and were now standing had been watching him and when he looked over they quickly looked away. Morgan started for the door. The man at the door was the messenger, the same one who had come over to him at the bar and he fixed Morgan with his dark eyes and then, with studied casualness, moved away from the opening and let him pass.

A beat-up gray Toyota Corolla of indeterminate age, the trim peeling off on the left side, was parked crossways to Morgan's truck and Morgan walked slowly over to the Dodge and as he did the passenger door of the Toyota opened and a young Mexican, looking barely 20, emerged and started for the door of the bar. He was wearing a white tank top and baggy black pants and long gold chains swung from his neck. His head was shaved and in the dark Morgan thought he could see a tattoo on his neck, the gothic script indecipherable. The driver of the car maintained a certain cool insouciance, his seat as far back as it would go and the seatback pushed back even further. Only the top of his head and his eyes were visible. His head was shaved as well and a few wisps of straggly hair sprouted beneath his lower lip and he turned small, dark eyes on Morgan.

Morgan unlocked the door of the truck and was about to get in when he felt the first kid on his left and he locked the door and slammed it shut and took two steps back trying to keep both of the *cholos* in his sight. The driver, however, had remained behind the wheel. "You know what?" the first one said to no one in particular, his attitude plainly aggressive. "I jus' go in to buy a six pack and I don' have enough money. Maybe you let me borrow a couple of bucks." With that, he grinned at the driver and the driver added: "Yeah, maybe you let us borrow a couple of bucks. Until payday." He laughed.

"I don't think so, boys. The IRS has already shaken me down. Maybe another day."

The first one moved closer and Morgan could see how strong he was but he could also see that his hands were empty. "This is not a donation, you *gabacho* prick. Give me your fuckin' money if you wanna walk outta this here fuckin' parkin' lot you fuckin' piece of shit."

The parking lot had emptied. The champagne colored Infiniti was gone and the traffic that went by on the highway was traveling too fast to be interested in what was going on in the parking lot of a sleazy bar. He took another step that brought him a little closer to the front of the Toyota and he heard the loud click of the door lock and then the driver was getting out. He was carrying a metal crowbar that gleamed in the neon lights from the bar. It looked to be heavy enough to do some serious damage.

Morgan looked back and forth between the two and made

a quick motion forward and planted his booted foot against the Toyota's door. The timing was perfect and the top of the door caught the kid on the bridge of his nose and he fell backward and grabbed his face with both hands, his nose sprouting a red smear. The crowbar clanged off the asphalt parking lot and Morgan bent to pick it up just as the first kid swung at him. His swing went wild over Morgan' head, and, off-balance, the kid caught himself on the hood of the Toyota. Immediately his left hand went to the back of the waistband of his baggy trousers and Morgan knew what was coming next and he came off the ground with the crowbar in both hands and caught the kid square across the forearm with the full weight of his body. The loud crack of breaking bone echoed across the front of the bar and the kid screamed out a stream of curses but the cheap pistol that he had taken from his waistband skittered harmlessly across the parking lot.

Morgan felt the rage take over his body and fought to control it but before he could help himself he had smashed the kid in the mouth with his bare hand and when the kid bent back, Morgan drove a kick into his groin and the kid went down. The driver was still clutching his nose, blood pouring from between his fingers and Morgan heaved the crowbar as far as he could and grabbed him, pulled him out onto the ground, fired up the car and put it in drive. It coasted slowly out of the way of his Dodge and as Morgan pulled out of the lot he saw both kids on the ground, not moving.

He went in the other direction first, away from Indio and toward the Salton Sea, until he was out of sight of the bar and then he turned south and west and headed back. When he hit a stretch where there was nothing but alfalfa fields, he pulled over and took a jug of water out of the truckbed and poured some over his hands and rinsed his face and dried himself on his red bandanna. As the adrenaline drained from his body he sat behind the wheel and took some deep breaths and used the time to put another call into Victor. There was no answer and again Morgan left no message.

He knew something now. He knew that someone was willing to pay for the journals he had written off as curiosities. The $5,000 was bait, of course. Someone wanted to entice him without letting him know exactly how much they were willing to pay. If they offered the 5K, he knew, they would pay a lot more. But why? Sixty-some years later what difference did it make?

He knew that most nights Victor frequented the American Legion Hall on Requa Street in Indio and he turned the Ford 180 degrees and headed off in that direction. A breeze had picked up off the desert that brought with it the unmistakable smell of sagebrush and with it a chill in the air and Morgan rode with the windows rolled up. The Hall looked like a thousand other Halls in a thousand other little towns, one story, brick and cheap granite or marble over cinderblock, vintage about 1920's. There were two old French 75's on the patchy green lawn pointed toward an enemy that had long since been vanquished, and a white flagpole with a tarnished brass ball at the top and a flag that was lighted with a spotlight from the corner of the building.

Morgan stopped the Ford in the red zone at the curb and took the steps two at a time. Inside the room it was quiet, a television set broadcasting CNN in the corner and a handful of people sitting around. He hailed the bartender, a pale anglo with thin, yellowing skin and a gray stubble. "Excuse me. You know Vic Gomez? The exterminator?"

"Yeah, what's it to ya?" the bartender answered, suspiciously.

"He's a friend of mine and…"

"I ain't never seen you before. How's come?"

"No, you haven't. But he's still my friend. Look…it's important. Have you seen him?"

"About two days ago. Maybe three."

"But not tonight?"

The bartender shook his head and hollered over to the group in front of the television set. "Anyone see Vic Gomez here tonight?" He was answered with a chorus of "no's" and turned back to Morgan. "Nope. We ain't seen him tonight."

Morgan nodded and was back in his car and out of the parking lot in record time. Once in the car, he dialed up information on his mobile phone and got Vic's address, then had Verizon's information service dial for him but again he got his message. He pressed the accelerator to the floor.

Vic's house was in north Indio, on 46th just off Arabia Street, in an area that had been built in the era before tracts, when there was more than 72 inches between houses and you could use the bathroom without your neighbor handing you a roll of toilet paper. He drove slowly down the street, checking addresses, and finally spotted Vic's truck at the very end of a driveway at the end of the block. He shut of the engine and coasted to a stop two doors away. It was close to nine o'clock but already the neighborhood was quiet, the stoopsitters having gone inside and the kids all in for the night.

Vic's lawn was neat and except for single palo verde tree in the front yard and some myrtle bushes up against the house there was nothing to block Morgan's view. The door was ajar two or three inches and a sliver of yellow light washed out onto the lawn but something nagged at Morgan and he circled the house on the sidewalk and went around to the back where he was screened by a low redwood fence and got closer to the house that way and looked inside where he could see under the blind. There was no movement, no sound. Nothing.

He continued around to the back. The door was open and

a screen door was all that blocked the doorway and he went up to it and knocked softly and when there was no answer, he called the man's name in a very soft voice. There was no answer and Morgan moved his hand forward to try the latch, thought better of it, and took his bandanna out of his pocket and grasped the latch with that and it gave under his hand and he pushed the door in.

A couch covered in chintz fabric protruded into the room and was placed so that it was in front of a small fireplace and Morgan could see Vic's hair on the armrest where the man had fallen asleep and he straightened out of the half-crouch he had unconsciously assumed and went around to the front of the couch. What stopped him was all the blood. Victor's eyes were wide open, his face, what he could see of it among all of the blood, was a mask of fear. Blood had sprayed from an obscenely wide slash that had almost severed his head and it covered everything and had even sprayed over the coffee table and as far as the fireplace in a garish decoration and Morgan stopped in his tracks. He had one thought now, how to get out without leaving any tracks.

First, however, he reached out and touched the body. It was cool. Vic had spoken to him two hours before and had obviously been killed right after that call. Somehow he had not stepped into any of the blood and he was about to back out when he thought about the answering machine and the message he had left. It wasn't anywhere in sight in the living room and he looked on the narrow kitchen counter and it wasn't there and he finally noticed it on the man's night stand, red light blinking, three messages showing. Morgan used one of his keys to tap the buttons.

Vic had obviously listened to Morgan's first message and erased it because the first call that played back was both sides of a conversation in Spanish, between Vic and someone else.

Both men spoke quickly and Morgan played it back a few times before he finally caught the gist of it. Someone that identified himself as Pablo had told Vic to stay home and Vic had argued that it wouldn't hurt anything if he went to the American Legion Hall and Pablo finally told him to shut up and stay home if he knew what was good for him. The last thing he said was that the patron would show him gratitude for the information and Vic reluctantly agreed.

The second call was from Leticia, Vic's long-time girlfriend. Her English was unaccented and she sounded concerned and she wanted to know where Vic had been and she was leaving the American Legion Hall and would he call her at home so she wouldn't worry. That was at 7:45, and Vic had probably been dead almost an hour by then.

Morgan's was the third call.

After he listened to the messages, he hit play again, and then erase, and watched to make sure the sequence went as he had set it. He debated calling the police and thought better of it and then it came to him that he was everywhere except where he should have been. Morgan was out the door and into the truck and he had it in gear and rolling down the street even before he closed the driver's door. At the intersection with Monroe, he fishtailed it so it slid around the corner and when it straightened out he firewalled the accelerator and the truck frame bottomed out at the crown of the road at 111 and he ran the yellow at Carreon and ran the stop sign at 50th and turned for the ranch.

The security light on the gallus gate out front had fired within the last ten minutes and it was still on. Morgan coasted by and parked in front of the next driveway behind some oleanders about 200 yards away and opened the truck door quietly and depressed the switch so the light in the cab wouldn't give him away. The last thing he did before he slid to the ground was pocket the Glock and take his penlight from the side pocket of his door.

The house was 300 or so yards from the road and from where he was he could see that nothing had apparently been disturbed, but from that distance, anything could be going on. The gate was still locked and that could be a good sign. He started to make a check of the perimeter and got as far as the telephone switching box on the pole at the street. The gray metal cover hung from one hinge, where it had been forced open. He shined the penlight on the wires and he could see three places where alligator clips had been used to bypass the alarm.

17

Okay, fuckers, he breathed. He felt to see that the safety was off the Glock and then he began to move closer to the house, placing each foot so as not to make a sound in the dead brush and the dry leaves under the oleanders. He kept to the empty field along the east side of the property where he could approach the house and remain concealed and he crept closer that way until he could see that the front door appeared closed. The plantation shutters in the sitting area were still secured and revealed nothing. There was no sound anywhere. In the pasture, there were only two dark shapes that moved slowly, heads to the ground.

Clearing the cover of the bushes he crouched behind the giant *nopal* cactus by the front door. From there he could see that it was open an inch or two and he counted to ten, moved closer, and eased it wider. Nothing moved.

The kitchen and the sitting area and the dining room were undisturbed and he moved soundlessly on the Saltillo tile floor to the door of his office. About half the file drawers in his desk and the contents of the two-drawer filing cabinet had been emptied into a pile onto the antique Russian rug in the middle of the room. The laptop was closed and the dustcover lay undisturbed. Like a baleful red eye, the message light on the phone blinked silently. Something had interrupted whoever it was that was doing the searching.

The alarm panel blinked ready and verified that everything was closed. Moving easily in the dark he went outside and checked the doors to the bunkhouse but they were all locked.

It was then that he realized the dog was missing. Morgan went from room to room calling, his voice just above a whisper. Outside near the pool equipment chanced a low whistle but there was no response. Nothing. The only thing that would keep the dog from answering his whistle was if he were gone or if he had been killed and he refused to think about either possibility just then.

He thought for a moment about calling the police and decided against that and called Burns instead. He used the handset of the bedroom phone and when he realized the line was dead he cursed to himself and pulled out his cell phone. It would be better than nothing. Just barely. There was no answer on the P.I.'s cell phone and he had to content himself with leaving a message. For good measure he left a message on Burns' machine at his house, which actually meant one of his massive computers. The detective would certainly discover it when he returned except that if he was off sitting at one of his bars up in Malibu, that could be a few hours, maybe not until the morning.

The next call was to the Indio P.D. Morgan called it in as a straight breaking-and-entering and the dispatcher asked him if he was in any danger and he answered that he wasn't. "Good," the cop said, "it's been a busy night. Seems like everything's happening."

He made sure the rest of the house was locked up, locked the front door, and retreated into the shadows on the side of the bunkhouse avoiding the zones of the automatic security lights. His vantage point would afford him an early warning and one against how ever many there were, he needed all the warning he could get. The light from his cell phone glowed on when he dialed up Amado and he shielded it with his body and waited. In a moment, the groom answered and Morgan whispered: "*Despierta te. Te necesito hoy. Es muy importante.*"

"*Seguro. A donde?*"

"*A mi rancho.* Bring Juan or Ramon or somebody. And do it quickly."

"*Si, pero que paso?*"

"I'm not sure. Someone tried to break into my house. And Max is missing. Be careful."

When nothing moved for five more minutes he let himself inside again and checked his answering machine. It was an old PhoneMate that had the quirky habit of saving messages instead of erasing them automatically. This time he was glad for it because someone had obviously listened to the two messages.

The first one was from Vic shortly after Morgan had left, his tone now anxious. "Listen, man. I'm not going to meet you at El Coyote Azul after all. And you definitely shouldn't go there by yourself, at least until I talk to you. Roger that for me ASAP, will *ya compadre?*"

The second was from Alexis at 8:30: "Hi, cowboy. I've been buried up here in San Fran and Jerome and I missed our flight. I'm going to try to get a later one but you know United. I'll call you when I get in. Love ya."

The familiar tugging at this heart was interrupted by a persistent knock on the front door that echoed throughout the foyer with a hollow sound. An unfamiliar voice called out: "Mister Morgan, you in there?"

"Who is it?"

"Indio Police. Would you please open your door, sir?"

Morgan braced his foot against the door and with his pistol at the ready he cracked it open until he could see that it was a uniformed officer. "Give me a sec," he said, and he closed the door and stashed the pistol under a couch cushion and only then did he open the door all the way. The policeman stood about five feet back from the door and held a silver metal .357 Magnum revolver loosely in his right hand, pointing down. "Would you mind stepping outside, sir? Away from the door, sir, please? And could you show me some I.D.? And please move slowly and keep your hands in sight."

Morgan extracted his wallet from his back pocket with one hand and flipped it open so that the cop could see his California Driver's License. The cop nodded and only then did the second policeman show himself from the darkness beyond the tangerine tree outside the well pump room. "Thank you, sir. Are you okay? I apologize for making you come out, but you can't be too careful."

Morgan took the two officers in tow and showed them the mess that was his office. With them in the house he could afford the luxury of looking carefully at the damage and he confirmed that nothing of consequence was missing. The younger of the two cops asked him if the intruders might have been looking for something specific but he told them he had no idea and that appeared to satisfy them. While they were talking, an 87 Olds Cutlass coasted up, a young man with a shaved head at the wheel. His passenger was built thick and had his cap set backwards.

Morgan stepped back but the cops and the *cholos* in the Olds exchanged waves and when he realized they were undercover detectives he relaxed. The undercover cops nodded at him almost as an afterthought and talked softly with the uniforms for a minute before walking off by themselves around the property. When they returned, the younger one came over to Morgan. He had a flashlight in his hand. "You got a minute? I wanna show you somethin'." He beckoned Morgan to follow and lead him to where the telephone switching equipment was attached to a thick short pole. The cover hung by one hinge. "Look here," he said, shining the light on where an alligator clip had been placed to jump a circuit. He reached over and disconnected the clip. "There you go…you got your telephone service back."

"Doesn't do a whole hell of a lot for my peace of mind."

"Most people don't realize how easily you can disable a telephone. And an alarm system. What you need is one of those wireless uplink deals, like they use on mobile phones. They got those now and they're pretty cheap…considering. But in any event, if you're a burglar you've got to know what you're doing. Which makes me think that the guy or guys that did this weren't just walkin' by. They were after something. You sure you have no idea what it was?"

"I can't imagine. Sorry."

The senior uniform gave Morgan a business card and said goodnight while the other one turned the car around and they drove off down the driveway. The Hispanic officers, however, hung back. The younger one, the one who looked as though he had spent ten years at Soledad, was about 35, and he asked Morgan: "Mind if I take another look around?" while the one with the backwards cap lit a cigarette and started back to the Olds.

"Not at all."

Morgan let him wander through the bunkhouse and showed him the corral and the small barn out in the back. A breeze had kicked up from the south and clouds were beginning to gather over Santa Rosa Mountain. They watched in silence and after a few moments the cop spoke: "You know, I would swear that I was here before. When I was a little boy, maybe in the 70's. This place belonged to an old Mexican guy that did some leather work and my father took me here with him once." Away from the car he dropped his cholo pose and his voice was soft. "I'm almost sure of it. Cosmetically it's completely changed, but it's got the same layout and the same feel. Ah, well. Maybe not. But you know how it is. My father died last year and I guess I think of him a lot. Thanks." And he threw a wave over his shoulder and started to walk down the driveway while the other one turned the car around.

"Wait a second." Morgan called after him. "My turn for a question. You know anything about *la familia* Gutierrez?"

The officer stopped and turned to him, a strange look on his face. "Sure. I guess everyone's heard of them. Maybe not your people, no offense intended. They're connected to most of the gang stuff that went on, and that still goes on. Loansharking, moving people, drugs, gambling. Mostly they stay clear of us. No way anyone's ever been able to prove anything, though. They're tryin' to become legit now, with that Indian gaming casino that they want to help the Indians put up. But that's bullshit. The Indians'll wind up getting' screwed anyway. Haven't you seen any of the pickets?"

"Guess I have. I just didn't realize that Gutierrez was into that."

"They are. That's why all the resistance by the locals. Gutierrez and his family has arm's length screwed most of the locals at one time or another over the past 80 or 90 years." He got quiet, remembering. "That's really a coincidence, you mentioning that. I told you I thought this place belonged to this old Mexican guy. Guy was old when I met him. I'm sure he's dead now. I remember my father telling me that the old guy had been one of the big lieutenants for Gutierrez but I thought he told me that just to scare me into behaving."

"Did it work?"

"Does anything work on a smart-ass seven year old?"

"Is Gutierrez still alive?"

"You mean the old man?"

Morgan shrugged. "I don't know who I mean. Shit, how many are there?"

"They really don't know who's in charge these days. Rolando was the boss man back in the 30's and he's supposed to be dead, but who knows? They weren't sure he was alive when he was alive. He was like a ghost. One of the things they called him was *fantasma*. The word on the street now is that even if he's still alive he's has turned most of it over to his son, Julio. The call him the hawk, *el halcon*. But like they say, *quien sabes*...who knows.

"Interesting." Morgan offered.

"Why?"

"No reason. I've just heard a lot about them lately."

The officer looked at him closely. "Those are some badass hombres. I wouldn't go messin' with them."

"I don't plan on it...I'm just curious. They're probably not local anyway."

"We hope not. Rumor is that they have some sort of estancia or something down van Buren way past Avenue 62 up against the mountains down there but that's unincorporated land still, and it's not in our jurisdiction and I'm just as glad. La Quinta's trying to annex that property but for now it's the Sheriff's Department that knows, probably. Although they're just as happy to let them be as along as they're not in anyone's face. There's an office in Palm Desert, contracting or building or some such, across from where

Jensen's is. It's supposedly legit but supposedly connected although there's never been anything obvious."

"What's the name of the company? The contractors, I mean."

"Don't know. I'd know it if I heard it but I don't recollect. Sorry."

"It's okay. Like I said…just curious."

"Don't get too curious…their protection comes from the reluctance of the illegals not to report them because they might get reported and deported themselves. Or worse. That, and a couple of hundred years of irrational fear of the peasants for the man. Not that man, but the man." He laughed. "All together it's a mighty impressive force, I'd say."

"Sounds like it. Thanks."

"Call if you need us. 911's the best way." This time he kept going down the drive to the gate. Morgan walked part way down with him and on his way back to the house a shadow detached itself from the oleanders. Than another one, and another. "Amado. Where the fuck did you come from?"

"I bring Juan. And Borrego."

"Thanks for comin' boys. I owe you."

"*No es problema*. What happen? Wha' you wan' us to do?"

Morgan filled him in while the three followed him into the bunkhouse and watched him carefully as he unlocked the antique gun cabinet. He removed a Remington 1200 12 gauge shotgun, opened the breech, and passed it to Juan and did the same thing for Borrego, and gave them each a box of 00 buckshot from the cabinet underneath. Then he took out his 12 gauge Belgian Browning, broke it open and handed it over to Amado along with a box of shells. "Make sure that the place stays quiet. Hang wherever, but don't stay together. Oh, yeah, and one of you should stay out of sight. Take turns sleeping. That'll get us through the night. Tomorrow we'll pay us a visit to this Gutierrez family."

The telephone was ringing when Morgan walked back in and he checked the Caller ID and saw an unfamiliar number and he lifted the phone, expecting the worst. "It's Don, Nick, from across the street."

"What can I do for you?"

"Well, fer one thing, Nick, we got yer dog." Marilyn said, on the extension, and Morgan felt himself relax for the first time since he had come home.

"He alright?"

"Looks to be. Plenty hungry, though."

"That's a big load off my mind. Thanks, you guys. How'd you get him?"

"Our dogs were barking and Don went outside to see why and there was yer yeller dog. He came right over to me and I tied 'im up and gave 'im some water and tried to call you but yer phone was busy. Fer another, what was all those cops doin' there? I don't mean to be nosy."

"I'll be right over and I'll fill you in."

"Don't have ta tonight. You're not going anywheres, are ya? We'll bring 'im over in the mornin'."

"Thanks, but all the same…he's family. I'll see you in five minutes."

Morgan and Max made the rounds of the buildings together, the dog at a close heel. The Mexicans were out of sight but they made smacking, kissing noises to Morgan as he went by in the dark so he knew they were there, and he made the noises back to them in answer. His last stop was the patio outside the master bedroom and he unlocked the glass doors and stepped into the shadows of the room. The only illumination came from the light in the living room and his first awareness that something was wrong came when Max halted two strides into the room and began a low, throaty growl. The smell of fresh quince was heavy in the air and at the same time he heard the icy, chilling rattle of a full-grown rattlesnake. The dog started toward the noise but Morgan grabbed him by his collar and pulled him back, out of the room and onto the patio. He slammed the door and took the dog the few steps to the mesquite in the middle of the yard where he chained him up. Then he went back to where Borrego and Amado were holed up. "There's a *pinche cascabel* in my bedroom," he whispered, "a fuckin' rattler."

Amado's face almost turned white in the darkness but Borrego simply grinned and pulled a long knife from somewhere in his belt. It glittered in the moonlight like a wicked jewel. "*Donde, patron? Ensena me.*" the man said.

"In my goddamn bedroom. "

With the light from a high-intensity flashlight, Morgan and Borrego slowly eased the door open. At the last minute Morgan took the jute doormat with him thinking it would make a good shield. "*Hueles muy mal.*" Borrego whispered. "It stinks."

There was no snake to be seen. Amado followed behind him, the Belgian Browning ready and Morgan turned back to him. "Don't shoot the motherfucker in my house if you can help it. I don't want to be picking pieces of snake out of my bed linen for the rest of my life."

Borrego stretched out on the floor and shined the light under the bed. "*Nada, patron. Solamente una caja pequeña.*" A small box, the size of a birthday cake, could be seen, its top open. "*Es un regalo.*" Borrego said, with a wicked grin. "A gift for you."

"Great. All I need is a snake in the fuckin' walls. Check under the television set."

There was nothing there.

Whether by sound or by intuition, Morgan and Borrego both looked up in time to see six feet of Diamondback rattlesnake launch itself from the top of the bed canopy, mouth open, jaws literally dripping venom, straight for Morgan's head. Morgan acted by reflex and he brought the doormat up just quick enough to deflect the snake and it dropped to the floor, rattling feverishly and striking again and again. Borrego motioned Morgan to back away and he moved to the side of the snake and when it struck air yet again he reached out and with one deft move severed a foot of snake from the front end of it. Morgan dropped the doormat on the part with the head and Borrego quickly grabbed the headless body and threw it outside.

When it was over they gave each other a high-five but Morgan was drenched with sweat. "We need *cervezas*," he said, trying to pass it off with a casual grin. Borrego was strutting around like a stud and finally he went outside to the body of the snake and examined it carefully with the flashlight. "*Es muy viejo.*" Borrego said, his voice full of pride.

Amado finally got up enough courage to speak. "*Yo pensar es un mensaje.* A message."

"Si," Borrego added, "*un aviso.*"

"What are you guys talkin' about?"

"It was a warning, Jefe. They carry the esnake in here and put under you *cama*. Next time…"

"There ain't gonna be no next time."

"*Primero Dios.*"

When they had cleaned the bedroom, Morgan and Borrego checked every corner of the house. "Okay," he finally said, "that's enough. There was only one. If they would have really wanted to kill me they would have been more efficient. I think you were right. This was only a scare."

But at the same time, when he went to bed it was in his

clothes and with his shoes on, on top of the covers.

If he slept during the night he wasn't aware of it. At 4:30 he had coffee going and by 5 he was outside. The sky in the east was barely lightening; here and there a wispy cloud was beginning to turn pink, reflecting the still-hidden sun. In the east, Venus shined like a beacon. The effect was soothing, peaceful, and it gave the tableau a sense that somehow the danger was past. Morgan sensed it was a false impression. Borrego was sitting at the glass patio table, his feet up on another chair, the shotgun across his knees, listening to the news in Spanish on a small portable. The night had gotten chilly and he had on a well-worn denim jacket, the collar turned up around his neck. On his head a dark blue cap with an embroidered Ralph Lauren polo player was pulled down low. When he saw Morgan, he gave a small lift of his chin and smiled his big grin.

"*Como esta?*" Morgan asked.

"*Como aciete, amigo.*"

"*Todos tranquilo?*"

"*Si. No mas cascabels.*" He grinned again.

"*Que es Nuevo?*" Morgan indicated the radio with his eyes.

"*No mucho. Un hombre muerto in Indio. Un burglary.*"

"*Si? Que?*"

"*No se.* They say only that he kill."

"You mean dead…"

"*Si. Lo siento.* Dead."

"And…"

"*Nada mas. Es Indio. Un otra murder…*" he didn't finish the sentence, but made a gesture with his hands, like brushing away a fly.

As it got lighter, Amado emerged from the darkness by the stables in back, looking like a moderately sized bear awakening from hibernation. Juan simply appeared. He seemed overnight to have grown a three day beard and his face was drawn, his eyes rimmed in red. He looked as though he hadn't slept and Morgan took all of them inside and poured coffee for them and they each poured milk and extra sugar in their cups. In the refrigerator, Morgan found most of a dozen eggs, a piece of chorizo, and an unopened package of tortillas and while they sat around and drank coffee and conjectured about who could have been behind the burglary and the snake episode Morgan fried the chorizo, scrambled the eggs, and warmed the tortillas. He put the finished product on a large platter and found the last of his home-made salsa verde and as the sun began to pour in through the now-open plantation shutters, they tore into their impromptu feast.

After they left, Morgan looked at the shotguns. They hadn't been fired in years and so he took them into the bunkhouse and opened his gunbox and opened the bottle of Hoppe's Number 7 and took a clean rag and the long fuzzy cleaning rod and swabbed out the barrels of each shotgun and then took out some thin gun oil and repeated the process and then he finished by rubbing a thin layer of oil over each weapon. It was almost 8 o'clock and when the phone rang his first instinct was to let the answering machine pickup but when he thought it could be Alexis he lifted the receiver.

"Whattup, bro?" Burns asked, his voice animated.

"Where the fuck you been?"

"Ah, my brotha, I met this divine young actress last night and she thought I was wonderful and I didn't get your message until just a minute ago."

"Fuckin' friend. I might have been killed and you're out fucking your fuckin' brains out."

"Vulgarity is the last refuge of the inarticulate motherfucker. But it was a good cause."

"Be serious. Things are getting a little nasty down here.

You got more than a minute?"

"I'll call you back in 10 minutes."

"I could be dead in 10 minutes."

"Five."

"Okay, five."

When Burns called back, Morgan filled him in with everything that had happened since last they spoke. "Bottom line," he finished, "is that Vic could've been murdered coincidentally, but it doesn't feel like that. And the kids in the parking lot could've been a coincidence but there were no other cars and they could've parked anywhere. And the burglary wasn't your basic hophead burglary. Shit, nothing was missing. They could have taken the stereo, the computer, the booze, for Chrissakes, and besides, no one in the area can even remember anyone getting burgled around here. It just doesn't happen around here. Someone took their time and cased the place and figured out the alarm and knew what they were looking for."

"And don't forget the snake."

"Like I could. I got out of bed this morning like I used to get out of a sleeping bag when I used to ride behind the cows."

"How's that?"

"Last thing you move is your legs. Just in case there's one curled up in your bedroll for warmth."

"Barbaric."

"Fuck you. Seriously. Someone cased the joint."

"Or someone had been watching the place since you moved in."

"Who?"

"Vic. You said he came with the place and you told me he cut you a real inexpensive deal from day one. Who better than an exterminator to wander around and look in closets and under beds without raising any suspicion?"

236

"So there was some unfinished business here. Or at least someone thought there was."

"Bingo."

"Is a..."

"Forget it. Sit tight, will you. I've got some stuff to finish up here and..."

"Like the actress."

"No. I left her at her place this morning. No. I was gonna call you anyway and head down there. I was going through some papers that Brooks left in the office before he was killed and for sure there's a connection in my mind with your Mexican mob. I'm not a hundred percent but a good, solid 75. Sounds to me right now that you could use some more firepower...it's as good an excuse as anything. There's definitely something about those journals they want and they'll be back for them. You didn't copy them yet so don't go out and do it now. Now they know you're not a pansy so they might come across more conciliatory."

"Or harder."

"Or harder. Either way, don't do anything dumb. Stay strapped."

"What?"

"You know...carry heat...a gun. You been outta the big city too long. I'll keep my cell phone on."

"Thanks. That's a big consolation here in cellphone hell."

Morgan hung up and called Alexis at the W Hotel but she had checked out the night before so he called her answering machine at home and left a "drop everything and call me" message and for good measure he left one on the voicemail on her cell phone even though he knew that she never checked that one. He used the cordless phone and paced back and forth between the main house and the bunkhouse by the Jacuzzi while he called the Boutique and told the Manager to have her call the minute he saw her. Then he left a message on her office voicemail. But all he really wanted to do was to get her near him so he could reassure himself that she was safe and then keep her that way.

He tried to sit down at his computer but he was too keyed up and finally decided to take a ride over to the club. He was turning the truck around by the basketball hoop in the corner of the driveway house when he noticed the skinny man sitting on the plain wooden bench, half out of sight under the pergola that ran around two sides of the bunkhouse. His feet were stretched out in front of him, his hands behind his head and his hat pushed forward. But he was clearly not asleep and he gave a wave to Morgan as soon as he realized he was noticed. It was David, one of Amado's endless supply of cousins. Primos, he called them. The boys were still watching.

When he got to the club, Amado and Juan were playing dominoes on a makeshift wooden board and Amado rolled his eyes when Morgan asked him how he was doing. "*Patiar in las nalgas.*" Juan laughed. "He's getting his ass kicked." Borrego was stretched out asleep on the floor of the tackroom.

His mobile phone hadn't rung and now it was almost two and this time when he called the Boutique, the Manager told him that they hadn't heard from her but they thought that she said that she might stop at the L.A. Mart for a moment before heading over to the Boutique and wasn't it just like her to get distracted. Her cell phone answered with a recorded message that said the call couldn't be complete.

When he got back to the ranch, Morgan settled into the couch in the living room and put his legs up on the camel saddle he used as a footstool. Shit, he hated not sleeping. The knock on the door broke his reverie and his heart began to pound. It seemed to bring him back from some far distant place. Max hadn't even barked and he sat instead in front of the closed door, his tail wagging as if it were Amado on the other side. Morgan opened it expecting the Mexican but what he saw seemed to suck the air out of the house and out of his body. A woman was standing there looking as though she had stepped out of a photo scrapbook from the 1930's, dark hair cut short, makeup a shade too dark, lipstick a touch too heavy.

"Aren't you gonna ask me in?" Alexis asked while Morgan tried to look casual.

"Of course," and when he took her in his arms the smell of lavender was so intense he became dizzy but he held her long enough to satisfy himself that it really was Alexis. At last he backed away and looked at her. "Like it?" she asked.

"I…yes. It's so different…such a different look for you."

"Who's to say a girl can't change her looks?"

"Not me, sweetheart. What are you doing here? I've been trying you all over L.A."

"I wanted to come down, to see you, especially after the way I took off the last time I was here." She whirled into the room and sat on the couch while Morgan got her a glass of water just to be doing something with his hands.

"How long can you stay?" he asked.

"Through the weekend. I squared it with Jerome. He said I needed the time off. And he's right. Whew, I've been like running a marathon." She drank most of the water and laid her head back on the top of the couch while Morgan went out to the Mercedes and retrieved her hanging bag, still confused about how she looked and not believing she was really there.

When he came back in her eyes were closed and she was breathing deeply, obviously in an exhausted sleep. He turned to the sink to rinse a glass for himself and that's when he heard his name behind him in a strange voice. The hair on his neck rose and he almost dropped the glass. "Nicholas." the voice, a woman's voice, sultry, smoky, repeated his name and he spun around but no one but Alexis was there.

She seemed to be in a deep sleep, yet her head moved from side to side, as if she were agitated. The voice appeared to be coming from her yet from someplace else, someplace on the other side and his mind raced to grasp the idea and promptly rejected it. He almost woke her but then remembered something about waking sleepwalkers and discarded the idea.

"Nicholas...please...you must help me. Scott's diary...in the middle of it...what you cannot understand...the numbers are changed around...backwards...please...my family is looking for me...please find the answer."

Now his hair felt as if it was standing straight up on his neck and back and he walked closer to the girl but already her breathing had changed and in a moment her eyelids fluttered and she woke up. "What did you say?" he asked, trying to regain his composure.

"Sorry. I said I was tired. I must have dozed off. Say? When?"

"When you were...Never mind."

The ringing of the cell phone interrupted and when Morgan saw Amado's number on the phone screen he answered it. "*Que paso?*" Morgan asked, without preamble.

"Nino. He hurt himself, on the leg. *Por favor*, come over and look me."

"Can it wait?"

"I no like that the leg, she's getting big. Maybe *un mordida de arania*, spider, you know."

"Okay, okay, I'll be there in five."

"*Gracias, patron.*"

She looked at him when he disconnected. It was Amado." he said. "Nino's hurt his leg somehow. Amado is worried, even more so than usual. Come with me...it won't take long to find out what's going on."

"No. I really need to lay down and rest. You go ahead. I'll be fine."

He hesitated and she said: "Don't be silly. You go. I'll be alright."

Another moment's pause, and then. "I'm gonna lock you in with Max. There's a skinny old dude back by the bunkhouse. You probably didn't notice him…it's David. Skinny, but tough. It's one of Amado's four hundred cousins. He's your protection. Just in case, though, don't let anyone in and don't go out. Remember, don't answer the door and don't go out no matter what happens outside, or what you hear."

18

Morgan bent over the bad leg. Amado was right. The only thing was that it didn't look like a spider bite. The gelding had probably kicked one of the metal stall rails with his lower leg and had given himself a good-sized hematoma for his effort but he could understand why Amado had mistaken it for a spider bite. The swollen area was warm, and when he palpated the pulse above the hoof with his thumb and forefinger it was more bounding than normal and he was dead lame on the leg. Together they applied a poultice to draw out the swelling and they followed that with a wrap over a white quilted dressing and for good measure they gave him a Bute.

At the barn, at least, he felt in his element. The horses were a commitment that couldn't be put off and the incident had been a timely distraction for him after what had happened with Alexis.

Morgan was on his way out of the barn area when he saw that someone had locked the access gate when it wasn't due to be locked for at least another hour. Mumbling softly about the dumb sonofabitch who couldn't tell time and knowing it would take him another ten minutes to go around the long way behind the Cantina he turned the truck around and by the time he turned west on Avenue 50 the sun was already dipping behind Santa Rosa turning the face of it a dark purple. He stopped at the gate to the ranch and unlocked it and eased up the driveway.

David wasn't on the bench by the bunkhouse. Morgan looked around but nothing else was out of place. The red Mercedes was still at the end of the circular drive where Alexis had parked it. Hummingbirds dive-bombed the feeder from the branches of the mesquite and a roadrunner was clicking in the back by the palo verde tree. He wrote David off as having gone to take a piss and why in the hell couldn't he piss in plain sight at a time like this? When Morgan started to insert the key into the lock the door gave way under his hand and swung open and Morgan felt a shudder go through his body. He pulled the door to without a sound and got the Glock from where it was on the front seat of the truck and with the weapon at the ready he crouched down and pushed on the door once again.

It swung open into a silent house.

He knew immediately that Alexis was gone and he cursed himself and cursed his stupidity and then he noticed the pool of blood on the floor. It went from near the front door to the door of his bedroom and he followed it, dreading what he would see.

The trail ended at a yellow mound of fur just on the other side of his bed. "My fuckin' God." he murmured, and he bent over the dog and put his ear against the animal's chest, relieved that it wasn't Alexis and broken-hearted at the same time. Max lifted his head and whimpered when Morgan touched him and when the man touched his face the dog wagged his tail in a weak gesture and began to struggle to his feet. "No…down." Morgan said. He probed his body. There was blood caked along Max's right shoulder and a small area where the flesh gaped. There was no way to tell how much damage had been done but for now it had already stopped bleeding. "You'll be alright, pard." Morgan said, trying to convince himself. "I'm proud of you. You were going straight for him. Good boy. Don't worry…I'll get you some help."

He found David's body behind the bunkhouse. They had tied his hands behind his back and slit his throat from ear to ear just like Vic and flies were already covering his neck like a writhing, buzzing black bandana.

This had gone way beyond the police. He would have to handle it himself.

The ringing of the phone would not be ignored and clamored for a reply and Morgan picked it up in the bunkhouse kitchen. "Señor Morgan," the voice began in a Spanish accent.

Morgan fought down his rage and managed to keep his mouth shut.

"*Señor* Morgan. I know it is you."

"Yeah, mother fucker. It's me."

"I'm so sorry, *Señor* Morgan, but I must be direct. We spoke of your rare book of great value last night…you remember? You didn't like my offer to buy it. Now I want to trade. I have something you want…"

"Julio, you Motherfucker…" Morgan began.

"This is not a time for you to talk, *Señor* Morgan. Listen. I am *la coleccionista*. How you say, a collector of rare books. I am looking for one rare book and I know now that you have it. It is a rare book of such value that I know you would be happy to trades for it…to have you lady friend back."

"You motherfucker," Morgan whispered, his voice coming from some primitive place inside, "what the fuck are you saying?"

"Relax, *Señor* Morgan. You lady friend, she is the honored guest with us. And we are hospitable, we no hurt our guests. Especially women guests." Morgan fought for control while Julio went on: "It is really very simple, you know. Easy, in fact. You have what we want, we have what you want. We get together and we make a trade. Everybody is happy. There is no problem, you see."

"I want to talk to her."

"Ah...*lo siente, Señor* Morgan. I'm sorry. That is not possible."

"I talk to her or there's no deal."

A hand went over the mouthpiece of the phone on the other side and he could hear muffled voices. Then the voice came back on, patient, parental. "You stay at you phone. We call you back in fifteen, maybe twenty minutes."

"I talk to her or there's no deal." Morgan repeated.

"Of course, *Señor* Morgan. But at the same time, I know you a smart man. You know there are times when you make, *como se dice*, the deal, and times when you no make the deal. This is the time you no make the deal. I think it is good if you be patient. We call back." Morgan was listening to his breathing, fighting to make it regular. "This one thing is *muy importante*. You tell anyone, there will be nothing for you to trade for. You understand?"

Morgan said nothing and the voice repeated: "*Usted entiende?* You know, *comprende?*"

"*Si, entiendo.*"

"*Bueno.*" And the line went dead.

Morgan held the handset in his hands, fighting the rage that was beginning to take him over, the all-too-familiar feeling that he thought had abandoned him years ago when doing something, anything, was better than waiting. The first thing he did was dial *69 but there was nothing, just a recorded message telling him that the party that had called could not be called back by that method. Then he checked the caller I.D. unit but all he saw on that was one word— "UNAVAILABLE."

The dog limped to him when Morgan came back inside the house and Morgan ordered him down and sat on the floor next to him. Somehow the bullet had missed anything vital. His leg seemed intact. "Don't worry, big guy," he said, "we'll get our licks in." But the words sounded hollow, the silence of the house broken only by the drumming of the air conditioner. He tried Burns and then Amado without making contact and then he touched the dog on the head and made him stay while he went over to the bunkhouse. The journals rested where he had stashed them, behind the stones of the massive fireplace, and he extracted them easily. What could possibly be in those old journals that was worth all of that killing, he wondered. All of the people in it had to be dead. So what if they screwed the locals out of their land and killed a few Indians and who gave a shit now if anyone had made big bucks from the goddamn All-American Canal. The only way it would make any sense was if someone was still alive and the only person at the ranch that day who could possibly still be alive would be the patron. Rolando, the cop said his name was. But he would have to be in his 90's. Why would he care who knew what happened then?

The daily journal seemed even more musty than it had been that day in Downey and he opened it and turned to the middle, to the cryptic notations he had noticed with Burns. The numbers are backwards, Alexis had said, or was it April who said it through Alexis. He read them off out loud. "52804." Backwards it was "40825". It was familiar, but why? Then all at once it came to him. That was the number of the house in Downey.

When the phone finally rang it was as if someone had thrust a cold hand in his solar plexus and he forced himself to let it ring a second time and when he answered it he kept his voice flat. "Hello." The hell with the goddamn journal, he thought, they could have the sonofabitch. All the same, he knew in his bones that if he just turned it over they'd probably kill both of them. He had to get Alexis out of their hands before he did anything else.

"*Señor* Morgan. You are ready to make our deal?"

"What are my choices?"

"*Señor* Morgan." The voice said, patiently. "You have no choices. You must do exactly as I say. *Usted entiende?*" Morgan didn't answer. "*Usted entiende?*" The voice repeated, sharper this time.

"*Sí.*"

"*Bueno.* You drive to Van Buren Street and Avenue 64 and we meet you there. If you bring anyone else, if you tell anyone else, if you even think of telling anyone else, there will be no deal. I mean that you can offer us that rare book, but we will have nothing to offer in return. *Usted entiende?*"

"I want to talk to her."

"*Señor* Morgan. *Usted entiende?*"

"*Entiendo, pero si hablo con ella,* then there's no 'rare book'."

A sigh on the other end and then he could hear a hand go over the mouthpiece of the phone again and some mumbling in the background and then a voice said: "Wait." and Morgan sat there, perched on the edge of his bed, helpless, filled with anger and powerless to do anything. Finally he heard her voice: "Nick!" she shouted, fighting for control of her voice then beginning to sob and scream. "Give them what they want and get me out of here. Please. They promised me that they'll let us go. Just give them what they want." Before he could say anything to her she was gone and the voice was back. "Van Buren Street and Avenue 64. In 30 minutes. *Entiendes ahora?*"

"*Sí.*"

And then the phone went dead.

He thought for a moment about getting the .357 but decided that the 9 mm Glock would be enough firepower and he shoved it into his belt behind the small of his back. Hefting the day book he realized again that both volumes were exactly the same size and when he realized that he also knew that the chances were slim that *la familia* or even the patron himself would know there were two of them. He would take one, the address book, leave the day book, the one that seemed to have the hot information, and no one would be the wiser. He wrapped the day book carefully in a plastic bag and replaced it in the cache spot and then he took the address book and put it under his arm. The last thing he took was a small stack of towels from the closet in the bunkhouse. Back at the truck he tucked the journal behind the bench seat in the truckcab and spread the towels on the seat for the dog. The dog was waiting at the door and Morgan bent down, lifted him up, and laid him in the front seat on the towels where he would be comfortable.

The polo club was empty, a vast, green plain bathed in that peculiar cerulean light that was left from the last rays of the dying sun. Shadows covered most of the desert floor and Morgan made the trip slowly, careful of the potholes on the dirt road that was Avenue 51 so as not to jar the dog. The thin sheen of dust that rose behind him hung in the air and swirled around him like sparkles in a souvenir glass globe or magic fairy dust.

The scene couldn't have been more normal when he turned into the barn area. The horses were just beginning to tear into their evening flakes of hay and at the end of the row

Amado and Borrego and Ramon and Juan and a few others sat on the decking of the wooden porch, their legs stretched out in front of them, their backs propped against the cinderblock wall. They each clutched a can of Bud Light and in front of them in a little pile like a surreal campfire three or four empties were piled and when they saw him they waved and called greetings and Juan held up a cold can of beer. He shook his head and then they saw the concern in his eyes and when they saw him lift the dog out they were all on their feet, trying to help.

"He was shot," Morgan said to no one in particular. "I'll tell you how later."

One of the men moved forward. "Give him to me." The man said. "I fix him up." The others seemed to defer to him and Morgan looked at Amado and the Mexican said: "'s okay, *patron. Esta hombre es Samuel. Es muy buen medico para perros.* He come from Monterey. They say he the best doctor for dogs."

Morgan laid the animal on the porch of his tackroom and when he stepped away the dog tried to get to his feet. Samuel went to his side and as soon as he did the dog laid down again and seemed to rest.

"*Gracias.*" Morgan said. "Watch him for me, *por favor, amigos. Para dos, tres horas. Es posible?*"

"*Seguro, jefe. Donda e vas?*"

Morgan exhaled. "I can't tell you yet."

The three men on the porch looked at each other. "*Necesita asistencia?*"

Morgan thought for a moment and then shook his head. "No...it shouldn't be anything I can't handle. But thanks. Watching Max *es bastante No te preocupas.*" He threw them a short salute and got back behind the wheel and spun out of the small parking area and went on through onto Monroe where he made a right and headed south, on toward the darkening mountains. Behind him, a small, grey Toyota pickup made the same turn.

Morgan never noticed.

The lights of the trailer park at 52 struggled half-heartedly with the darkness and then were gone, dropping behind him like a stone into a murky pool as he traveled south and before he knew it the sky was almost completely dark in the east and where the date palms towered except that back from the road in quiet places a waxy yellowish light from a porchlight or from a window here or there struggled against the heavy darkness.

Avenue 56 was the logical place to hook on over to Van Buren and he made a left there and when he made a right onto Van Buren, an unlined asphalt two-lane, he glanced at his watch and saw that almost 20 minutes had already elapsed and when he looked up again there was a blue Chevy pickup filling his windshield so close in front of him that he had to jam on his brakes. Its truckbed was filled with rakes and brooms and folded tarps and Morgan cursed and began to accelerate to pull out and pass. But the Chevy began to move faster and he backed off on the accelerator. "Fucking asshole..." he thought, and he looked in the rearview mirror before pulling back in and this time the gray pickup was right on his rear bumper and then it was in the other lane parallel to him and the Chevy was beginning to slow down and Morgan realized that he had been boxed in and buttoned up like a squirrel in a trap.

He tried to jam on the brakes but the driver of the gray pickup anticipated somehow and slowed and squeezed over into his lane as the car in front tapped on his brakes and the three of them moved to the side of the road that way, an odd, twelve-wheeled monster, off the black top and onto the sand and he felt the wheels react to the change in terrain and the steering wheel jerk in his hand.

The passenger door in the grey pickup opened when they stopped and in the dome light he recognized the driver, one of the kids that he had encountered at El Coyote Azul the night before. His eyes, however, were really on the taller man that got out from the driver's side, a beefy dude in a black t-shirt with cut-out sleeves. Someone else emerged from the Chevy in front and stationed himself at the right side of Morgan's truck in the darkness where he couldn't see his face and stood there, arms folded.

"*Señor* Morgan." The tall man was young and when he got closer Morgan realized what he had seen as beef was really muscle. The man had a thick neck and a tattoo on his neck that said something in Spanish. He came up to Morgan's window and when he bent over the gold chains around his neck cascaded out of the t-shirt. He made rolling-down motions and when Morgan cracked the window he spoke, but with exaggerated politeness. "Get out of your car, *Señor, por favor*, and keep your hands where I can see them." The Glock pressed reassuringly against the seat but he knew he had virtually no chance of going for it just then.

It was the time before moonrise and the warm velvety night sky pressed down all around them in the darkness of the desert. Off to the east side of the road, a date palm grove seemed to suck up what little light remained and nothing moved on Van Buren in either direction even though with the flatness of the land you could see for several miles. The Chevy had cut its lights, and the gray pickup showed parking lights, unnaturally bright. Morgan had no sooner emerged when the tall man stood in front of him and pantomimed his hands up and when Morgan complied, he patted him down expertly, wasting no motions. When he came to the Glock he shook his head and Morgan could feel the barrel of a gun in his ribs so he stood there as the man extracted the weapon and pocketed it. "Do not worry, Señor, we must take this precaution. It is for your safety. We will return your weapon when you leave."

Morgan was motioned into the gray pickup. "You understand, of course, that the patron treasures his privacy and does not want many people to know where he lives. We will take care of bringing your truck but you must go in this car. And, oh yes, I am sorry that we must take this precaution to cover your eyes. You have what the patron wants, of course. Do you not? So that he can conclude this business with you."

"I have it."

Morgan estimated that they drove another ten minutes in the same direction. Once or twice the truck slowed and Morgan assumed that the Mexicans were running stop signs and he tried to remember how many but he soon lost count. All he knew for sure was that he was crowded in the front bench seat, between the kid from the bar the night before and the man with the thick neck and there was a vague smell of stale sweat and body odor in the pickup, partially edged out by the sickening smell of a strawberry deodorizer, the kind you'd buy at the Indio Car Wash or at the Wednesday night swap meet at the Date Festival Grounds.

After that they made a left, then a right, and in a few moments Morgan heard the tires grinding on stones or shells and then the pickup stopped and he heard voices talking and a few shouted words in Spanish outside the truck, making no effort to keep quiet. Then there was the sound of a gate opening, metal scraping on metal, like hinges, and the pickup moved on again and this time when it stopped, the engine shut down and a moment later, the passenger door opened and Morgan felt the thick-necked man get out.

"Please, *Señor Morgan*, I am sorry to inconvenience you in this manner." This was a different voice, the language colloquial. "The patron, he is very careful of his, you know, his privacy. And so, of course, must we be. Please come out." Someone took his arm when he emerged from the cab of the pickup and he felt hands patting him down again then the blindfold came off.

He was standing in a large courtyard or compound surrounded by a masonry or stucco wall that was at least eight feet tall. Beyond the walls to the south and to the east it was dark, dark and quiet, and mountains loomed in the blackness, their heavy presence felt as much as seen. In the dim light of the few bare bulbs he figured the space enclosed by the wall to be at least 100 by 100 feet. The roughhewn wooden gate had been closed behind him. In one of the corners a fire burned low and around it a half dozen or so figures clustered close against the evening chill and a couple of them were smoking and they looked like any group of vaqueros taking their leisure and he looked to make out their faces but he could not.

A man in dark slacks with a white *campesino* shirt fastened at the neck came out of what seemed to be a door in the wall. "My name is Fernando." He appeared to be in his late 30's. There was a scar that started on his forehead and went over one eye socket that gave his face a puzzled expression. "You have what el patron wants, of course." On his upper lip there were a few wisps of what could have been a moustache or an afterthought and on his lower lip in the center another tuft of hair so that in better circumstances he could have been a Mexican D'Artagnan. The handle of a revolver stuck out of his waistband.

"Of course."

"Let's go, then." he said, and then, "Follow me," lifting his chin in the direction he meant for Morgan to go, a portal toward the back into some kind of building that looked to be part of the wall. With every step Morgan felt as though he was descending into a pit, a black hole out of which there would be no escape.

He had to bend his head to step inside, and once inside he was in a dark hallway, the air rich with the faint but unmistakable smell of mold and frying pig fat. The man behind him pushed him firmly into the first room off the hallway. There was a window at the back of the room, well off the ground, cut through an adobe wall that looked at least to be a foot thick, perhaps more, but it opened only onto blackness. In front of the window there was a heavy wooden desk of a dark wood and a high-backed leather chair and a sideboard of the same dark wood. After a moment he could make out a man in the chair. His face was shadowed but there was something familiar about him." *Señor* Morgan." He had a flat voice, and he chose his words carefully. "You say you have brought what we spoke about the other night but here you are and I see nothing in your hands. And it would be so sad if you had nothing to trade, to swap, as it were, because then I would have nothing either, *entiende?*"

"I'd like to tell you that it was in my pants but your boys took care of what I was carrying. What I have to trade you can see, but first I see the girl. The deal."

Julio held up a hand. "Yes. All of you big-shot Hollywood types know the deal. But you are in no position to, *como se dice*, make the terms, Señor Morgan. You have involved yourself in something in which you should have no interest. It is the business of the family only. *La familia*. We believe in the family. To you *gabachos* the family is nothing but to us it is everything." He made an indolent wave of the hand, and for the first time Morgan realized there was a third man in the room off to the left of the man behind the desk. That man went to the door and opened it and a shaft of light sliced across the room and he said something softly to someone outside and then closed it and stepped back inside. The shaft of light was gone as quickly as it had appeared.

"You are *el halcon*, the hawk." Morgan ventured, to the man behind the desk.

"That is not important. You will see that we would never hurt anyone without cause. But at the same time it is my duty to act to protect the family. That is my responsibility. So I have to balance how I feel against what I must do. For example. I would personally never hurt a woman. If you, however, could not produce what we are looking for it would make it difficult to honor that conviction." He made a shrugging gesture. "It would have been taken out of my hands."

"How convenient"

"I am just being realistic. If I am forced by your actions to do something that I personally do not want to do it is not my fault, is it?"

"Tell me, Julio, what is so damned important about a 65 year old day book? What's important enough to kill over?"

"I don't know what you mean, kill, *Señor* Morgan. We are merely businessmen...all of us. So I don't know what you mean. I'm sorry you don't..."

"If you don't have the woman...or if you've hurt her..."

"You are an intelligent man, *Señor* Morgan. You know when you have been outmaneuvered, yes? And you know when you have no place from which to bargain." They all turned simultaneously as the light from the opening door split the room again and Alexis was silhouetted in the light, except, of course, that she looked like April. She saw Morgan immediately and closed the distance between them quickly and when she hugged him he knew three things—that she was terrified, that she hadn't been hurt yet, and that this was not going to be resolved by handing over any journal and then holding hands, singing Kumbayah, and going home. She whispered in his ear: "I'm okay. Give the bastards what they want. Get us out of here."

"What you want is behind my seat in the truck, in a plastic bag. Now let…"

The man held up his left hand to silence Morgan and snapped the fingers of his right hand in the direction of the man off to the side. "Not so fast, *Señor* Morgan. Make yourselves comfortable and when Raul returns from your truck we will see if you brought what we agreed upon." The man reached across his desk and opened a small wooden box and removed a thin, black cheroot and then lit it in a careful and deliberate way with his face turned away from them. The smoke had the peculiar aroma of mesquite and pinon and it curled slowly up the ceiling.

It seemed to take forever until Raul returned and when he entered the room he held the journal in his hand, but in front of him and gingerly, like it was a kind of bomb ready to go off. The man behind the desk took it and then Raul whispered something to him and handed him something small, placed it in his hand, and then took up his station off to one side.

"One moment more, I'm afraid. I will be right back. In the meantime, I think you will want to have this." And he flipped the small object that Raul had given him to Morgan, a casual, underhanded gesture, and Morgan caught it in midair and realized in a horrifying heartbeat that the object was Amado's gold pendant, the anchor with the saint. It was encrusted with blood. He felt himself stiffen and felt Alexis' hand on his arm and he heard the man say, as if from a distance: "A pity. You were, after all, asked to come alone. Sometimes we are not the ones to suffer for our mistakes. I am sorry, but as I say, I have responsibilities. To my family. They are more important than anything. Now, you wait."

He arose, journal in hand, and moved swiftly and

smoothly, almost gliding, out the side door and Morgan remained standing, his breath caught in his throat.

"God, God, how did they get Amado's gold chain?" She was almost crying. "What happened to him?"

Morgan shook his head. "He would never have given it up willingly."

A moment later Raul took Alexis' arm and moved her away from Morgan, out the door from which she had entered, and when Morgan began to protest, the third man moved in front of him with an automatic weapon, a TEC-9, and gestured for him to be quiet. "Don't worry." he said, and when she had gone out the door the man with the TEC-9 began to laugh.

Just then the other door opened with a rush and a wooden wheelchair emerged, propelled by a tall, thin man dressed in loose white pants and a floppy white shirt in the *campesino* style, as though he might have been a retainer for an old Mexican family in days gone by. The wheelchair held an old man, small, almost dwarfed by the size of the chair. The skin on his head was strangely transparent, and stretched tight over the bones of the skull. But whatever appearance of weakness there evaporated when he stuck a finger in Morgan's face, quivering with rage, and in an instant Morgan knew he had come face to face with Rolando, the original patron. "*Donde esta el otro libro?*" How in the fuck did he know there was another goddamn book? The old man continued to rave. "This one is *pedazo de mierda*." He waved the volume in the air in front of Morgan. "It is worth less than nothing. I myself saw the *pinche abogado* write things that are not here. *Donde esta el otro libro? Yo quiero el otro libro.* I want it!"

"My father says you brought him the wrong book." Julio said. "He says that there was another book."

"*Yo hablo Español?*"

"Well?"

Morgan ran through his options in his mind, one after another, and realized he had none. Getting Alexis out of there and back to who she had been was all important.

"Well?" the man repeated.

"There is another volume..." he exhaled. "I assumed it was of no importance..."

"A bad assumption." He turned to the patron. "*El otro no esta aquí.*"

"Get it for me." Rolando said, and he threw the address book at Morgan's face and motioned to his retainer to take him out of the room.

Julio spoke in a quiet voice. "Señor Morgan, you have no idea how important it is that we correct this unfortunate situation right away. My father will have both of you killed and your ranch burned to the ground if you do not provide this book. I can assure you of this. You must tell me where this other volume is immediately and we will send a few men to get it. As soon as we get it, you will be free to go."

"That's not possible."

"Why not?"

"Because it's in a place only I can find. Look, take me back with a few of your men and I'll hand it over. What've you got to lose? You've got the girl for a hostage. Why not?"

The man thought it over for a long, silent moment. "If you try anything, I can promise you won't succeed. And that my father would be consumed by his anger. You he would destroy. And the woman..." he left it in the air. "I will send you with Fernando and someone else. And your woman will stay here. With me. She will be safe. Now you must go. Quickly. The old one is beyond being annoyed."

19

Fernando motioned for Morgan to hold out his hands and the Mexican wrapped baling twine around his wrists and with the blood supply cut off his hands began to tingle and slowly go numb. Then the Mexican took a red bandana out of his pocket and went around behind Morgan and tied it over his eyes. The cloth stunk of a mixture of chickens and motor oil and when Morgan began to say something Fernando shut him up. "*Callate el hocico, cabron. Andele ahorita.*" and someone else shoved Morgan forward so that he almost lost his balance. Another man took his arm in a rough grip to steady him and the procession went outside like that, walked a few steps, and stopped. What sounded like a car door creaked open in front of him and he was bent down and in and onto the seat of a small vehicle, the upholstery of it worn so that he could feel the springs almost pushing through. Another man got in after him so that Morgan finished up sandwiched in the front seat.

A voice shouted at them, hurrying them out of there: "*Andale. Rapidito…rapidito,*" and the car chugged off into the night, the engine noise echoing off of the courtyard walls until they were out of the gate. Morgan tried to count stop signs but he gave up when he realized they were rolling most of them. One of the men lit up a joint, and soon the truck cab was filled with heavy, sweet smoke and a second later he heard pop-tops open and smelled beer. Still the truck went on.

It might have been twenty minutes but eventually the vehicle stopped and a hand reached over and pulled the blindfold down and Morgan could see the front gate of Spirit Ranch. Fernando had been on his right and he got out of the truckcab first and leaned back in. "Hey, man," he said, breathing old garlic in Morgan's face. "Get out and open the *pinche* gate for us. Don't do no fuckin' shit either, man." and he twirled the cylinder on the revolver in his hand and then waved it in front of Morgan's eyes.

A man had been riding in the truckbed and at Fernando's signal he got out and stood quietly while Morgan emerged and then Fernando gestured at the chain and the combination lock that secured the gate. "Open the motherfucker."

It was almost as if he was watching the scene from the side somewhere, watching himself unable to do anything and he held his bound hands up toward Fernando. "Take 'em off."

"Aw c'mon, man," the Mexican said, his voice a mocking whine, "don' be a pussy. You can open the lock with those on, man. My people do it all the time." His three captors laughed.

In the silence of the night they could hear the deep booming resonance of a stereo as a car made its way south on Jefferson, the sound rising first and then falling as the car drove on in the night. It was just after 9 PM but nothing else moved on Avenue 50 and there were no lights in any direction. Morgan bent over and twirled the combination lock in the glow from the gatelight and as soon as it opened Fernando pushed him out of the way and took the chain off and the heavy blue iron gate swung open. He motioned to the driver and the pickup rolled inside, its lights out and then he closed the gate and secured the chain without locking the lock so that it looked undisturbed. He motioned Morgan back into the truck, stationed the third man just inside the oleanders, and climbed in the bed of the truck. "Andale." he said, smacking the roof with the flat of his hand.

The car moved down the right side of the driveway and when they went past the front door of the main house the security light flared and the driver cut the engine and rolled the pickup to a stop in the darkness beyond the basketball hoop. After a moment the light dimmed again and all was silent and the driver restarted the engine and turned the truck so that it faced back down the driveway. Fernando placed the muzzle of his revolver against Morgan's neck and walked him a few paces from the truck.

"Now find this fuckin' thing, man. We've got 20 more minutes and after that the patron is going to be one pissed-off hombre, and if he gets pissed, I get pissed, and if I get pissed, you die."

"This way." Morgan said, starting for the bunkhouse.

The door to the bunkhouse was closed but unlocked and when he opened it the alarm began to beep a warning. Fernando was right behind him and again he felt Fernando's revolver against his neck. Morgan thought for a moment about inputting the panic code but he knew that would be the end of Alexis and instead he input the standard code on the pad and the beeping stopped, leaving a heavy silence in its wake.

The interior of the bunkhouse was cool, colder than he had known it for days. The weak exterior security light by the garage cast a feeble glow up against the windows but the interior was impenetrable darkness. Nothing had happened but Morgan noticed that Fernando was acting edgy, as though something was making him nervous. "Okay, man." Fernando said. "Turn on a fuckin' light." He pushed Morgan with the gunbarrel again.

The light switch was in the hallway to the right of the fireplace and Morgan flipped it with his tied hands. There was only a small bulb in the fixture on the ceiling and it barely illuminated the hall and Morgan said: "There it is. Have at it." indicating the paneled wall with a lift of his chin.

"There what is, fucker." Fernando said. "I don' see nothing there."

"Open that closet door."

The Mexican complied and looked inside quickly. There was nothing but blackness. "Don' fuck around wit' me, *gabacho* prick. I don' see nothin'."

"Reach inside. Towards the front there's a hole in the fireplace stones you can feel with your hand. It's in there." and he backed off a few steps to give the Mexicans room.

A cooler breeze seemed to swirl around them carrying the scent of mold and lavender, a mortuary smell, and the light seemed to flicker as if it were a candle flame. Fernando noticed it as well and was darting his eyes this way and that, and telling the other man in Spanish what to do. The other man hesitated and Fernando cursed at him and pushed him forward. In the area behind the fireplace the blackness seemed to absorb all the light there was. The Mexican put his hand inside, felt around for a second, and withdrew his hand in a panic as if he had been scalded. "I can feel nothing." His face was a pasty white.

Fernando pushed his compadre aside. "*Estupido!* Let me." he shouted at the man and replaced his revolver in his belt and reached inside himself and immediately he withdrew his arm. "*Chinga. Hijo de puta.* Here. You. You do it." When he pointed to Morgan, his hand was unsteady but Morgan held his bound wrists forward and Fernando extracted a long switchblade knife with a black handle from his pocket, snicked the blade out, and cut the twine.

Morgan's rubbed some feeling into his wrists and then he put an arm into the blackness and felt around. The cache place was deeper in than he remembered and he had to lay his face up against the paneling to reach it and when he did so he could sense the faint aroma of lavender that grew stronger and then he became aware of the sound of breathing, loud, louder than he had ever heard it before and he seemed to be drawn down into a whirling vortex of air.

The journal was still there, wrapped in the plastic, just the way he had put it in. Just as his hand was about to close on it he felt a warmth to the left and when he moved his hand ever so slightly in that direction he realized it was his .357 and his fingers closed on the grip.

Fernando wasn't paying attention. The man was leaning against the other wall in the hallway looking as though he was going to be sick and the other man, the driver, seemed to be sweating, his skin gray. In one motion Morgan pulled the revolver from the hiding spot, pointed it at the driver's head, the closest target, and pulled the trigger and where there was the pasty-white diaphoretic face one moment there was nothing but a red, spongy mass the next. He turned the weapon on Fernando but the Mexican was one millisecond quicker and had his revolver against Morgan's temple.

"*Pinche gabacho cabron.*" he said, pushing the dead man's body away as it fell and pulling the hammer back on his revolver. You've got one breath to get me the fuckin' book."

"Not so fast, motherfucker." Burns stepped through one of the side windows looking to Morgan just then as if he were the 7th Cavalry, a dull black Israeli Galil assault rifle in his hands and a shiny .357 on his left hip. He slammed the bolt of the Galil home for emphasis. "Don't even think of it." He motioned Morgan away. "If you do, you might live. Might...I'm not sure. If you don't, I'm sure of one thing...I'll fuckin' drop you where you stand and there won't even be enough left to mop up. Nick...you ever see one of these babies?" Burns asked innocently, as though they were at a gunshow. "Fires a hunert rounds a minute. Hardly has any kick. Watch, I'll show you."

Fernando lowered his weapon and Morgan kicked it out of his hand. Burns moved quickly and slammed the Mexican with the butt of his weapon and the man fell to his knees.

"What in the fuckin' name of everything were you tryin' to do, Nick? Jesus fuckin' Christ, I told you. You're the writer, I'm the fuckin' dick. You didn't have a Chinaman's chance of gettin' 'em both. I'll give you that this brave soldier over here looked a little green around the gills. But still...what did you think you were doin'?"

Morgan inclined his head in the direction of the main gate without speaking.

"Don't worry about him. I fitted him with a wire collar that got a little tight and then I asked him where you were but he couldn't tell me anything so I left him in the oleanders for your gardener to clean up."

"You're a sweet kid. Where did you come from?"

"Malibu...of course. I was originally going to come down tomorrow but something nagged at me after we spoke and I decided to drive down tonight. Of course I couldn't get your mobile to pick up. Good goddamn thing. I get here in time to see you and your friends driving in. It didn't look like you had invited 'em over to shoot pool. It looked like y'all was fixin' to have a party without me." Fernando began to stand up but Burns gestured at him with the barrel of his weapon. "Down on your fuckin' knees, asshole. Be thankful you're still alive."

"They've got Alexis."

"Fuck. That's enough to piss off the Pope. Where?"

"Their compound. Wherever that is. I don't know. They snatched Alexis from here a little while ago and I tried to go after them myself. Not the best idea I've ever had. Amado followed me, I think, to try to cover me but it looks like they found him. They had the holy medal he wears and they would have had to pry that off him."

"I'm sorry, bro. Let's get back to their compound and get Alexis before some more shit happens."

"Into the compound. Right. I'm not sure I could even find it."

"Ah, but we have a guide. Right, Fernando?"

"Go fuck yourself."

"Listen, fuck face," Burns stuck the barrel of the Galil near Fernando's left eye. "You're alive as long as you're useful. No help, no alive. You dig? *Comprende* motherfucker?" Fernando glared at him and Burns pushed the weapon into his skin. "Answer me, shithead."

"I understand that you'll never make it out of there."

"We're not askin' your fuckin' opinion." Burns said. "This ain't fuckin' talk radio, you know." He turned to Morgan. "How many guys were there?"

"At least 15."

"So now there's 12. And if we stop by the barn and pick up some of your boys that'll help. You've got enough shotguns in here to arm a few guys. And from what you say, they'd love a shot at these badboys."

The compound was surrounded by an eight foot high stucco and adobe wall set back from the road. Only a few small windows and orderly rows of heavy wooden vigas broke the expanse that faced the street and it could have been anyone's idea of a southwestern estate, or maybe something that had been build in the 1920's for one of the reclusive Hollywood types. A row of cottonwoods lined the back wall, and inside the walls an invisible campfire reflected an inviting glow against the buildings toward the back.

The pickup looked almost as it had when it left, Fernando in the right hand seat, Morgan in the middle with his blindfold back on, and behind the wheel a nondescript head covered by the blue baseball cap the original driver had worn. But this time the head belonged to Rigoberto, another of Amado's endless supply of cousins. Morgan's hands were bound with the same baling twine they had used originally. Still wrapped in plastic, the journal rested on Morgan's lap and Burns himself slouched in the shadows of the back seat, almost invisible. In his left hand he cradled the assault rifle; his .357 was in his right, its muzzle at Fernando's ear. An old tarp they found at the polo club lay rumpled in the truckbed and concealed Borrego, Tomas, and Angel, four of Morgan's shotguns, and a few boxes of 00 buckshot.

Just a few minutes ago the boys had been drinking beer on the porch of Morgan's tackroom, wondering how they were going to spend the next few hours. Now they knew.

"Do we go up and knock on the door?" Rigoberto asked. His voice was nervous.

Burns prodded Fernando with the .357. "What do we do, dickhead?"

"Find out for yourself, *gabacho*. You so smart."

Burns hissed a warning to the boys in the truckbed. "Get ready. Rigoberto, you hit the horn once. And you, dickhead," he said, to Fernando, "you will be the first to die if something happens so if I were you I'd take my chances on cooperating. If we get lucky and someone comes out, tell him to take Morgan to the patron. Tell him you're tired or you gotta take a piss or something. And remember, Morgan understands

Spanish. Oh, yeah, and this little handgun is peanuts. This nice little kosher salami I'm holding behind you will ventilate your ass like a fuckin' Swiss cheese. *Queso* Swiss. I've heard it's good on nachos. *Comprende?*"

"Fuck you, *gabacho* motherfucker." Fernando spit out the words. "I fuckin' *comprende.*"

Rigoberto tapped the horn button and the gate opened a crack and one man emerged wearing a wrinkled Hawaiian-style shirt outside his pants and looked as though he had been sleeping somewhere. He was carrying a sawed-off 12 gauge. When he saw the truck he nodded without looking and sauntered up to Fernando's side of the pickup. He held the shotgun casually, barrel pointed to the ground.

"Take the *gabacho* to Rolando." Fernando said to the man. "*Voy a ir a echar una meada.*"

The man nodded and Burns managed a whisper to Morgan. "Okay, Nick. Go with this motherfucker and stall. We'll be along."

"I'll set a place for you."

"Keep your fuckin' seat." Burns said to Fernando in the passenger's side, and Rigoberto slouched out from behind the wheel as though it was the most natural thing in the world to do with Morgan after him. The Hawaiian shirt came up close to him and examined his blindfold and when he was satisfied that Morgan couldn't see, he poked him in the back with the shotgun and pushed him in the direction of the door.

Burns, Rigoberto, and Fernando were suddenly alone in the courtyard. Rigoberto got behind the wheel and drove the pickup into the shadows behind the low building that looked to be part of the wall and Burns got out and stationed himself at the open door of the truck. From somewhere they could hear guitar music, totally inappropriately lush and romantic, and then a loud noise as one of the doors in the building slammed behind them. Without thinking, Burns glanced in the direction of the noise and the distraction was all that Fernando needed. Quick as a cobra, he produced a smaller knife that had been concealed in his boot and started a killing thrust at the detective's neck. Borrego picked just that moment to roll out from under the tarp and when he saw the gleam of the knife he moved just as quickly and grabbed the handle of a jack and brought it down across Fernando's forearm. There was a dull crack as his arm shattered and the knife clattered to the ground and then Rigoberto was on him in a heartbeat with a knee on his face and he picked up the man's knife and swiftly cut Fernando's neck from one side to the other and then grinned at Burns as he wiped his bloody hands and the knife on the dead man's shirt. *"Ahora no es posible que el hablando."*

"What? Ah, fuck...forget it...tell me later. You're doing great."

Inside, someone had taken the journal, still in its plastic wrapping, from Morgan and he was moved down what smelled to him like the same corridor or hallway but it seemed to him as though they were going much deeper into the fortress. He stumbled once and almost lost his footing and one of his escorts cursed at him but in the process they bandana was moved so at least he could see something in the dim light. Morgan recognized none of his escorts this time. At last they came to an unmarked door and he was pushed inside where two men waited and when one of them turned around he knew him immediately. Unfortunately. It was the kid from El Coyote Azul the night before, the one whose arm he apparently had broken with the tire iron.

"*Pinche gabacho,* motherfucker, let's see how fuckin' tough you are now." The kid spat at Morgan and as quickly hit him in the jaw with his good fist. The sudden blow staggered him and he tasted warm blood in his mouth. With his hands still bound Morgan lunged at the kid but the two that had brought him in grabbed him and the kid punched him again. This one was harder and caught him on the side of his head and with the next one he lost his footing. The men that had been holding him let him slump to the ground and when he lay there the kid began to kick at him, landing a few hard ones on his chest and one to the side of his head and the pain in his ribs was almost too much for him to bear. And then everything went black.

20

The first thing he became aware of was a circle of yellow light, a bright hole in an inky firmament that pulsed and pulsed to a primal rhythm. It was the most beautiful color he had ever seen and as he watched it seemed to grow and expand until it took form until he could see that the light was a flame and the flame was in a kerosene lamp and the kerosene lamp was suspended from a roughhewn beam that looked to be in a stable. It was then that he felt the pain in his head and when he tried to take a deep breath he almost passed out again. He was lying on a hardpacked dirt floor in an enclosure with rough wooden walls that smelled like a stable and Alexis was stroking his face and tears were running down her cheeks.

He started to get up, to shake his head, to clear it, but even the thought of that hurt and he let himself back down. "You okay?" he muttered.

She managed a grimace. "You come in looking like you were dragged behind a car and you ask me if I'm alright?"

"Well are you?"

"Better than you."

"You were right. Polo would kill me sooner or later."

"No jokes. Look over there." She indicated something in the corner and he lifted himself on an elbow, the movement exquisitely painful. It was a man, his face an unrecognizable mass of purple welts and dried blood. Only when he saw the black boots with the silver tips did he realize it was Amado.

He knew then that the chances of them getting out of there alive had just been cut by half but it wasn't something he felt he needed to tell her just yet. Or wanted to. He motioned her closer. "Burns and some of the boys are here." he whispered, but in his heart he knew that if there was any chance of rescue it would have happened already.

She brightened at his words: "Where?"

"Good question. I was the decoy…"

"Some decoy."

"Yeah, well, anyway, I don't know. We need to hook up. It shouldn't be more than a couple of minutes more."

"That's too long. Amado needs to get to a doctor fast. He's done nothing but moan since they threw him in here and he's been quiet for the last few minutes. I'm not a nurse but his pulse doesn't feel too strong to me."

"All we can do is sit tight now and wait for Burns to make his move."

With that, the door slid to the side with a grinding sound of metal on metal and the hall smell of stale cooking swirled in but the head that poked was on a burly torso and behind him another man of greater girth and as little grace and without a word they both went to Morgan and pulled him to his feet. "Andale, andale," they commanded.

"Where are we goin' handsome?" Morgan asked. There were blank looks. "*Donde vas, guapo?*" The larger man pushed him against the wall and was about to punch him when the second man stopped him. "*Alto. No. El patron dice que no necesita. Tenemos que llevarlo a la patron. Immediatamente."*

They pushed Morgan into the hall and Alexis followed, determined not to be left behind, and when they tried to shove her back in she drew herself up to her full 5 foot 3 inches and put a finger in the smaller man's face. "Look, you bastard," she screamed, "I've been in that fuckin' stable for hours and I'm damn tired of it and you'd better take me to see your fuckin' boss, too, or else I'm gonna fix it so that somebody kicks your ass." Confused by her outburst, the men looked at each other and laughed, a silly, incongruous, nervous sound, but they made no more moves to stop her.

The patron's living quarters were large, a combination office and sitting area and bedroom. The only light in the room came from a light on the desk, an old brass lamp with a green glass shade, and it cast the furniture into a deep gold. At the desk, the patron himself sat in his wooden wheelchair apparently lost in thought, oblivious to the people in the room and the sudden commotion of Morgan's entrance. His shoulders were slumped and his head on his chest as if asleep.

The two guards pushed Morgan ahead of them, into the light and when the patron saw them he motioned the guards out of the room and beckoned Morgan closer. That close, Morgan could see again how old the man was. The patron might have been imposing in his youth; now his head appeared too large for his frail chest and the skin on his nose and forehead was blotchy and stretched taut but Morgan was again impressed by the presence he radiated.

He fixed Morgan with a clear stare for a moment and then he began to speak in English. "You are Morgan, the writer." he said.

"Si. Yo soy Morgan."

The patron shook his head. "You *norte Americanos*. You think because you espeak *Español* that you understand the

Mexican. But it needs more than to espeak *Español* to understand the mind of the Mexican. It take many hundred years. Because you have to know the *corazon*, the heart of the *campesino*, the mind of the *Indio*. So we will espeak English. And you will think you understand. But you will not.

He had unwrapped the plastic bag but had gone no further and was pointing at a shiny object. "So now I ask you. Where you get this?"

On top of the closed journal Morgan could see the gleam of a silver object that had to be the dead girl's marcasite brooch, the one he had seen in his dream. He drew in his breath before answering. "I never saw it before, close up. It was probably with the journals when I got them."

"No. That is not possible. I myself saw this thing on the dead girl on that day. I myself covered her with the sand. That is not possible." He took a deep, wheezing breath. "I no mean for her to die." He was speaking to himself as much as Morgan now and behind him he could feel Alexis move closer. "I no mean for her to die." He put his hands over his eyes and bent down and spoke softly. "The man I send there that day, Ernesto, he is very stupid. Very stupid, very careless. I know his family from Guanajuato and they say give him a job but he is the stupid one. I send him to kill the lawyer. The lawyer think he smarter than *la familia* and he wan' more money or he go to the police. So it is time for him to die. But the *pinche* lawyer bring a girl with him. And the girl was..." his voice trailed off.

Alexis had been moving closer with each breath the old man took and now she had come to stand next to Morgan. Her voice seemed to come from somewhere else, a place years away. "Who was the girl, Rolando?" she whispered.

"It was you," he said, seeing Alexis for the first time and hardly breathing.

276

"It is you," he said. "Here...take this and go away," and held the brooch out with both hands and when she took it the patron slumped back into the chair.

The gunshots that exploded in the hall outside the door shattered the moment and Rolando closed his eyes and leaned back, already in a different place. Morgan held his bound wrists out to Alexis. "Here, help me get these damn things off my wrists."

She stuffed the brooch into the pocket of her slacks and fumbled with the knot and when it finally gave way Morgan opened the door and eased his head out low where no one would expect it. One of the guards was running toward the patron's office but just as he saw Morgan and began to raise his weapon, his mouth filled with blood and with a surprised look he fell forward. Morgan could see Borrego's knife protruding from his back, the one he had used on the rattler the day before. There was a kissing sound from an alcove behind the man and Morgan looked over in time to see Borrego perched on the sill with Morgan's most expensive Belgian Browning raised in a pantomime of celebration. The guard lay still and Morgan got out of his crouch just as Burns stepped out of the shadows.

"That's two," Morgan said. "I owe ya."

"We'll settle up later."

"Very funny. How long have we been here anyway?"

"Not that long, but the odds aren't much better than they were before. Ten to five. Rigoberto, and Tijo are outside. It's you, me, and Borrego here. We've got to figure out how to get out of here."

"Minor detail."

"Right...here...take this." Burns produced Morgan's 9 mm from somewhere and underhanded it to him and watched while he checked the chamber, checked the clip, and undid the safety.

"Amado looks awful." Alexis said to all of them. "He's in the stable. We've got to do something."

Burns drew in a deep breath. "We just came from the stable. Too late...Amado's dead. I'm sorry."

"Goddamn." Morgan said, his voice soft. "I..."

"It's time to get the fuck out of here." Burns said. "Follow me."

"You know where you're goin'?"

"More details."

After that it was sheer confusion and they tried one door after another, edging each one open, unsure of what lay beyond, until they came to the one that opened into Julio's office. Two of his guards were still there, one of them armed with a TEC-9 automatic weapon and Borrego saw that, hollered for everyone to get down, pulled the door shut and threw himself on the ground in a microsecond. A heartbeat later the wood dissolved in a sustained burst of lead that filled the corridor with chips of wood and ricocheting bullets, taking the small overhead light with it and plunging the area into darkness while Morgan and his team tried to make themselves as small as possible. There was no chance to fire back and the noise of the weapon blocked everything else and pressed them down with a physical force.

When it stopped they heard nothing for a second but ringing in their ears and when the ringing subsided they could hear Borrego cursing rapidly and earnestly in Spanish. Burns and Morgan kept silent, eyes on the doorway, while they located Borrego in the dark but as they did one of Julio's guards appeared in the doorway. Julio's voice was prodding him from behind. "Andale, Andale." The backlighting through the smoke from the gunshots made it look as if he filled the doorway. Burns and Morgan remained silent, playing possum, knowing the man could see nothing in the dark hall.

"*Da me una luz.*" the man said and Julio passed him a flashlight and when he turned it on, Morgan could just see that Burns was plastered along the wall near the door, where the man couldn't see him. As he watched, Burns reached out of the darkness and pulled the guard by the arm that held the light and the man lost his balance and tumbled forward to the floor.

"One for you, one for me. Don't fuck it up, Nicholas." Burns said, and he stepped into the doorway with the Galil at his hip and fired a short deadly burst into the room as Morgan fired two shots from the 9 mm into the guard's head.

"Alexis." Morgan said out loud.

"Over here." She had somehow gotten the TEC-9 from the guard and was crouched down now along the corridor, the piece at the ready.

"Where'd you learn that?" Burns treased.

"Too many Nancy Drew mysteries."

"Good, 'cause I'm sure it sure wasn't at FIDM." Morgan's voice was full of relief and he reached a hand over to Alexis and touched her arm.

"Okay," Burns said, his voice low, "there's nobody left alive in here but us chickens. I can't speak for the rest of this shithole."

Outside they could hear pistol shots and a shotgun blast but no more automatic weapons.

"Don't forget Rolando, the patron."

"He ain't goin' nowhere in that wheelchair. Borrego…are you okay?"

More curses. "It's my *pinche* leg. Hurts like fuckin' shit but I'm not bleed too bad."

"Can you walk?"

"Shit, yeah. I no stay here."

"Now comes the hard part...gettin' out." Burns said. "It's quieter outside. Anybody hear any automatic weapons lately?"

They all shook their head's no and Morgan offered: "That's either good or bad. Ready?"

"Say when."

"Why do I feel like this is the last scene in Butch Cassidy?"

"Cause you're a writer. Fuck it...let's go."

They rushed the last door.

Outside there was almost complete carnage in the courtyard. Bodies of the members of *la familia* lay here and there and the two grooms, Rigoberto and Tijo, huddled next to the pickup, smoking. Rigoberto had four empty bottles of Corona beer that he was filling with gasoline from a milk carton while Tijo stuffed rags into the bottle openings.

Morgan stopped in his tracks. "Don't even breathe...if you do, we'll all go up. "*Que haces?*" he asked.

"Making little *bombas*. You know, *la bomba*." Rigoberto cackled.

"You no wan' no *chinga* evidence, right *jefe?*" Tijo added.

"*Donde esta* Amado?" It was Rigoberto's question. Morgan hesitated and finally answered: "Dead. Killed in the shootout."

The grooms looked at each other. "That is what he say." Tijo said, his voice controlled.

"What who say?" Morgan asked.

Rigoberto answered slowly. "What Amado say. Before he follow you tonight. He say he go make up for his cousin, what his cousin do back then. He say his *abuelo* tell him."

Borrego had not said anything, but now he spoke. "Burn this *pinche lugar* to the *pinche* ground."

"Take Amado's truck and Morgan's." Burns was directing

things outside. He pointed at the Toyota they had come back in. "Leave this one here."

The last thing they did before they drove off was to pitch the lighted Molotov cocktails around in the compound where they glowed behind the walls like a crucible and before they reached Avenue 64 the night was shredded with three massive explosions. Morgan hunched his shoulders involuntarily. The patron was going to the hell he had created for everyone else all those years ago.

21

Burns drove Morgan's truck, and with Morgan and Alexis piled into the front seat they followed the grooms deep into the barrio of Coachella where they found an old *curandero* who could be relied on to treat gunshot wounds discreetly and they left Borrego there, with a wad of bills stuffed into the healer's hand and a promise to be back for him in the morning. Max was in the tackroom on a pile of saddle blankets where Santiago had left him, his shoulder wrapped with vetwrap. They lifted him into the truckbed, saddle blankets and all, and continued down 50th, back to Spirit Ranch.

As soon as they were sure Max was comfortable, Morgan, Burns, and Alexis opened a round of Coronas and went outside where they sat by the pool in the light of the waning almost-quartermoon. Some of Amado's *compadres* had come out while they were gone and had taken David's body to a mortuary in Coachella and had gotten rid of Fernando's dead guard up against the mountains where the coyotes would have the body gone before sunrise.

The blue iron gate to the ranch was closed and locked and

for the first time in a long time Morgan felt safe inside. When Alexis went off to take a shower, Morgan found two black cheroots in his desk drawer and brought them out and he and Burns lit up in silence and walked slowly down to the pasture fence.

It was absolutely quiet without a breeze, the two of them draped over the fencerailing while the smoke from the cigars curled straight up in the night air. No traffic moved on Avenue 50, and the darkness hung like velvet from the cactus gardens to the back oleanders. Here and there a coyote yipped at the moon and by the salt pines in back an owl called. The almost incongruous sound of water running in the shower carried to them in the night air like a Zen fountain.

After a while, Burns spoke: "What happened in there before?" He indicated the bunkhouse with a nod of his head.

"I don't have a clue. I've got some ideas but it's all guess. I brought the Mexicans back here stalling for time, hoping you'd show up, or something, and then once we got here I realized there was nothing I could do. Your basic deep shit situation."

Morgan shook his head and took a puff on the cheroot and let the smoke slowly out. "When the light began to flicker and they got weird behind the fireplace I got this feeling that I could handle things. How? I don't know. Why? I'm not sure. But they both chickened out of putting their hands in there and that made Fernando cut my ties. I put my hand in the hole and felt the .357. Unless I'm losing my mind, I know I didn't leave the .357 in there, I would swear I never had that piece even near there, but there it was anyway, somehow calling me by the warmth of it."

"And then I showed up."

"The 7th Cavalry. But something definitely happened in the five or ten minutes between when we drove on to the ranch and when I shot that first asshole. Even now I'm looking for a logical reason."

"Maybe there isn't one."

"Maybe. And then I'm left with what I never believed in. But there's no friggin' way to deny what happened. But there was something stranger that happened. The old patron found that brooch, the one from my dreams, wrapped in the package with the journal."

"How could that be?"

"How, indeed? He tried to give her the brooch and told her he was sorry she had been killed. It was as if no time had passed. Like when Alma, the psychic spoke. It was as if it was happening right now. It was if he knew her."

"So you think…"

"I don't know what to think. Maybe she reminded him of someone... I really think she reminded him of his sister, but I can't tell you why except that she had that beautiful cinnamon-colored skin and auburn hair."

"That would have explained why he killed his hired gun. It was not the shot he wanted. None of it."

"Anyway and more to the point, if you ask me we'd better clear out for a while." Morgan said.

"I don't think that's necessary."

"The police…"

"The police will never trace anything to you. They'll treat it like some kind of gang thing, drugs, whatever. Like they did that incident in Baja last year where they found 12 or 13 dead including the wives, kids, dogs, you name it, scattered around a hacienda. That was in the paper exactly two days. This might make three, you don't know. It's Palm Springs and nothing ever happens in Palm Springs. Those boys weren't saints, you know. You probably did a whole bunch of people a big favor. I'm sure everyone from the police to the hombres they were loan-sharking would bless your name."

"Yeah…Saint Nicholas."

"Not for about six months."

"Very funny."

"How about *la familia?*"

"There are so many gangs and branches of gangs that they'll never get around to thinking a *gabacho* did it."

The two of them walked back up to the house, pulled the white chaise lounges next to each other in front of the low adobe wall outside his bedroom, and relaxed that way, listening to the pool bubbling in the background. "All the same, I think we'll go up to the city for a few days in the morning, Alexis and I. Just for a few days, to let things cool down. I need to have some time with her…figure out where we're going. And I need to write some things down. I'm sure there's a story worth writing here and writing has always been my way to deal with things."

Burns stubbed out his cheroot and popped an Altoid. "Nobody would believe you…"

"It's fiction, man. All just a figment of someone's imagination. Nobody has to believe it. It just has to be a good story. It's called the willing suspension of disbelief. People will read it on an airplane or watch it on the Hallmark channel and forget about it as soon as it's over. It's not like it's WAR AND PEACE or something."

The detective shrugged. "I guess…"

"Who knows anyway?" Morgan offered. "After that, I'll be back, never fear. I don't know about Alexis. After all she's been through I wouldn't blame her if she never wanted to see this place again. It's different for me, though. I fought for this place and probably, on some level, was ready to die for it. Maybe it was just my Montana stubbornness. I wasn't ready to give it up to any threats before this and I'm sure as shit not ready to give it up now."

"Why do you think I am?" Alexis had come outside wrapped in one of Morgan's fluffy white robes, a towel around her head. Standing in the shadows he knew she had heard most of their conversation. "I don't think it will bother me any more." She took the towel off her head and shook her head and they saw immediately that she had done something to her hair so that the auburn color was less apparent and the way she sat and combed it then she looked almost like her old self and she could see that they noticed.

"I don't know what came over me. All I know is that from the time I was here last to now I had a whole different concept of how I should look, maybe even who I was. And no matter what, I wasn't going to go near that bunkhouse. Completely irrational, I know, but I wasn't going to go in it no matter what. Now I don't think I care. In fact, I'm sure I don't care. It feels like just another building to me."

"Since..?"

"Since we came back here tonight. From that house of horrors."

"Something else we can add to the category of great unsolved mysteries."

Burns and Alexis looked at Morgan. "I can't believe you said that." Burns said.

"I can't believe I said that. Maybe it's just that I'm ready to admit that some things just can't be explained. Just don't push me too far on that." He got up and stretched. "Anyone want another beer?"

They both passed on his offer and Morgan got one for himself and after he came back out Burns went in and crashed on the daybed in Morgan's office. Morgan laid back down on the lounge chair and Alexis came and sat next to him in silence and after a while she said: "I'm sorry about Amado."

"That hasn't even sunk in. Won't for days. Of course I'll go down to Guanojuato and tell his parents myself after a while. Take Borrego or someone. Funny, Amado and I were always going to go down there so his mother could cook for me. And something always came up. Now it's too late. Good argument for the Don Juan philosophy."

"Which is..?"

"Live like a warrior."

She gave him a quizzical look.

"It's from THE TEACHINGS OF DON JUAN. The writer was a guy named Carlos Castenada, something of an enigma himself. In the book he meets a Yaqui Indian sorcerer, Don Juan Matus, and Don Juan is always telling him to live like a warrior. It's living with the certain knowledge that each day could be your last. Not putting things off."

Morgan shifted his position. "I know I don't live that way, much as I'd like to, much as I try. I'm not sure Amado lived that way either, not in any conscious way at least. But in his own unsophisticated way he managed to get the maximum enjoyment from each day. I guess I always envied that, his ability to live in the present and not worry too much."

"You do some, too. Live in the present, I mean. You ever think that it may be one of the reasons you play polo? When you play you're forced to be in the moment. You've always said that. If you're not in the moment when you play you don't get anything done. Or worse. You get hurt."

She reached for his bottle of Corona and took a long swallow of his beer. "You two were more alike than you know, I told you that before. And it wasn't just your sixth sense with the horses."

"I wonder if he ever found the answers he was looking for."

"Which answers?"

"How he related to this place. If, in fact, the original killer was the man his *abuelo*, his grandfather told him about. I think maybe his *abuelo* was trying to warn him away from this place. Whatever, it had the opposite effect and drove him closer to it, the moth to the flame."

"So you mean you can't avoid your fate?"

"Influence it, maybe, alter it, perhaps, but avoid it, no. I don't think so. You ever hear the old tale about the man who travels to a distant village when he hears that the Angel of Death is looking for him? And then his servant sees the Angel of Death in the village square and tells him he won't find his master there, that he's gone to a distant village. The Angel of Death says: 'I know…I'm supposed to meet him there later today.' No. I don't think you can avoid your fate completely. All you can do is twist and turn and maybe strike a bargain with it."

They stopped talking and a comfortable silence filled the space between them, and finally he laughed quietly. "But then again, maybe life isn't like a river."

"Which means what?"

"A punchline to an old joke. I'll tell you when you've forgotten it."

She bent over and kissed him. "Let's go to bed."

Alexis' warm naked body wrapped around him in bed and even though she tried to avoid his sore ribs and his sore neck he couldn't get comfortable and after a while he got up and slipped on a pair of shorts and started outside and as an afterthought he pocketed the marcasite brooch Alexis had left on his dresser. Max shifted in his sleep and moaned softly but made no effort to go with him. Morgan crouched at his side for a few moments.

The air was still warm and he went across to the bunkhouse and opened the door and for the first time the place felt warm, and smelled like it had been closed up for some time. Amado's cousins had cleaned the great room of blood. He went to where the journals had been hidden and sniffed the air but there was no lavender, only the faint odor of sage where it had blown in off the desert. In the room where Alma told him the girl had been murdered all was quiet, and hardly breathing, Morgan listened for anything but there was nothing.

He walked outside and down the slope to the orchid tree behind the bunkhouse, in front of the two horse barn where she said the three of them had been buried. Was it really too late? Could they ever find anything digging there? He knew he would never test that theory.

The heavy branches of the tree blocked most of the moonlight and there was almost complete darkness under it. The brooch felt warm in his pocket and he took it out and looked at it carefully, marveling at how it reflected what little light there was or created its own light, he wasn't sure. He turned it over and over thoughtfully for a long time and finally started slowly back to the main house. After a few steps he stopped and turned around yet again and walked back down to the foot of the tree. There he laid the brooch in the grass.

In the morning it was gone.

The End

ACKNOWLEDGMENTS

People who have taken the time to read SPIRIT RANCH invariably ask me how I found the time to do the in-depth historical research. The fact is, I didn't. The information, like the mystery and magic of the Coachella Valley, seeped in through my pores after years spent riding the desert, playing polo, socializing with the locals, and listening. I cannot ever thank all of them enough, desert rats one and all, not just for what they did for my book but for enhancing the love affair I have had with my adopted home.

The Mexican grooms, the horsemen, the Mexican-Indians, all exist in much they same way as I have described them. They brought me into their homes, their churches, their festivals, and taught me their dances and how to cook their food. Their culture is as deep and mysterious as I have portrayed it and their love of horses humbling. I was privileged to be part of it.

Polo players are larger than life, whether American, Argentine, Mexican, or Chilean. The intensity of the game and of how they live their life defies description. Being a part of that world for more than 20 years still defines my life.

My attempts at putting down on paper the peculiar patois known as Spanglish were helped by my dear friend Alba Xochihua. She read the book in its early form, sent me an email full of corrections, and was sweet-talked into proofing the entire book. Be careful what you volunteer for.

The cover was designed by long-time friend Peter McMahon of www.petermcmahonstudio.com. He is an unparalleled graphic designer and photographer and all-around good guy.

My daughter, Michelle, a sports journalist, read the book early on and offered many good suggestions (and a lot of sidebars about USC). My gratitude to her and to my son, Loren, another unrepentant Trojan, whose encouragement meant a lot to me.

The horses in the book are real and their influence on me continues to be felt every day in every way. Some of them have gone to what a Hawaiian polo-playing friend calls *lio lani*, horse heaven. *Maui, E.T., Macho Man, Buddy, Barbara*, continue to live in my heart along with some who continue to play for other players, *Rosa, Mescalito*, and *Perla Negra*. The three retired polo ponies I still have and continue to ride, *Macarena, Groovy*, and *Nino*, look deep into my heart all the time and try to make me a more honest person. Sometimes they succeed.

I cannot even find words to describe the importance of my wife, JoAnn, to my life and to SPIRIT RANCH. Take the best friend you ever had, someone who is confident enough in your relationship to tell you when you are way off base, way out of line, or when your writing isn't up to par, multiply it by a gazillion and you will understand what she means to me. I have seen her change out of a very expensive Ralph Lauren black business suit after returning from a buying trip to Milan or Paris and fix a PVC pipe ten minutes later. I have watched her take an abused young horse who wouldn't give any two-legged creature a chance and have it following her around the pasture. I have seen her, after not having sat a horse for two or three weeks while off on a business trip, outride so many people I've quit counting. She is the Bacall to my Bogie, the person you want at your side with a loaded rifle when a crazed Cape buffalo is charging and your weapon just jammed; the someone you want to share a beer with at the end of the day. If you like SPIRIT RANCH, you have her to thank.

People say that the desert is gone now, covered in golf courses and housing tracts. It's not true.

Thespirit of the desert is still there…you just have to listen and let it find you.

ABOUT THE AUTHOR

Richard Foxx has at various times been a successful ocean-racing navigator, a rated polo player, a trainer of winning field-trial retrievers, a sometime trainer of polo ponies, a physician, and a US Army surgeon. He has written for numerous equestrian magazines and yachting publications. Now Medical Director for the aesthetic medical spa he founded in 2003, Foxx has authored many articles on aesthetic and spa medicine and is considered an authority in that field.

A full-time desert resident, Foxx lives at the east end of the Coachella Valley with JoAnn, his wife and companion of 25 years, and Sammy, a black Lab, close by the horses that remain from his polo playing days.

www.ingramcontent.com/pod-product-compliance
Lightning Source LLC
Chambersburg PA
CBHW031600240626
47153CB00002B/585